Praise for the novels of Robert Littell

"Besides being hugely entertaining, *The Company* is a serious look at how our nation exercised power, for good and ill, in the second half of the twentieth century."
—Patrick Anderson, *The Washington Post Book World*

"*The Company* reads like a breeze . . . guaranteed to suck you right back into the Alice-in-Wonderland world of spy vs. spy . . . a ripping good yarn—entertaining, chilling, insightful."
—Andrew Nagorski, *Newsweek*

"Since his Cold War classic, *The Defection of A.J. Lewinter,* Littell has been steadily creating his own subgenre, the counter-thriller, witty and highly original tales that play off the clichés of the Cold War thriller and subvert them."
—Joseph Finder, *The Washington Post*

"*The Sisters* is so clever, so outrageous and cynical that your breath is taken away. . . . We're seduced by the game of who's controlling whom . . . and by his amusingly quirky characters. . . . Ultimately, we are hooked by the story, which it is not much of an exaggeration to call the plot of plots."
—Christopher Lehmann-Haupt, *The New York Times*

"*The Debriefing* is beautifully plotted . . . with a clever, ironic twist at the end. . . . Littell's craftsmanship shines through."
—*Chicago Tribune*

"A fast-paced satire . . . [*The Visiting Professor*] is by turns bawdy, cerebral, and touching."
—*Publishers Weekly*

ABOUT THE AUTHOR

Connoisseurs of the literary spy thriller have elevated Robert Littell to the genre's highest ranks along with John le Carré, Len Deighton, and Graham Greene. Littell's novels include the *New York Times* bestseller *The Company* (rights sold in eleven countries, film rights sold to Columbia Pictures), *The Defection of A.J. Lewinter, The Once and Future Spy, The Amateur, The Sisters, The October Circle, The Revolutionist, An Agent in Place, Mother Russia,* and *The Visiting Professor.* His novels have been published in eleven languages. A former *Newsweek* journalist, Littell is an American currently living in France.

THE VISITING PROFESSOR

A NOVEL

ROBERT LITTELL

PENGUIN BOOKS

PENGUIN BOOKS
Published by the Penguin Group
Penguin Group (USA) Inc., 375 Hudson Street, New York, New York 10014, U.S.A.
Penguin Group (Canada), 90 Eglinton Avenue East, Suite 700, Toronto,
Ontario, Canada M4P 2Y3 (a division of Pearson Penguin Canada Inc.)
Penguin Books Ltd, 80 Strand, London WC2R 0RL, England
Penguin Ireland, 25 St Stephen's Green, Dublin 2, Ireland (a division of Penguin Books Ltd)
Penguin Group (Australia), 250 Camberwell Road, Camberwell,
Victoria 3124, Australia (a division of Pearson Australia Group Pty Ltd)
Penguin Books India Pvt Ltd, 11 Community Centre,
Panchsheel Park, New Delhi – 110 017, India
Penguin Group (NZ), 67 Apollo Drive, Rosedale, North Shore 0632,
New Zealand (a division of Pearson New Zealand Ltd)
Penguin Books (South Africa) (Pty) Ltd, 24 Sturdee Avenue,
Rosebank, Johannesburg 2196, South Africa

Penguin Books Ltd, Registered Offices:
80 Strand, London WC2R 0RL, England

First published in the United States of America by Random House, Inc. 1994
Published by The Overlook Press, Peter Mayer Publishers, Inc. 2006
Reprinted by arrangement with The Overlook Press, Peter Mayer Publishers, Inc.
Published in Penguin Books 2009

10 9 8 7 6 5 4 3 2 1

PUBLISHER'S NOTE
This is a work of fiction. Names, characters, places, and incidents are either the product
of the author's imagination or are used fictitiously, and any resemblance to actual persons,
living or dead, business establishments, events, or locales is entirely coincidental.

THE LIBRARY OF CONGRESS HAS CATALOGED THE
RANDOM HOUSE EDITION AS FOLLOWS:
Littell, Robert.
The visiting professor / Robert Littell.
p.   cm.
ISBN 1-58567-816-3 (hc.)
ISBN 978-0-14-311553-3 (pbk.)
I. Title.
PS3572.I782V57   1994   813'.54—dc20   93-26109

Printed in the United States of America

FOR HENRI BERESTYCKI
IN MEMORY OF SUZANNE, HIS SISTER

So where is the visitin' professor visitin' from, huh?
And when he gets his act together, what is his act?
—Word Perkins

Order. Routine. Chaos. Joie de vivre.

—M. Ravel

Hey, I like your music. C major, wow! Rock 'n' roll.
—The Tender To

Contents

Part One

TENDER TO

Chapter One

Lemuel Falk, a Russian theoretical chaoticist on the lam from terrestrial chaos,
threads thick, callused fingers through a tangle of ash-dirty hair that
manages to look wind-whipped even in the absence of wind. He leans
his brow against an icy pane as the train spills through the marshaling
yard toward the terminal; departures he can cope with but arrivals
give him indigestion, migraines, shooting pains in his solar plexus. An
implausible fiction stirs in his brain: he is the Great Headmaster, circa
1917. Long shot of a train creeping into the Finland Station. Tight on
the paramount *Homo sovieticus*, seen through a rain-stained window,
worrying himself sick he will be lynched or, worse, ignored. Vladimir
Ilyich's edginess infects Lemuel. His headache presses against the back
of Lemuel's eyeballs; his cramps pinch Lemuel's intestines.

The fiction ebbs as Lemuel's train docks at the quay. Shabby bill-
boards advertising budget rental cars, mint-fresh toothpaste, a local
MSG-free Chinese restaurant, graffiti denouncing plans to establish a
nuclear waste dump in the county, piles of freight stenciled THIS SIDE
UP drift past the window. In any given country, who gets to decide
which side is up? Lemuel wonders. Under foot, there is a hiss of hy-
draulics, a shriek of wheels. The train shudders to a stop. On the overhead rack, an enormous cardboard valise teeters. Lemuel, with

improbable agility, reaches it in time and wrestles it to the floor. Outside the window, a figure Lemuel instantly identifies as a *Homo antisovieticus* is stamping his feet to ward off frostbite. Immediately behind him, two men and two women breathe great clouds of vapor into the night as they eye the passengers descending from the train.

Lemuel recognizes a reception committee, as opposed to a lynching party, when he sees one. Heartened, he raises a paw and salutes them through the rain-stained window. A woman wearing fox cries, "That has got to be he," and holds aloft a cellophane-wrapped beacon to guide him to the Promised Land. Shrugging a worn strap of his old Red Army knapsack onto a shoulder, clutching the cardboard valise in one hand, a duty-free shopping bag in the other, Lemuel lurches up the aisle to the vestibule, spots the reception committee milling on the platform in a brackish pool of light cast by a naked overhead electric bulb. Struggling with his luggage, he backs down the steel steps, turns to confront the reception committee.

The Director, tall, thin, abstemious, floating in a ski parka that makes him look lighter than air, peels off a sheepskin mitten, cracks several knuckles and offers a cold hand. "Welcome to America," he declares with manifest sincerity. "Welcome to upstate New York. Welcome to the Institute for Advanced Interdisciplinary Chaos-Related Studies." He tries to smile but his facial muscles, frostbitten, only get as far as a smirk. His lips, which appear to be blue, barely move as he pumps Lemuel's hand. "I am delighted the Commie bastards finally let you out."

"Out is where they let me," Lemuel agrees fervently.

"To tell the truth, I never thought I'd see you on this side of the Iron Curtain."

Lemuel mumbles something about how there is no Iron Curtain any more.

A gust of Arctic air brings tears to Lemuel's eyes. The woman wearing fox lunges forward and thrusts six cellophane-wrapped red roses under his nose. "Russians," she emotionally informs the others, misreading his tears, "wear their hearts on their sleeve."

Until he misplaced the book, Lemuel taught himself rudimentary English from a *Royal Canadian Air Force Exercise Manual.* At a loss to see how it is possible to wear a heart on a sleeve, he pushes the bouquet back to her. "I am allegoric," he explains. He is desperate to make a good impression, but he is not sure how to go about it. "I break out in tears in the presence of flowers or cold."

The woman wearing fox and the Director avoid each other's eyes. "Summers must be living hell for you," the Fox remarks in a language Lemuel takes to be Serbo-Croatian. "Winters too, come to think of it."

The Director serves up a formal introduction. "D. J. Starbuck," he informs Lemuel, "teaches Russian Lit 404, which is mostly but not all Tolstoy, at the university. She is here in her capacity as chairperson of the local Soviet-American Friendship Society."

Lemuel, bowing awkwardly over the Fox's hand, mumbles something about how there are no Soviets any more.

Impatience flares in D.J.'s eyes. "We are looking for a new name," she admits in her guttural Serbo-Croatian Russian.

The Director, whose name is J. Alfred Goodacre, waves forward the committee. A man wearing windowpane-thick eyeglasses, an astrophysicist studying cosmic arrhythmias, is introduced. "Sebastian Skarr, Lemuel Falk." Skarr angles his head and addresses his remarks to a distant galaxy with a mysteriously irregular pulsar throbbing in its core. "I was stunned by Falk's insights on entropy," he says, almost as if Lemuel were not there. "I was mesmerized by his description of the relentless slide of the universe toward disorder; toward chaos."

An older man stumbles forward, removes a fore-aft astrakhan, exposing a scalp covered with a crewcut gray fuzz. "I'm Sharlie Atwater," he announces, slurring consonants so that Lemuel has trouble following what he says. "When I'm sober, whish is weekdays before noon, I do surface tension of water dripping from faucets. Your paper on the relationship between deterministic chaosh and what you call fool's randomnesh took my breath away."

A handsome middle-aged woman speaks up in a clipped English accent. "Matilda Birtwhistle," she introduces herself. "I cultivate chaos-related snowflakes in the Institute's antediluvian laboratory. We followed your exploit with pi—calculating it out to three billion, three hundred and thirty million decimal places. Your formulation about how if pi were truly random it would seem at times to be ordered struck us all as incredibly elegant. None of us had given much thought to the enigma of random order being a constituent of pure randomness." She flashes a thin smile. "The faculty are keen to have one of the Western world's preeminent randomnists join the staff."

Lemuel, roused, seizes Birtwhistle's hand and, bobbing, brushes his chapped lips against the back of her hand-knit Tibetan glove. The gesture is mean to convey old poverty as opposed to the newer, sweatier, more desperate poverty of the proletarian masses. Straightening, Lemuel coughs up a nervous rasp from his throat. Dealing with abstract ideas, he likes to think he can hold his own with an Einstein; he is less sure of himself and easily intimidated when it comes to dealing with people. On this occasion he ducks for cover behind memorized phrases: He begs them all to presume he is elated to have been named a visiting professor at the Institute, to believe he is eager to plunge into its chaos-related waters.

Searching the faces of his interlocutors, Lemuel slips into a delicious fiction: The Swedish embassy has turned out to inform him that he has been awarded the Nobel Prize for his pioneering work in pure randomness. Close in on the ambassador, wearing sheepskin mittens. Pan to a certified bank check for three hundred and eighty thousand United States of America greenbacks as he hands it to Lemuel. Negotiated on the Petersburg black market, that should bring roughly 380 million rubles. Set for life, set for the next one too, Lemuel sniffs at the cold; it burns his nostrils. The pain reminds him who he is and where he is. The members of the reception committee are staring at him as if they expect an encore. Traces of alarm appear in the corners of Lemuel's bloodshot eyes. His brows arch up, his nostrils flare as he departs from his prepared text, memorized during the interminable hours of the Petersburg–Shannon–New York flight. The voyage has exhausted him, he says. He desperately needs to urinate. Would it be imposing on their hospitality to ask for a cup of authentic American instant coffee?

Charlie Atwater, who has been holding his breath to extinguish hiccups, says, "How about shomething with a teeny-weeny bit more alcohol content?"

Muttering "Falk badly needs a hat or a haircut," the Fox pivots on the spiked heel of a galosh and stalks off in the direction of the station's coffee-vending machine. With a toss of his head, the Director invites Lemuel to follow her.

And follow her he does. With listless gratefulness, Lemuel permits himself to be sandwiched between the people who are proposing to deliver him from a fate worse than death: chaos!

The last thing Lemuel expected when he applied for an exit visa was to get one; the last thing he wanted was to leave Russia. It was an unpleasant matter of fact that the former Soviet Union was spiraling into chaos; shelves in stores were bare, people had taken to trapping cats and pigeons, to brewing carrot peelings because tea was too expensive, inflation was running to three-digit figures a year, the ex-Communists who claimed to be governing in Moscow were distributing money as fast as they could print it. Lemuel's salary at the V. A. Steklov Institute of Mathematics, where he had worked for the past twenty-three years, had tripled in the last four months. The price of a loaf of bread, when bread was available, had quadrupled. Pretty soon he would need a fifty-liter plastic garbage sack (impossible to find) to bring his ex-wife her monthly alimony. Still, the chaos had the advantage of being Lemuel's chaos. The English scriptwriter Shakespeare had put his finger on it: Better to bear the chaos we know than fly to another chaos we know not of. Or words to that effect.

This being the case, what prompted someone as viscerally cautious as Lemuel (he has always taken the position that two plus two *appears to be* four) to head for allegedly warmer climes and allegedly greener pastures?

He had applied for an exit visa every year since he began working as a randomnist. It was his way of taking random samplings of the political climate. Come September, he would fill in the appropriate forms in triplicate, stick on the appropriate government tax stamp and drop the application into the overflowing in basket of the appropriate time-server at the Foreign Ministry's visa section. Every year the application would come back with a bold red "Refused" stamped across its face, proving to Lemuel that the world he knew but did not necessarily love had the saving grace of being in order. For Lemuel, it seemed, had a working knowledge of state secrets. Because of this, he was not permitted to stray beyond the state's frontiers.

When, this year, a stamped, certified visa miraculously appeared in the communal mailbox, he panicked. He fitted his eyeglasses over his eyes and read it twice, removed his glasses and cleaned them with the tip of his tie, put them back on and read it a third time. If they were letting Lemuel Melorovich Falk—winner of the Lenin Prize for his work in the realm of pure randomness and theoretical chaos, member of the elite Academy of Sciences—slip through their usually sticky fingers, state secrets and all, it meant that chaos had infected the rotting core of the bureaucracy; it meant that things were worse than he had imagined.

Because they gave him permission to leave, he decided the time had come to go.

He had made the acquaintance of the Institute's director a dozen years before at a Prague symposium on the relatively new science of chaos. Invited to deliver a paper, Lemuel had dazzled the assembly with his work on pi, the Greek letter that represents the transcendental number arrived at by dividing the circumference of a circle by its diameter. In his quest for pure, unadulterated randomness, he had programmed an East German mainframe and calculated pi out to sixty-five million, three hundred and thirty-three thousand, seven hundred and forty-four decimal places (a world record at the time) without discovering any evidence of order in the decimal expansion of pi. The Director, impressed not only by the originality but the elegance of Lemuel's dissertation, had arranged for the paper to be published in the Institute's prestigious quarterly review. One article had led to another. Already eminent for discovering potentially pure randomness in the decimal expansion of pi, Lemuel, essentially a randomnist who dabbled in chaology, began patrolling what he called, tongue in cheek, Falk's Pale: the gray no-man's-land where randomness and chaos overlap. Every time someone put forward a candidate for pure, unadulterated randomness, he would subject it to the rigorous techniques of chaology, then advance proof that what looked like randomness was in fact determined albeit unpredictable, and therefore not pure randomness at all. Nature, according to Lemuel, generated complexities so vast, so unpredictable, that they appeared to the naked eye to be examples of pure randomness. But this "fool's randomness," so he argued in a paper that gilded his reputation in America, was nothing more than the name we gave to our ignorance. We did not know enough. Our instruments were not sensitive enough. Our sampling was not spread over a long enough period—something on the order of a million years. Once you burrowed under the surface—once you perfected the instruments with which you measured randomness, once you increased the period over which the measurements were taken—you discovered (to Lemuel's bitter disappointment) that what passed for pure randomness was not random at all, but a footprint of what physicists and mathematicians had taken to calling chaos.

For several years there had been a standing offer of a visiting professor's chair from the Institute for Advanced Interdisciplinary Chaos-

Related Studies; the Institute would be thrilled to have Lemuel patrol his Pale on its turf. The day Lemuel discovered the exit visa in his mailbox, he remembered the Institute's offer of a chair at the same moment he realized that he badly needed to sit. He had been on his feet for forty of his forty-six years, queuing for food, for toilet paper, for windshield wipers for his beloved Skoda, for permits to Black Sea spas, for mud baths at the spas, for the apartment he shared with two couples eternally on the brink of divorce, if not murder. He had joined queues simply because they were there, without knowing what was for sale until his turn came. He had queued to get married and queued to get divorced a decade later. Over the years his ankles had swelled. His heart, too.

With the exit visa tucked into his passport, Lemuel had slipped out of Russia without a word to his ex or his colleagues; without even telling his daughter, the common-law wife of a black marketeer who had cornered the market in computer mice. The only person he confided in was his occasional mistress, a bleached-silver journalist for *Petersburg Pravda* named Axinya Petrovna Volkova, who devoted Monday afternoons and Thursday evenings to conjuring erections from Lemuel's weary flesh. Axinya, a creature of routine who invariably spent half an hour putting Lemuel's room in order before allowing him to fumble with the zippers and clasps and buttons of her clothing, took the news of his impending departure badly.

"You are trading one chaos for another," she told him, "in the mistaken belief that someone else's chaos will turn out to be greener. Your pal Vadim told you American streets are paved with Sony Walkmans. Admit it, Lemuel Melorovich, in your head you know it's a fiction, but in your heart you think it may be true. In any case, the trip is bound to end badly—you have always been more fascinated by the going than the getting there."

When this argument failed to impress him, she trotted out the big guns. "People kill for tenure at Steklov. How can you abandon it like that?"

"Everyone in Russia has tenure," Lemuel observed crabbily. "The problem is they have tenure in Russia."

Ladies first, the visiting professor (still clutching his duty-free shopping bag) and the reception committee crowd into the Institute's minibus for the twelve-mile drive back to the village that is home to both the university and the Institute. Word Perkins, the Institute's factotum (he doubles as a chauffeur, night watchman, switchboard operator, plumber, electrician, carpenter, ice-salter and snow-shoveler), brings up the rear. "So what'cha got in here, huh, Professor?" he wants to know, struggling with Lemuel's enormous valise. "Bricks maybe?"

"Books maybe," Lemuel replies in a voice that conveys remorse.

Matilda Birtwhistle flashes a supportive smile. Lemuel grins back uncertainly.

Perkins, huffing, slides in behind the wheel, raises the earflaps on his mackinaw cap as if it is a preflight requirement, adjusts the hearing aid hooked over an ear, works the choke and guns the motor. Snow chains on all four tires set up a rattle that renders conversation difficult. "So where is the visitin' professor visitin' from, huh?" he calls over his shoulder. "And when he gets his act together, what is his act?"

The Director twists in his seat and blinks his eyes rapidly—his way of apologizing for the egalitarian nature of American society that permits chauffeurs a degree of impertinence. "He has come from St. Petersburg," he shouts to Perkins. "As for his act, he happens to be one of the world's preeminent randomnists."

"I can't promise I know what a predominant randomnist does for a livin', but if it's got anythin' at all to do whit snow, he's come to the right place, huh?" remarks Perkins. "What whit all this snow we got, we got us a randomnist's paradise. Hey, professor from Petersboig, in case yaw the athletic type, the village staw under Tender To rents out lightweight cross-country skis."

D.J. rolls her eyes to the tops of their sockets. Matilda Birtwhistle suffocates a smile in her Tibetan glove. Lemuel, mystified by the conversation—why would a randomnist need skis? And what or who is tender to?—stares morosely out a window. Now that he has finally gotten where he is going, he finds himself struggling against a persuasive postpartum depression. His first glimpse of America the Beautiful does not help. The minibus rattles down a wide, bleak main street paved with cracking volcanic tarmac, not Sony Walkmans, past mountains of plastic garbage sacks that look as if they have washed ashore on a tide. Long stalactites of ice trickle from lampposts and store signs and the giant clock over the revolving door of a bank at an intersection. The minibus, making its way between drifts of dirty snow, crosses a bridge with rusting girders, passes darkened, dead gas stations and supermarkets and cut-rate furniture stores and an all-brick drive-in savings-and-loan next door to a gray-washed wooden church with a movie marquee advertising CHRIST SAVES, without specifying what. Lemuel spots an illuminated billboard at the side of the road that makes him wonder whether he can get by with his Royal Canadian Air Force Exercise Manual English.

He leans forward and taps D.J. on the shoulder. "What does it mean, 'Nonstops to the most Florida cities'? How can one city be more Florida than another?"

"Hey, professor from Petersboig, take a gander at them trees," Perkins calls before D.J. can dredge up a Serbo-Croatian translation for the billboard's message. "They all been turned into weepers, huh? We just had us the woist ice storm since 1929—rained cats 'n' dawgs mosta yesterday, huh? Last night the temperature went an' plummeted on down to five."

"Five degrees Fahrenheit," Sebastian Skarr notes, "is the equivalent of minus fifteen degrees Celsius."

"Cats? Dogs?" Lemuel, bewildered, asks.

"That's an American idiot," Charlie Atwater explains. He hiccups sheepishly.

Up ahead, a pulsating light atop a vehicle sends tiny orange explosions skidding across the ice-lacquered pavement. The minibus catches up with a truck spewing sand over the highway. Squinting through his window into the night, Lemuel begins to make out the branches and power lines coated with ice and sagging under its weight. Slipping into a tantalizing fiction, he conjures up a night moth batting its wings somewhere in the vast wasteland of Siberia. The trivial turbulence created when its wings flail the air sets off tiny ripples that amplify with time and distance to produce the swirling tempest of ice paralyzing the east coast of America the Beautiful.

Another footprint of chaos!

D.J. points out the road sign planted at the spot where the countryside ends and the village begins. The sign, encased in ice, reads: "Backwater University—founded 1835." Underneath is a smaller sign: "Home of the Institute for Advanced Interdisciplinary Chaos-Related Studies." Moments later Perkins eases the bus to a stop in front of a green clapboard house with a wraparound porch set back from Main Street. A gust of icy air invades the bus as Perkins, his mackinaw buttoned to his jawbone, his earflaps down, opens the door and, gripping the rope handle of Lemuel's cardboard valise, picks his way along the sanded path toward the house.

The Director twists in his seat. "What with the cold et al., I think I'll pass up the chance to go in with you." Leaning toward Lemuel, he lowers his voice. "Who cuts your hair? You don't mind my asking?"

"I cut my hair. In a mirror."

The Director slips an envelope into a pocket of Lemuel's faded brown overcoat. "Some cash to tide you over until you deposit your first paycheck." He clears his throat. "Uh, you won't resent a suggestion?"

"If you please."

"There's a barbershop in town over the general store." He treats Lemuel to a conspiratorial wink. "It's open mornings until noon." The Director speaks again in a normal voice. "The professor you'll be sharing the house with is expecting you. Tomorrow there's a faculty luncheon in your honor, after which I'll show you your office and introduce you to your girl Friday."

"That's what we call a secretary," D.J. explains in her Serbo-Croatian.

Wondering who will take his letters Monday through Thursday, Lemuel makes his way up the aisle, mumbling his thanks, shaking hands right and left, thinking, as he approaches the door, that he is about to parachute from a plane into an icy abyss. He gives his khaki army-surplus scarf another turn around his neck, tightens the straps on his Red Army knapsack and steps into the void. Making his way up the footpath, he crosses Perkins duck-walking back to the bus. Perkins attempts to high-five Lemuel, but gets only a puzzled look for his trouble.

"Don't they high-five folks in Russia, huh, professor from Petersboig?" the chauffeur calls cheerily.

Lemuel pauses on the front porch to watch the minibus pull away from the curb. The red brake lights flicker and vanish around a corner. In the stillness, Lemuel raises his right hand over his head and stares up at his fingers.

High. Five. Ah! High-five.

The whetted air knifes through Lemuel's corduroy trousers, numbing his thighs. He turns and reaches for the corroded brass baseball, but the door flies open before he can rap the baseball against the corroded brass catcher's mit. A hand shoots out from a starched cuff. Powerful fingers grip Lemuel's khaki scarf and haul him inside. Lemuel gets a whiff of a vinegary deodorant, a glimpse of nicotine-stained teeth, a thick scraggly beard, coillike sideburns dancing in the air, bright Talmudic eyes bulging with carnal curiosity. The door slams closed behind him and Lemuel, pulled almost against his will into an outrageous fiction, decides he has come face to face with Yahweh.

On the short side—his head comes up to Lemuel's shoulder blades—but heftily built, Yahweh appears to be in his early thirties. He is decked out in scuffed black lace-up high shoes and a tieless white-on-white shirt buttoned up to a magnificent Adam's apple. Where the starched collar chafes his neck there is a ringworm of a welt that makes it look as if he is sporting a dog's collar. He has on baggy dull-black trousers, a rumpled vest, a loose-fitting jacket that droops open. Above a bulbous nose, black beetle brows sky-dive toward each other with delicious abandon. Defying gravity, an embroidered black skull-cap perches on the back of his large head. Eyeing his visitor through perfectly round silver-rimmed spectacles, murmuring *"Hekinah degul, hekinah degul,"* backpedaling across threadbare carpets as his guest advances, Yahweh lures Lemuel through the vestibule into the over-heated house.

"What language is *'Hekinah degul'*?" Lemuel asks.

"It is Lilliputian," Yahweh says. "Roughly translated, it means 'What in the Devil.' I have a theory the Lilliputians, metaphorically speaking, are maybe one of the lost tribes of Israel." He half circles Lemuel, sizing him up from one side, then the other. "It's me, your colleague and housemate," he finally says in a singsong rasp. His bony hand closes over Lemuel's gloved hand in an iron grip. "The bush, burning or otherwise, I do not beat around—it is not my shtick. In academic circles I am known as Rebbe Asher ben Nachman, the Gnostic chaoticist. In religious circles I am known as the Eastern Parkway Or Hachaim Hakadosh, the holy man from Eastern Parkway, which is in the heart of the heart of Brooklyn. To situate myself in the rabbinical spectrum, I am what Jews from the Venetian ghetto would have called a *traghetto*—a gondola plying the murky waters between the ultra-orthodox and the ultra-un-Orthodox. To situate myself in the historical spectrum, I am the last but not least in a long line of rabbis who trace their lineage back to the illustrious Moshe ben Nachman, alias Ramban, may he rest in peace, who met his Maker in Eretz Yisrael circa 1270." He nods approvingly. "You are trying not to smile at things which strike you as pompous. Your discretion is a tribute to the parents who raised you."

Dancing back a few steps, the Rebbe pulls an enormous handkerchief from the inside breast pocket of his jacket and opens it with a theatrical flourish; for an instant Lemuel is convinced his host is about to produce a white dove or another bouquet of roses. He is disappointed when Yahweh, deftly manipulating the handkerchief with one hand, noisily blows his long nose a nostril at a time.

"Coming from Russia," Yahweh says, his tone suddenly nasal, "you have probably not heard of me, believe me I am not insulted, but you have maybe heard of Brooklyn?" As he prattles on he inspects the handkerchief, looking for a bulletin on the state of his health. "Standing with your back to the Atlantic Ocean, sitting too, Brooklyn is immediately to the right of Manhattan."

Folding away the handkerchief, laughing at his little joke, the Rebbe dives for Lemuel's valise, hefts it as if it is filled with feathers and starts up the stairs. "Before I became a rebbe and a holy man, I worked as a longshoreman on the Brooklyn docks." He beckons Lemuel with a crooked finger. "Come. I keep a kosher house, I will not eat you. Upstairs is the apartment the Institute has put at your disposition." He flashes a shy, asymmetric grin, transforming his face into something closely resembling a cubist guitar. "When you have settled in and down," he tells his wary visitor, "I invite you for tea and sympathy."

Hefting his knapsack onto a shoulder, carrying his duty-free shopping bag, Lemuel trails after the Rebbe past waist-high leaning towers of books stacked, spine outward, against the walls. "Tea I take with a lump of sugar between my teeth," he remarks gloomily. "Sympathy I take with a grain of salt."

Rebbe Nachman turns to stare quizzically at his housemate. "That we can become friends is within the realm," he announces. "You have maybe heard of male bonding?"

Lemuel stops dead in his tracks. He remembers his mistress criticizing him for thinking someone else's chaos would be greener. Axinya turned out to be right about the Sony Walkmans. What did she know that he only suspected? "In Russia," Lemuel notes in a voice that attempts to convey unflinching heterosexuality, "that kind of thing is definitely against the law."

"In America," Rebbe Nachman declares zestfully, "male bonding is nothing more than a respectable way of hating women."

Peering through a magnifying glass, the Rebbe studies the fine print on the page of the newspaper spread out on the kitchen table. "Oy, IBM is down seven and a quarter. I should have maybe sold short months ago. General Dynamics is up four and a half. Is this the time to sell or should I maybe hang on? Explain me this, please, how am I going to set up a yeshiva if I don't make a killing?"

A tinny rendition of Ravel's Concerto for Left Hand comes from an old Motorola balanced on a stack of books. Sighing, the Rebbe goes back to shredding dried brown buds into a rectangle of cigarette paper. Observing him from across the table, Lemuel helps himself to another lump of sugar from the pewter bowl, peels away the paper advertising the restaurant it was stolen from and clamps the cube between his front teeth. Filtering herb tea through the sugar, he watches in fascination as the Rebbe's fingers knead the rectangle of paper into a perfect cylinder.

The Rebbe notices Lemuel noticing. "Before I was a longshoreman, I worked in a cigarillo factory in New Jersey." He flicks the spongy tip of his pink tongue along the edge of the paper and seals the cigarette. Frisking his pockets, he comes up with a book of matches, also filched from a restaurant. He strikes a match and holds the flame to the joint. When the tip is smoldering, he shakes out the match and takes a first tentative drag. Exhaling, he asks casually, "With a biblical name like Lemuel, which signifies, correct me if I'm mistaken, 'Devoted to God,' you are maybe Jewish?"

"My father's father, who was an ardent *Homo sovieticus,* called his son Melor, which stands for 'Marx, Engels, Lenin, organizers of revolution.' My father, who was a ardent *Homo antisovieticus,* claimed Lemuel stood for 'Lenin, Engels, Marx, undersexed exhibitionist lumpen-proletarians.' " Coughing up a snicker, Lemuel goes back to sipping tea through the sugar cube.

The Rebbe persists. "With a name like Falk, you are maybe circumcised?"

Worried that they are returning to the subject of male bonding, Lemuel offers an evasive grunt.

The Rebbe is not put off. Looking Lemuel in the eye, he demands,

"Do you believe in Torah? Do you fear Yahweh?" He articulates the sacred name of God, daring Him to strike him dead for the transgression of pronouncing it out loud.

"What I believe in," Lemuel mutters, in no mood to be drawn into a theological discussion, "is mathematics. What I love is pure randomness. What I fear, what I detest, is chaos, though on a theoretical level, I admit to being fascinated by the possibility of discovering a seed of order at the heart of chaos."

"So tell me this: If you do not believe in Yahweh and Torah, in what sense are you a Jew?"

"I never said I was a Jew." Lemuel shrugs. "I am a Jew in the sense that should I happen to forget, every twenty or thirty years the world will remind me."

The Rebbe takes a serious drag on the joint, holds the smoke in his lungs before breathing out. "If you are Jewish enough to be reminded of it that easily," he says with a shrewd glint in his eye, "how come you did not wind up in Eretz Yisrael?"

Lemuel grimaces. "For me, America, not Israel, is the Promised Land." He snorts under his breath. "I have a friend in Moscow who swore me the streets here were paved with Sony Walkmans."

"My father's grandfather, may he rest in peace, came over from Poland in 1882 thinking they were paved with Singer sewing machines." The Rebbe sucks smoke into his lungs. Holding his breath, he offers the joint to Lemuel.

Lemuel shakes his head. "I am allegoric to cigarettes."

The Rebbe exhales. "This is not a cigarette. Cigarettes I gave up for Chanukah, after smoking two packs a day for sixteen years. This is what they call a reefer. A joint. Dope. Marijuana. Mary Jane. The lady who supplies me calls it Thailand truffles."

Sniffing delicately at the smoke hovering like a rain cloud over the stock-market pages, Lemuel discovers that marijuana has a surprisingly pleasant odor. "No offense intended . . ."

"Ask, ask."

"I am curious what kind of a rabbi smokes dope."

"Ha! No offense taken. Fortunately for mankind, for womankind too, the happy few are always tempted, like Eve in what the Prophet Ezekiel called the Garden of God, by forbidden fruit. In the sense that Eve defied God in Eden, I smoke dope. It permits me to better know wrong and right." The Rebbe's eyes glaze over as he again offers the joint to Lemuel. " *'Ta'amu ure'u,'* " he mutters. "I'm talking Psalm 34:8. Roughly translated, it means 'Taste it and see.' "

Lemuel waves the cigarette away along with the smoke.

The Rebbe tugs at the top button of his shirt, loosening the collar, runs a finger between the collar and the welt on his neck, takes still another drag on the joint. "Oy, oy," he murmurs, his head rolling from side to side in agitation, "this Eden, this Garden of Yahweh, what is it but a swamp of randomness? How come Adam is molded from *adamah* or clay, and Eve from rib? Explain maybe why Adam and Eve can remain in the garden on condition they do not eat from one particular fruit tree? What in God's name does fruit have to do with good and evil? And what could have been going on in that head of His that Yahweh had to invent murder?"

"Yahweh invented murder?"

"The first recorded death in what we Jews call Torah and goys call the Old Testament comes when Yahweh slays an animal so Adam and Eve can hide their bodies. I'm talking Genesis 3:21. 'Unto Adam also and to his wife did the Lord God make coats of skins.' Come at the problem from another direction: What coded signal is God sending to the resident scholars and visiting professors at the Institute for Advanced Interdisciplinary Chaos-Related Studies when He identifies Himself to Moses at the burning bush?"

Lemuel, who sharpened his *Royal Canadian Air Force Exercise Manual* English on the King James Bible, Raymond Chandler and *Playboy,* remembers the standard King James translation for Yahweh's answer to Moses. "I am that I am."

"Ha! In Hebrew, 'Yahweh' is written 'yod-he-waw-he,' which is derived from the root letters for the verb 'to be.' What Yahweh tells Moses at the burning bush—*'ehyeh asher ehyeh,'* which is the future tense of the verb 'to be'—is a play on words based on His name." Nachman rambles on excitedly. "Yahweh should maybe be translated 'I will be that I will be.' I am personally reading this to mean 'I will be when and where I will be.' So who is this Yahweh who refuses to be pinned down to a specific time or a specific place? I will tell you who He is. He is the incarnation of randomness. And what is randomness—how did you put it in your paper on entropy?—what is randomness but a footprint of chaos? What does it tell us about the Lord God that He created a universe governed by the laws of chaos and peopled it with us?"

The Rebbe uncrosses and recrosses his legs. Lemuel catches a glimpse of pale, hairless skin glistening above his lace-up high shoes. "Ha! After the destruction of the Second Temple, Rebbe Judah ha-Nasi, may he rest in peace, is said to have asked, 'If God really loved man, would He have created him?' " Pulling at his beard, the Rebbe rocks back and forth in a kind of delirium. "It is not only a good question, it is maybe the only question." Wincing, he brings his hands up to his temples. "Oy, in the words of the illustrious Rebbe Akiba, my head is spinning from all these questions without answers."

"Your head is spinning from all the marijuana." Lemuel leans forward. "Are you all right?"

"I am not all right, but I will be all right. You maybe know the Jewish proverb: If you want to forget questions without answers, put on a shoe that is too tight." The Rebbe's bulging eyes flick open and focus intently on Lemuel. "Do not make the mistake of thinking you can tell a rebbe by his cover any more than you can a book." He melts back into his chair. His lids drift closed. When he speaks again, his singsong voice is barely audible. "You maybe know the story—the famous Vorker Rebbe, may he rest in peace, said you could distinguish an exalted person by three things." Rebbe Nachman thrusts a fist into the air and raises a finger for each item. "One: He weeps without making a sound. Two: He dances without moving. Three: He bows down with his head held high."

The Rebbe's fist drops back onto the table, his head nods forward onto his chest, the joint slips out of his fingers. Lemuel scoops it up from the stock-market pages, passes it under his nose as if it were a Cuban cigar. He is tempted to follow the Rebbe's example, to come at the world of chaos from another direction. In the end he decides he has had his ration of chaos for one day and stubs out the joint in an ashtray that bears the name of the hotel it was stolen from.

Removing his shoes, glancing over his shoulder at the Gnostic chaoticist snoring fitfully in his chair, Lemuel pads softly out of the room.

Like every insomniac, I have learned to use the night. When St. Petersburg was still Leningrad, I would pace my room into the early hours of the morning, contemplating the whiteness of the night, scribbling differential equations on the backs of envelopes, squaring circles, following elusive threads of randomness to their chaotic origins on the off chance of stumbling across a single example, one would be enough for a lifetime, of pure, unadulterated randomness.

I did some of my more imaginative thinking in man-made near-randomness during these insomniac patrols, discovering, to give you a for instance, the idea of programming a computer to dip almost randomly into the infinite chain of pi decimal places in order to create a three-number key which, in turn, generated ciphers that came remarkably close to being random and thus, for all practical purposes, unbreakable. But this is not something I want to go into in any detail right now.

All this is by way of saying there was nothing extraordinary in the way I spent my first night in Backwater. Inspecting my American living room furnished in what I took to be Mexican modern, there was a great deal of straw, I tipped a wicker rocking chair forward and observed it swinging back and forth. It reminded me of several applications of the mechanics of the pendulum I had worked on years before; it reminded me also of my mistress leaning over my body, her sagging breasts swinging like pendulums as she coaxed erections from my reluctant flesh. Suddenly memories of Petersburg I had been hoping against hope to leave behind invaded my brain cells: Faceless men were spilling out of doors and windows; thick-soled, steel-toed shoes were kicking at figures on the ground; a little boy I did not recognize was cringing in a corner. Oy!

Proust, Marcel, somewhere said the only paradise is paradise lost. Or words to that effect. Petersburg, lost, still did not seem like a paradise to me. Nor, for that matter, did Backwater, found. Which left me, like the Rebbe plying between two shores in his *traghetto*, en route . . .

Now that I think of it, it is probably true what my mistress said me about my being more interested in the going than the getting there. Arrivals give me migraines. If only someone would invent a journey without an end.

Feeling out of place, out of time, out of sync, I prowled the apartment over the Rebbe's head, stepping off the distance from wall to wall, from window to door, from bookcase to fireplace, from one end of the corridor to the other, from toilet to tub, calculating square meters, almost swooning when I came up with 120, which was twice the size of the apartment I had shared with two other couples in Petersburg. I explored closets and nooks and the crawl space under the staircase leading to the attic, all the while flicking switches—I turned on the toaster, the microwave oven, the dishwashing machine, the electric knife sharpener, the electric can opener, the Toshiba T3200SX computer. On a bookshelf I came across a Sony hi-fi that would have cost me a year's salary on the Petersburg black market. I pushed buttons, I twirled knobs. A radio came on. What turned out to be a local early-morning call-in show was under way, with a host who talked so rapidly I had to shut my eyes to follow what he was saying.

If I understood the situation correctly, the host was in the process of interrupting the program for the hourly news bulletin. I remember some of what he said. A clerk transcribing the number of the winner of the South Dakota lottery had made a typing error, a seventy-seven-year-old man was informed he had won twelve million dollars. The next day, when the error was discovered, he died of a heart attack. On the local front, residents protesting against the construction of a radioactive-waste dump in the county were assured by a state commission that the dump site posed no health hazard. Federal law required every state to have a place to store radioactive waste from nuclear power plants, hospitals and industry by 1993. Residents opposing the dump site claim that radioactive waste would seep into underground rivers, eventually polluting the county's water supply. And this item just in from the tri-county newsroom: State police today discovered the body of the latest victim of the serial killer who has been stalking the tri-county highways and byways. The most recent victim, a thirty-seven-year-old septic-tank cleaner, brings to twelve the number of people mysteriously murdered in the last sixteen weeks. A police spokesperson stressed there was no pattern to the crimes; the age and occupation of the victims, the sites of the murders, the intervals between the crimes were never the same. The only thing connecting this grisly series of killings, aside from the .38 caliber dumdum bullet rubbed with garlic and fired at point-blank range through the victim's ear into his or her brain, was the signature of the killer—

which is to say, the lack of a signature, the utter randomness of the murders. "And now," the host rasped into the
microphone, "we'll take some more calls." He repeated a
telephone number several times.

Without thinking I snatched the cordless telephone off
the hook and punched in the number. I could hear a
phone on the other end buzz. A recorded announcement
informed me I was seventh on a waiting list. You must understand that for someone who has spent half his life
queuing in Russia, being seventh in line is as good as being
next. After a while the recorded announcement informed
me I was second, then first. A moment later the voice of
the host came over the phone and the radio at the same
instant.

"Hallo."

"Yes. Hello," I shouted into the phone. A staticky voice
that sounded vaguely familiar echoed back at me from the
hi-fi speakers. "Yes. Hello," it said.

"I just now arrived in America," I shouted into the telephone.

"I just now arrived in America," I heard myself shout over
the speakers.

"Turn down your radio. That's better. What's your handle?"

"Handle?" "Handle?"

"What's your name?"

"Yes. Falk, Lemuel." "Yes. Falk, Lemuel."

"Which of the two is a first name, Falk or Lemuel?"

"Lemuel." "Lemuel."

"Well, now, Lemuel, welcome to the U.S. of A. So, uh,
where did you say you hailed from?"

"I am not for sure." "I am not for sure."

"What you are is not for real. Ha ha! Only kidding.
How's that, you're not sure?"

"I was born in Leningrad . . ." "I was born in Leningrad,
but I came here from St. Petersburg. Physically the two occupy the same space. Emotionally they are light-years
apart."

"St. Petersburg, that's, uh, in Russia, right? So what
brings you to America, Lemuel?"

"Chaos brings me to . . ." "Chaos brings me to America."

"Are you running away from it or toward it? Ha ha ha ha!"

"Both. I thought your chaos ..." "Both. I thought your chaos was greener. Dumb as it sounds, I thought your streets were paved with Sony Walkmans."

"Well, Lemuel, you are one funny son of a gun. What are you doing, trying out a comic routine on me? Or have you had one too many for the road? Only kidding. So tell me something, Lemuel, as someone fresh off the boat, so to speak, what hits you as the biggest difference between America and Russia?"

"First, your towns, the distances ..." "First, your towns, the distances between them, even your citizens are smaller than in Russia, though maybe they only seem smaller because I expected larger than life. Second, your apartments do not smell of kerosene."

"Mine smells of cat litter. Ha ha! If you're listening, I was only joking, Charlene, honey. Okay, so Lemuel, what'cha wanna get off your chest?"

"Off my chest?" "Off my chest?"

"Why didja call in for? What'cha wanna talk about?"

"I want to talk about ..." "I want to talk about the serial murders. I want to say you this—the crimes may look random, but this seeming randomness is nothing more than the name we give to our ignorance."

"If I read you right, you're saying there's a pattern behind the murders the police aren't aware of."

"There is a pattern ..." "There is a pattern waiting to be discovered. Randomness, pure, unfortunately does not exist. At least nobody has been able to come up with an example. I should know. I have been looking everywhere—"

"Well, I'm afraid I'm in over my head when it comes to anything pure. Ha ha ha ha. But we'll be sure and pass your tip on to Chester Combes, the county sheriff. Listen, Lemuel, we're counting on you to keep an eye peeled for this pure randomness—it's got to be out there somewhere, lurking in the bushes, hiding in the shadows of an alleyway. Nice talking to you, Lemuel. Enjoy your, eh, stay in America. I'll take another call ..."

I sensed he was about to hang up. "I need answers to questions," I shouted into the phone. "I figured out the high five. You explained me *handle*, you explained me *get-*

ting off your chest. But how is it possible to wear a heart on
a sleeve? What does it really mean, Nonstops to the most
Florida cities? How can one city be more Florida than another? My *Royal Canadian Air Force Exercise Manual,* King
James, Raymond Chandler, *Playboy* never used such an expression. Concerning which side is up, who gets to decide
that in America? I have a last but not least, here it is—what
or who is *tender to?*"

It dawned on me my voice was no longer echoing from
the hi-fi speakers. Then I noticed the phone had gone dead
in my ear. On the radio, the host was saying, "If you've just
joined us, you're listening to WHIM Elmira, the station
where talk is cheap and sex is the number-one topic of conversation. Hallo." He began chatting with a lady barber
about something called the G-spot.

Feeling frustrated, unable to get a grip on this America,
I hung up the phone and turned off the radio and switched
off the overhead light and the desk lamp and wandered
over to stare through a pair of French doors opening onto
an ice-covered sun deck built over a garage. Outside, a brittle stillness had settled over the piece of America the Beautiful I could see. Above the sun deck, the branches of a
gnarled oak creaked like a ship's rigging under the weight
of the ice. Contemplating the winter wonderland, the part
of me that is theoretical chaoticist started fashioning questions. Should one take the accumulation of ice on
branches, like the serial murders, as yet another footprint
of chaos? If the weight of the ice caused a branch to snap
off, should one interpret this pruning of dead wood as a
random event or an act of God? Is there such a thing as
God? Was Eden, as the Rebbe claimed, really a swamp of
randomness? If so, was the randomness pure and unadulterated? Or was it garden-variety fool's randomness, and
thus nothing more than a footprint of the order we call
chaos?

Assuming both God and pure randomness exist, what is
the relationship between the two?

If God created man, should this be taken as evidence that
He loathed man? Or was Creation simply a random event
that went unnoticed by everyone except man?

Oy—I heard the Rebbe's voice in my brain—my head too
was spinning from all these questions without answers.

Feeling drained for the first time since my arrival in America, I turned away from the French doors and made my way to the bedroom at the back of the apartment. Kicking off my shoes, sliding fully dressed under the sheets, I quickly sank into a fitful sleep. I dreamed the usual dreams: thick-soled, steel-toed shoes kicked at figures on the ground; faceless men began to dismantle a piece of furniture; a little boy I did not know cringed in a corner, barely able to breathe. . . .

What seemed like minutes later, with the first rays of first light flecking the walls of the room, I was roused by the sound of a car pulling slowly into the driveway. A door slammed shut. There were footsteps below in the Rebbe's apartment, then muffled voices, then for a long while absolute silence, then a hoarse cry that broke off abruptly, followed by someone moaning "Oy, oy, oy." Moments later a toilet somewhere downstairs flushed.

Intrigued, I padded over to the window in my stocking feet in time to see a woman wearing fox climb back into a car. She started the motor, let it idle until the engine was turning smoothly, then pulled slowly out of the driveway.

Smiling to myself, I leaped to a conclusion: marijuana was not the only forbidden fruit the Gnostic chaoticist had an appetite for. Again I heard the Rebbe's voice in my head. " *Ta'amu ure'u,* ' " it said. " 'Taste it and see.' "

Chapter Two.

Freshly shaven (though not well shaven), a patch of toilet paper clinging to a coagulated cut on his chin, reeking from a few dabs of duty-free after-shave, Lemuel drifts at midmorning down South Main Street, past emergency crews repairing overhead telephone wires, past teenagers chipping away at the ice on the sidewalk, into the village of Backwater, population (not counting students) 1,290. With each breath the cold dry air stings his nostrils, bringing tears to his eyes. He glances furtively at one sleeve, then the other, looking for evidence of a Russian heart, is vaguely disheartened when all he sees is frayed sleeve.

Dozens of young people Lemuel takes for students scramble up narrow paths toward the campus, which clings to the side of the long hill that dominates the village. Colorful scarves trailing behind them, they move with that distinctive rolling duck walk he first saw when Word Perkins tried to high-five him the night before. Lemuel is struck by the fact that the students appear to want to get where they are going. He decides that Americans may walk strangely but, unlike their Russian counterparts, they are not put off by journeys that end in arrivals.

Continuing on, Lemuel passes a post office, a drugstore, a pool hall, a bookstore. The buildings strike him as being on the puny side, groundscrapers where he expected sky. He scales a frozen snowdrift and picks his way across the sanded street. On the far corner he stops to inspect a low-roofed hangar with a gaudy neon sign that reads "E-Z Mart" suspended from a gallowslike structure planted in the frozen lawn. Lemuel remembers hearing rumors about hangars with interminable aisles. His son-in-law claimed to have gotten lost for several hours in such a hangar in a suburb of West Berlin, a story Lemuel took, at the time of its telling, as metaphor.

Clutching his briefcase under one arm, Lemuel shoulders through the swinging door and catches sight of endless aisles. The heart he does not wear on his sleeve misses a beat, then accelerates. He is startled by a burst of hot air from a grill built into the floor. Flinging himself through the wall of heat, pushing through a turnstile, he sets off down an avenue of an aisle. Both sides, as far as the eye can see, are lined with shelves—and the shelves, without exception, are crammed with things to eat!

If only the Great Headmaster could see this. Lenin always claimed that quantity could be transformed into quality, and here, in the aisles of a food store, was the living proof.

Inspecting cans of corned beef and creamed corn and baked beans, Lemuel discovers that his fingertips have grown numb. Examining jars of low-calorie peanut butter and plastic containers of Hershey's chocolate syrup and vats of Vermont maple syrup, he feels his knees begin to buckle. Suffering from what he suspects may be a terminal case of vertigo, he clings to a shelf, inhales and exhales deeply several times, brings a hand to his face, is relieved to find that his nose is cold and wet. Or (a sudden doubt) is that a sign of health only for dogs? Disoriented, he plunges on, fingering cellophane packages filled with spaghetti of every imaginable size and shape and color. His lips sounding out the letters, he reads the labels on jars of spaghetti sauce with or without meat, with or without mushrooms, with or without calories, with or without artificial coloring. It hits him that there are people in this miracle of a country who spend time and money *coloring* spaghetti sauce red.

At the vegetable counter he fights back tears as he runs his fingers over a crisp iceberg lettuce. He starts to caress a cucumber, but drops it back into the bin when a stout lady with a mustache, pushing a shopping cart heaped with detergents, clucks her tongue at him. At the fruit counter Lemuel completely loses control of his emotions. Seizing a lemon—he has not laid his bloodshot eyes on a lemon in more than two years—he brings it to his nose and sucks in a long, drunken draught of its perfume.

Dazed, dazzled, blundering from side to side, Lemuel turns a corner so abruptly he almost collides with a dirty blond ponytail. He notices the young woman attached to the ponytail slip a tin of fancy sardines over her shoulder into the hood of her duffle coat.

"What are you doing?" he blurts out.

The girl, wearing tight faded blue jeans and ankle-length lace-up boots under the duffle coat, turns on him. "Yo! I'm scoring sardines," she announces innocently. She bats enormous seaweed-green eyes as if she is having difficulty bringing him into focus. "What are you scoring?"

Lemuel has the eerie feeling he has looked into these eyes before. . . . Nonplussed, he thrusts out his empty hands, palms up. "I am not scoring nothing. I am not even playing."

The girl flashes a deliberate smile, half defiant, half defensive; freckles dance on her face. "Hey, don't be a doorknob. Score something. Everyone knows supermarkets pad their prices to make up for shoplifting. Which means someone's got to shoplift to keep the supermarkets honest, right? To make sure they don't profit by people *not* shoplifting."

"I can say you I have never looked at it that way."

The girl hikes a shoulder. "Hey, now you know it like a poet." Smiling dreamily, she wanders off down the aisle, inspecting labels, casually stealing the cans that appeal to her.

Lemuel meanders on to the beer area, where he is overwhelmed by the choice. Confronted by cans and bottles and six-packs and twelve-packs and cases of every imaginable size and shape and color, he rolls his head in bewilderment. A young man with a three-day blond beard, long hair tied back with a colorful ribbon, granny glasses, and a small silver ring dangling from one earlobe, struggles past pulling a dolly loaded with cases of alcohol-free beer. A tag pinned to his flannel shirt identifies him as "The Manager" and "Dwayne."

"If you don't see what you're looking for," Dwayne says, "ask."

Lemuel works up his courage. "Do you by any chance sell kvass?"

The manager scratches at his beard. "Is that a brand name or a generic?" When Lemuel looks back blankly, he asks, "What exactly is kvass?"

"It is a kind of beer brewed from bread."

"If someone out there's smart enough to make beer out of bread," Dwayne declares with an engaging laugh, "we sure as heck want to market it. In case the word hasn't reached you, at the E-Z Mart the customer is king." He produces a pad and a stub of a pencil. "How are you spelling kvass?" he wants to know, licking the point of the pencil, staring at Lemuel expectantly.

"I am spelling kvass K, V, A, double S."

Dwayne looks up from his pad and peers at Lemuel through his granny glasses. "You speak with some kind of an accent."

"You think so?"

"Yeah, babe, I think so. An accent's nothing to be embarrassed about. America is a melting pot of accents. Where is it you're from?"

"St. Petersburg, Russia."

Dwayne brightens. "That's cool. When I was working toward a master's in business administration at Harvard, I did my thesis on the disadvantages of central planning on a non-market-oriented economy. It had a catchy title—'Trickle-Down Incompetence.' "

"With a master's in business administration from Harvard, what are you doing running a supermarket in Backwater?"

Dwayne pulls a pack of Life Savers from the pocket of his shirt, offers one to Lemuel, takes one himself when he shakes his head. "I did the Wall Street bit for a while," Dwayne says, "analyzing the infrastructure of companies for a *Fortune* 500 brokerage house, making big bucks, washing my hands in corporate bathrooms where they got real towels, living in a condo on Third Avenue, the whole Manhattan scene. Then Shirley, she's the cashier with the naturally wavy hair, Shirley and me, we decided we'd rather be ordinary fishes in a small unpolluted pond than minnows in a sewer. So here we are"—Dwayne makes swimming motions with his arms—"swimming away." He stuffs the pad back in his jeans, sticks out a paw. "I'm Dwayne to my friends."

Lemuel shakes his hand. "I am Falk, Lemuel, to everyone."

"So it's been nice talking to you, Lem, babe. See you around the pond, huh?"

Back in the street, Lemuel experiences something akin to rapture of the deep—he feels like a skin diver who has surfaced from giddy depths. A melody he does not recognize fills his head. It takes a minute or two before he discovers, to his relief, that it comes from the steel carillon tower on the wood line of the hill. Further down Main

Street, he ducks into a Kampus Kave with something called "A Money No Object Pizza" advertised in the window, hikes himself onto a stool, orders coffee from the woman reading a comic book behind the counter.

She looks up. "With or without?"

Afraid of appearing ignorant, Lemuel replies, "If you please, one of each."

The woman snickers. "Now there's one I ain't heard before."

Warmed by the coffees, one with, one without, Lemuel asks directions to the general store. He winds his khaki scarf around his neck and sets out. Passing a modern, one-story glass-and-brick building, he spots an electric billboard flashing the hour and the temperature and something called "Today's Money Market Rates." He notices a line snaking out from the building's vestibule. Without giving the matter a second thought, he joins it.

"If you please, what are they selling?" he asks the girl in front of him.

Her jaw stops working on a stick of gum as she uncorks an earphone from an ear. "Huh? Sorry?"

"Could you say me what is for sale." Lemuel gestures toward the vestibule with his chin. "With such a line, it is undoubtedly something imported." He rummages in his pockets for the small notebook that he always carried in Russia, opens it to the page containing his mistress's measurements—brassiere size, glove size, shoe size, pantyhose size, hat size, shirt size, inseam, height, weight, her favorite color (crossed out, with a note in Axinya's handwriting next to it saying "Any color will do").

The list arouses in Lemuel an aching nostalgia for the familiar chaos of Petersburg.

"The line's for the ATM," the girl explains in a whiny voice. Plugging the earphone back in her ear, she executes a little shuffle with her feet, almost as if she is dancing to a snatch of music.

Lemuel turns to a young man who has joined the line behind him. "If you please, what is an ATM?"

"Automatic Teller Machine." He notices the bewilderment in Lemuel's eyes. "It distributes bread, as in money?"

Lemuel assembles the pieces of the puzzle. The phrase "Money Market" on the electric billboard, an ATM that distributes bread as in money, the twenty or so people queuing patiently despite the minus ten degrees Celsius. What could be more logical? In Russia you queue for bread, in America the Beautiful you queue for another kind of bread. The streets may not be paved with Sony Walkmans in this Promised Land he has come to, but it is nevertheless a country full of wonders.

Lemuel turns back to the young man to confirm his suspicions. "When my turn comes, *bread*"—he winks to show that he has caught on to the code—"will be distributed to me?"

"You have to have plastic." The boy holds up a credit card for Lemuel to inspect.

"You need plastic to get bread?"

"Yeah. That's the deal."

"Where can I acquire plastic?"

"Inside. But the bank only gives plastic to people with bank accounts."

Lemuel eyes the building. "This does not look like a bank."

"It looks like what?"

"It reminds me of a dacha I once saw in the Crimea."

"What's a dacha?"

"A dacha is where the nomenklatura spend their weekends."

"What's a nomen-whatsis?"

"In Russia, they are the ones who decide which side is up. If I can offer you a word of advice, young man, in any given country, the single most important thing you need to know is who decides which side is up."

Lemuel startles the young man with an awkward high-five, then slips away from the line to continue exploring the Promised Land.

Lemuel's *Royal Canadian Air Force Exercise Manual* vocabulary is growing by leaps and bounds; he knows expressions Raymond Chandler, may he rest in peace, would have to look up if he were alive. High-five. Handle. Money market. Bread. Plastic. Ah, he must not forget the chest off of which you get things. Not to mention doorknob, which is clearly something you do not want to be. Pushing through a door into the Village Store, which takes up the ground floor of a worn, gray, peeling, century-old two-story clapboard building on the corner of Main and Sycamore, Lemuel walks up to the counter. "I am looking for the barbershop," he tells the teenage clerk, who is trying to pry open the drawer of an old-fashioned cash register with a screw-driver.

The clerk jerks his head in the direction of the back of the store. Lemuel makes his way between racks of ski jackets and cross-country skis and track suits to a rickety wooden staircase. A large hand with its middle finger rudely extended in the direction of the second floor is painted on the barn-side planks of the wall next to the staircase.

The steps creak under Lemuel's weight as he starts up. The silvery snip-snip-snip of scissors comes from behind the curtain that has been nailed up in place of a door at the top of the stairs. Pushing through the curtain, Lemuel finds himself in the barbershop.

The young woman who was stealing sardines in the avenue of the E-Z Mart aisle is ducking and weaving around a young man sitting in an old-fashioned chrome-and-red-leather swivel chair. Her ponytail flailing, she leaps back to survey her work, then bounds forward and attacks the hair over an ear. Snip-snip-snip-snip. Behind her, beams of speckled sunlight knife through a large plate-glass window with faded letters arched across it. Lemuel sounds out the words, reading from left to right. OT REDNET. It dawns on him that the letters form words, and the words are meant to be read from the outside, his right to left.

" 'Tender . . .' Ah!" he mutters. "So this is a Tender To."

The woman cutting hair nods toward the straight-backed chairs lined up against one wall. If she recognizes Lemuel from the E-Z Mart, she doesn't let on. "With you in a min," she murmurs. Turning back to her client, she plants herself behind the chair and studies him in the mirror. "Yo, Warren? You look almost but not quite beautimous."

"My sideburns suck."

"You want a second opinion, they make you look sort of . . . Rhett Butlerish."

"You think so?"

"Hey, you know my motto—'My haircuts grow on you.' "

Lemuel jams his scarf into the armpit of his faded brown overcoat, folds it and his jacket over the back of a chair and settles into a seat next to a low table piled high with copies of *Playboy*. He picks up one that has been read so often its pages have the texture of cloth. Glancing at the barber to make sure he is not being observed, he leafs through it to the center spread. When Petersburg was still Leningrad, he had browsed through a copy of *Playboy* in a streetcorner flea market. It had been selling for what amounted to a week's wages, which had not prevented him from purchasing it in order to improve his English. He thought then, he thinks now, that the stark naked ladies smiling out from the magazine's pages, their pubic patches neatly trimmed into goatees, the nipples on their flawless breasts aimed like artillery at the reader, look about as erotic as frozen fish. The nudity, in his view, is only skin-deep.

Across the room the sardine thief crouches in front of her client and, using the point of her scissors, delicately snips away the hair protruding from his nostrils. That done, she dusts talc across the back of his neck with a soft brush, then whips off the blue-and-white-striped sheet and shakes it out on the floor, which is covered with a thin layer of hair that swirls around her feet as she moves.

"Yo," she summons Lemuel.

The student hands a bill to the lady barber. "Keep the loose change, Rain. Are you signed on for the Delta Delta Phi bash tonight? I hear they've booked some good flicks for the occasion."

"Maybe."

"What does 'maybe' mean?"

Suddenly defensive, she says, " 'Maybe' means maybe not."

Lemuel hefts himself into the barber chair.

"Like you must be new in town, right?" the lady barber comments. "So did you take my advice and score something to keep the supermarket honest?"

Lemuel has been hoping she would recognize him. Flustered, he answers, "I tried to score kvass, but I could not find any on the shelves."

The sardine thief shrugs. "It's a good thing I scored enough for the both of us."

With a laugh, she deftly slips the striped sheet over his head, tucks the end under his collar. She stares at him queerly for a moment, then leans forward and gently peels the patch of dried toilet paper away from his chin. Her face is so close to his he can smell her lipstick. Once again he has the impression he has looked into her eyes before.

He brings up an embarrassed grunt. "I cut myself shaving."

"I didn't think you cut yourself dueling." Brandishing the scissors in one hand and a comb in the other, Rain surveys the tangle of gray hair on Lemuel's head. "So what do you want?"

"A haircut."

"No kidding. What kind of goddamn haircut? How do you want to come on? Intellectual? Academic? Athletic? Woody Allenish? Rhett Butlerish? I do a Renaissance man that'll have you beating off the Renaissance women."

"There is a faculty lunch," Lemuel says stiffly. "I am supposed to look like a *Homo chaoticus,* as opposed to a *Homo sovieticus.*"

"I know what a homosexual is. But a *Homo chaoticus* . . ."

"It is man in his role as chaoticist, which means a professor of chaos."

"Yo! I get it. You must be one of the suits from the goddamn Institute tucked away in that dilapidated building behind the library. Hey, if you want to look like a professor of chaos, you ought to go and leave your hair like it is."

Using her fingers as a comb, she struggles for several minutes to untangle his hair. At one point Lemuel winces.

"Sorry about that." She unfurls the half-defiant, half-defensive flag of a smile he saw on her face in the E-Z Mart.

Tentatively at first, then with growing confidence, she snips away at his hair. "Like you must have a name."

"Falk, Lemuel."

Rain stops cutting and talks to Lemuel's reflection in the mirror. "L. Falk. You're the Russian dude from the talk show last night. I remember you said something about randomness being ignorance. I wasn't sure what you meant, but it sure sounded goddamn cerebral. Hey, check it out—it's a small world, right? I mean, I was the person who called in right after you."

"You were saying about a G-spot . . ."

"So you heard me?"

"What in the name of God is a G-spot?"

Rain positions Lemuel's head and continues snipping away. "I suppose it was discovered by S. Freud and Co. It's an extremely sensitive spot about the size of a fingerprint on the face inferior of the . . ." The scissors hesitate. "You're pulling my leg, right?"

Lemuel understands that he is not even touching her leg, which means that "pulling someone's leg" is another idiom he has to reckon with. He also understands that "G-spot" is a sexual term. He tries to recall if his mistress back in Petersburg had one, decides the subject is a mine field and tiptoes around it.

"Is Rain your first name or your family name?"

"First. My family name's Morgan. I happen to have the same name as a dude you're probably not familiar with, you being Russian and all. J. P. Morgan? No. I didn't think so. He had something to do with money, which is what I want to have something to do with." Pursing her lips, she peers over Lemuel's head at his reflection in the mirror. Apparently satisfied, she begins trimming the other side.

"How did you acquire a . . . handle like Rain?"

"I was named after the weather the morning I was born. My full name, it's written in on my birth certificate, is Occasional Rain, but I only use the Occasional occasionally. I have a kid sister named Partly Cloudy. Hippie parents. Go figure."

"And what is the significance of 'Tender To'?"

Rain gazes at the

ＴＥＮＤＥＲ ＴＯ

painted on the window. "I sublet from the Village Store. 'Tender To' came with the lease. The way I see it, 'tender to' is how women see themselves—we're tender to men, in the sense that we are gentle and loving and sympathetic to them. But men have a tendency to see us as *the* tender to—the small boat that services a big yacht." Rain shrugs. "I try not to let men depress me. I don't always succeed."

Her legs spread wide, her knees flexed, Rain circumnavigates Lemuel's scalp, chattering away as she shears his hair. "Dudes who don't know each other usually start off talking horoscope. You've heard of the zodiac in Russia, haven't you? Personally speaking, I don't believe in all that Capricorn crap. It's all right for ice-breaking, but after that what are you left with? Ascending this, descending that. I'm a practicing Catholic, though what I practice is not Catholicism. The last time I attended Mass it was because I was hitchhiking through Italy and needed to steal money from the collection basket to eat. I also scored candles and sold them on streetcorners."

"If you do not practice Catholicism, what do you practice?"

"I practice hairstyling, but only part-time—I cut hair to work my way through college. I practice the French horn in the Backwater Marching Band even though I can't march and I can't read music, I play by ear. I practice safe sex, which I also play by ear, though these days safe sex more often than not means no sex. I practice home economics, which is my major, and motion-picture history, which is my minor. I practice . . ."

Gradually Lemuel finds himself tuning out. He hears her voice droning on, but no longer makes out what she is saying. It is like watching a film without a sound track. From time to time he mutters "Uh-huh," which is an American expression he has never been able to locate in a dictionary, but everyone seems to understand. It occurs to him that having your hair cut by a lady, and an attractive one at that, is a curiously intimate business. He has not been this close physically to a woman he does not know since the KGB handcuffed him to the lady movie reviewer after his arrest for signing a petition. When Rain leans diagonally across his chest to trim the hair falling over his eyes, he feels the air stir, he gets a whiff of female flesh, of rose-scented toilet water that has almost but not quite worn off. Out of the corner of his eye he inspects her narrow hips, the line of her thigh, her wrists, the shape of her fingernails, the rings she wears on almost every finger, no two are alike. When she turns away to reach for a comb, he takes a long look at her ass, which strikes him as nothing less than glorious, encased as it is in washed-out, skin-tight jeans. At moments her breasts are level with his eyes, and only centimeters away. With his peripheral vision he sees the buttons straining at her shirt, catches the barest glimpse of flesh, the faintest swell of breast between the buttons. She is obviously not wearing a brassiere, something unheard of in the workers' paradise he fled. Once the soft tip of her breast grazes his ear—or is he merely slipping into an agreeable fiction?

Oy. *Ta'amu ure'u.*

If only he could.

And then she is snipping away at the hair jutting from his nostrils and loosening the sheet and brushing talc on the back of his neck and pulling the sheet free. Lemuel climbs stiffly to his feet, fixes his glasses over his eyes and studies himself in the mirror.

"So?"

"I feel . . . couth."

"Couth is the opposite of uncouth, right? So it must be a goddamn compliment."

Lemuel threads his fingers through his hair. "I suppose I will not be mistaken for a student." He produces a small zippered purse, counts out five one-dollar bills and hands them to her. "I have read how you are expected to offer gratuities in America, but I am not knowing how much."

"The haircut's four-fifty. Most people give me five and tell me to keep the goddamn change."

"If you please," he says with a faint smile, "keep the goddamn change."

Rain bats her eyelashes. "Not many dudes say please when they tell me to keep the goddamn change." As Lemuel starts to climb into his overcoat, she edges closer. "Here's the deal: I've never met a live Russian before. And I was invited to this frat bash tonight. I'm not thrilled at the idea of staying home, also I'm not thrilled at the idea of turning up alone and getting pawed, right? All those goddamn jocks casually running their hands over my back and shoulders to see if I'm wearing a bra." She takes a deep breath. "Like I won't beat around the bush—"

"You are the second person I have met in America who dislikes beating around the bush."

"Who's the other?"

"He is a rabbi."

"Asher Nachman, the swinging rebbe?" Rain pulls a face. "It's me who supplies him with dope. I once asked him if there was oral sex in the Old Testament. You know what he told me? He told me what I called the Old Testament and he called something else, I forget exactly what, had a goddamn oral tradition. He also told me that this dude Onan, you know who I mean, right? the one whose name is the sophisticated word for jerking off, this dude Onan was only practicing coitus interruptus, which according to the Rebbe is what people did for birth control B.C., which means before condoms. Hey, where is it written a clean young rabbi can't be a dirty old man? On the other hand a rabbi who smokes dope can't be all bad. Especially one with sideburns teased into springs. I know girls who'd kill for sideburns like that. I offered him haircuts on the house if he'd give me the secret, but he said no deal. Anyhow, to get back to the bush I'm not beating around: Would you be interested in being my date?"

Lemuel does not trust his ears. "You are asking me to escort you to this fraternity party?"

"So I wouldn't mind if you wouldn't mind."

Lemuel considers the invitation, then nods carefully. Rain, unsmiling, holds out her hand. Lemuel, unsmiling, takes it. They shake. "Right," she says as if they have negotiated a contract.

Like I'll try and play it back like I remember it.

I must have heard someone coming up the stairs because I remember turning my head and seeing the curtain billow towards me as if it could feel a warm body approaching. And then this suit who almost ran me over in the E-Z Mart pushed through the curtain into the shop. Talk about needing a haircut, he had this tangle of steel wool that comes, take it from someone who knows, from years of having your hair cut by amateurs using dull sheep shears. Your average Neanderthal man probably looked civilized compared.

Apart from the hair, there was something, like, *foreign* about him. I'm not talking cheap after-shave, I'm talking the way he wore his clothes, I'm talking the clothes themselves. They were so nondescript I'm not sure I could describe them if my life depended on it. If I concentrate, I can just about remember a faded brown overcoat skimming the tops of his shoes. I can remember a scarf, khaki, wound twice around a thickish neck. He obviously had on trousers, but I don't remember the color or whether he hung right or left, which is the kind of detail I usually notice. He had on a shirt buttoned up to the top button. I don't think he wore a tie. No, I'm positive he wasn't wearing a tie. A tie, which is the exception as opposed to the rule in Backwater, I would have remembered. He wore a sleeveless sweater under his jacket, I don't remember the color of either of these items except the sleeveless sweater could have been used to shine shoes, it was that ratty. Under one arm he carried a shapeless imitation-leather satchel. The reason I assumed it was imitation as opposed to the genuine article was somebody dressed like that had to be into imitation.

So now I'll do his face. He had a funny as in bizarre glint in his eyes which I couldn't place until I happened to look in the mirror when I was sweeping up after him and recognized the same thing in my eyes. I read somewhere, it probably comes from a *National Geographic* I browsed in my gynecologist's waiting room, how every face is a map of a country we vaguely remember visiting. Anyhow, I'm here to tell you it's so. My Neanderthal, I'm talking haircut, right? not intelligence, my Neanderthal had been startled at some point in time of his life and the traces of fear, of alarm, of surprise, of agony even, were printed on his face, in his eyes. Which were bloodshot. Which meant he drank too much or didn't get enough shut-eye or all of the above.

When I see clients carrying bags, imitation or not, I keep an eye peeled to make sure they don't swipe my goddamn *Playboys*, which is not the same thing, excuse me if I anticipate what's going through your head, as scoring sardines from the supermarket because I don't pad my prices to cover lost *Playboys*. So he'd know I had an eye peeled, I hit him with my usual line. "With you in a min," I said. I watched him jam the scarf into the armpit of his overcoat, which happens to be a gesture I can relate to—it reminds me of my ex-husband, who I divorced after two months of marital grief because he arranged for his relatives to throw rice instead of birdseed at my wedding. Uncooked rice, in case nobody's given you the word, swells in the bird's stomach, right? which brings on acute indigestion and, if the bird has eaten enough rice, which they tend to do at weddings, an excruciating death.

Where was I?

I saw him fingering the *Playboy*, I saw him look up with his eyes as opposed to his head to see if yours truly was watching, but I averted my eyes—lah-di-dah, I get off on words like *averted*, they make you sound so . . . educated—I averted the aforementioned eyes and he casually flipped through the pages to the centerfold. Which brings me to the first thing about him I *liked*.

For me he was an open book, most men are, and what I read was he didn't have any religious or otherwise scruples against nudity, what sane person does? but he didn't find the Julies sexy. I was intrigued, I admit it. I mean, in my experience women fuck dudes they basically like who happen to come equipped with a cock; men on the other hand fuck cunts which may or may not be attached to someone they even know, forget like. But my Neanderthal seemed somehow different. He was twice my age, which is twenty-three, if he was a day and I could hear the goddamn brothers at Delta Delta Phi needling me about robbing the grave as opposed to the cradle, but since when do I care what people think, assuming you put Delta Delta Phi brothers in the category of people who think.

Like there were other reasons in the back of my brain for asking L. Falk, which turned out to be his handle, to escort me to the bash. They say everything over thirty is downhill, but I'm beginning to wonder if I wouldn't be better off with a main squeeze headed downhill. I've had it up to here with the uphill jocks who think they're doing you a favor when they fuck you, who actually say thanks when it's over, as if you're the goddamn Tender To who has serviced their goddamn yacht, right? who roll out of bed and dry their dicks on your goddamn towels and mumble "So I'll call you, huh?" on their way out, when you both know they don't have your phone number.

I'm tired of one-night stands that end up with me waiting for the goddamn phone to ring.

So what else about L. Falk intrigued me? He didn't smoke, for starters. I could tell from his breath, which I got a whiff of when I leaned over to pull off the toilet paper sticking to the shaving cut. I never smoked neither until I found out that some goddamn admiral or general of surgery was shooting off his mouth about how the dudes who smoked were killing the dudes who didn't. Like they're getting ready to dump their goddamn radioactive atomic garbage on Backwater's doorstep and the state commission has the goddamn nerve to say this is *not* hazardous for your health, right? but it's my goddamn cigarette that's killing off the human race! You have to know I started in smoking as a sort of one-woman protest. I hated the smell of tobacco on my breath so much I gave up after a few days, but not before I sent this admiral or general of surgery a handwritten blast about the goddamn radioactive atomic garbage dump and the killers who feed uncooked rice to birds at weddings.

So he never answered me. So what?

Where was I?

I was explaining what was going on in that brain of mine when I asked L. Falk to, uh, escort me to the bash. Like it's true what they say about safe sex being the same as no sex, right? I mean, thank God for the Hitachi Magic Wand. The last time I got laid was seven, count them, seven goddamn weeks ago when I broke a cardinal New Year's resolution

and smoked my own dope instead of selling it and wound
up in the sack with this Polish-origin nose tackle on Backwater's football team. The dialogue went from baaaaad to
woooorse. "So get the condom," I told him when the kettle
started boiling. I remember all motion suddenly stopped.
"What condom?" the nose tackle asked in panic. I didn't
beat around the bush. "Hey, I hardly know you, Zbig," I
told him. "I can't even pronounce your last name. You
don't expect me to fuck you without a goddamn condom."
He was pathetic. "I don't use needles," is what he said. "I
don't fuck boys," is what he said.

I don't fuck boys! What a chuckle, right? when you need
to educate an adult nose tackle as to the facts of life. So I
rolled off him and read him the goddamn riot act. "The
last girl you screwed could have fucked boys that fucked
boys. Come on, Zbig, you have got to have a condom
stashed away for a rainy day."

My goddamn luck, he didn't. "The least you could do is
blow me," he said, as if safe sex was oral sex. Like I don't
usually say no to dudes when they ask politely. I mean,
where's the advantage to being a consenting adult if you
don't consent? And what's a blow job between friends anyhow? What I don't like, *what I can't deal with,* is when they
push your goddamn head down south and then start moaning before you get there to show how much the mere idea
of getting sucked is turning them on.

You have to know I get off on turning dudes on. My ex-
husband, the bird-killer, once informed me I was a
fellatrice. I tried looking it up in the library's Random
House dictionary, but it wasn't there. I'm talking about the
word, not the dictionary. But you'd need to be birdbrained
not to figure out what fellatrice means, and I had to agree.
With my ex. About me being a fellatrice. I love what in polite circles is called oral sex. I enjoy giving head. I don't understand why more women don't do it more often. Like
what could be more natural than feeling a cock grow hard
in your mouth? I mean, talk about being influential! Talk
about being in control of the situation!

I guess what I'm saying is that sucking and fucking are
goddamn amazing activities. I gave my first blow job when
I was thirteen and a half, and to show you how jaded I am
I still remember who and where—it was a pimply basketball

player I had a crush on, his name was Bobby Moran, he happened to be my first cousin but that's another story, the dirty deed took place in the stage squad's projection booth at the back of the junior high auditorium. That was ten years ago, holy Jesus! when I think how time zips by, and you have to know I've given my share of blow jobs in the intervening years, but I have definitely not become blasé. For me sucking and fucking never lost their mystery—that totally awesome mix of giving pleasure, right? and taking pleasure from giving pleasure.

Which is why we spend our lives spreading our legs and opening our mouths to the single most original thing men have going for them, which is a goddamn erection.

Go figure.

Which brings me back to L. Falk and the fraternity bash. I don't automatically assume we're gonna wind up in the sack, him being twice my age and not knowing a G-spot from a hole in the wall. But you have to deal with the possibility that sex will be the ultimate outcome of any date— why else go to frat parties, right? I mean, why do all these dudes spend all that goddamn energy trying to convince you they're nonviolent? I'll tell you why—to get you to collaborate in what is basically a very violent act is why. So if they're convincing enough, I collaborate. Or at least I used to until the goddamn Black Plague struck. Which is where L. Falk comes into the picture. I'd be lying if I didn't say straight out I considered the possibility, I'm still considering it now, that he might be the answer to my prayers.

As usual in cases like this there are pluses and minuses. On the minus side you have got to deal with the fact he's definitely toast, burned out, washed up, over the goddamn hill. Christ, he's pushing forty from the wrong side. He's about as far as you can get from my image of the great lover. On the plus side is the fact he wouldn't need to be a great lover, I tend to be good enough for two. Also, he is definitely nonviolent, which makes it easier for a girl to collaborate. Even him not being able to put his finger on the G-spot can be interpreted as a plus—exploring uncharted waters can be fun for the navigator as well as the helmsman, right? By far the most important plus in his quiver is that L. Falk comes from Russia, where (I am a *Backwater Sentinel* subscriber, which is how come I am familiar with this particular item of information) along with practically no meat and practically no bread, there is also practically no AIDS.

Hey, safe sex might not be great sex, but at least it would be sex, right?

My last but not least for being interested in him is the business of the serial murders, which seem random to me even if they don't seem random to the *Homo chaoticus,* the professor of chaos, L. Falk. Look at it from my point of view: If the murders weren't random, if someone was killing blonds who stuttered, say, or left-handed lesbians, or sexy women barbers who deal Thai truffles on the side, at least I'd know where I stood. I'd know whether or not I was a potential victim, right? What I'm saying is, because the crimes are random, I could become an actual victim without even knowing I was a potential victim. Random murders are the worst kind—you can't be sure you're not next.

Not knowing I'm not next, I'm not thrilled about living alone. Which is why I decided to go to the Delta Delta Phi bash tonight. Which is why I don't mind if someone who isn't familiar with the G-spot escorts me. To the bash. And back home afterwards.

Right?

Right.

Munching olives, sipping martinis, talking shop or stock market or weather, the fifteen permanent scholars, along with the dozen visiting professors and the handful of fellows at the Institute for Advanced Interdisciplinary Chaos-Related Studies circle the parenthesis-shaped tables in the faculty dining room looking for their names on hand-lettered tags. As they settle into their seats, co-ed waitresses wearing spotless white aprons begin filling the wineglasses from decanters. The Director, J. Alfred Goodacre, grips Lemuel's elbow and steers him to the head of the parenthesis.

"Bravo for the haircut," he whispers. "She's quite a number, our lady barber."

Lemuel is confused. "In what respect can a lady barber be compared to a number?" he asks, but the Director, shaking hands with a visiting professor from Germany, doesn't catch the question.

Down the table, Matilda Birtwhistle is deep in conversation with her neighbor, Charlie Atwater. "They didn't use to decant the wine at faculty luncheons," she remarks.

"They decant it," Atwater, nursing his fourth martini, replies, "so we won't dishcover what sheep wine they're serving us." He sniffs the wine in his glass and screws up his face in disgust.

Matilda Birtwhistle laughs. "Oh, Charlie, come off it."

"You think I'm making this up?" Atwater takes a sip of the wine, rolls it around in his mouth as if he is gargling, then swallows. His eyes bulge. "Oh my God! It's *nouveau vinaigre!*"

Holding a wineglass by its stem, Rebbe Nachman, sitting across the parenthesis from Matilda Birtwhistle, carefully swirls the liquid around in the glass, then watches as it seeps back down the sides. "You maybe want an independent opinion," he calls across the table, "it was *mis en bouteille,* as we say in Yiddish, in the basement of the E-Z Mart on Main Street, after which it did not travel well." Flashing a lopsided grin, he calls *"Bolshoi le'hayyim!"* and treats himself to a healthy swig.

Later, as the coeds clear dessert dishes from the tables and serve coffee and mints, the Director climbs to his feet and clangs a spoon against a glass. "Gentlemen, ladies?" The luncheon guests are so busy talking to one another they don't notice that he is trying to get their attention. "First off," Goodacre pitches his voice higher, "I want to welcome you all to this faculty luncheon." Gradually the guests simmer down.

"Let me tell you," Charlie Atwater, mimicking the Director, whispers to his neighbor, "how impreshive it is to shee sho much chaosh-related brain power in one room."

"Let me tell you," Goodacre continues, "how impressive it is to see so much chaos-related brain power in one room."

Matilda Birtwhistle snickers appreciatively.

"As Albert Einstein once noted," the Director goes on, "the most incomprehensible thing about this universe of ours is that it is comprehensible. It gives me a great deal of pleasure to welcome into the Institute's ranks someone who has done more than his share to make the universe comprehensible. He needs no introduction. You are all familiar with his work on entropy, as well as his search for pure randomness in the decimal expansion of pi. Many of us suspect that if there were a Nobel Prize awarded in the field of mathematics, he would surely have received it by now for pushing back the frontier of randomness. Let's have a welcoming hand for the visiting professor from St. Petersburg. Gentlemen, ladies: Lemuel Falk."

The permanent scholars, visiting professors and fellows are on their feet now, applauding. Lemuel, his head bowed, his cheeks burning, stares at his briefcase, which is leaning against one leg of his chair. Old habits die hard. At the V. A. Steklov Institute of Mathematics faculty luncheons, especially the ones with foreign guests, were occasions to steal onion rolls and tins of caviar and half-liter bottles of Polish vodka. Lemuel has abandoned any hope of appropriating one of the wine decanters, which are surely counted before and after the luncheon, but he has his heart set on transferring the seeded roll that has been overlooked on the small plate in front of him to his briefcase. But with everyone gazing at him, how is he to pull it off?

The applause dies down. The guests settle back into their seats. Lemuel, at the head of one curving parenthesis, thrusts himself to his feet, adjusts his eyeglasses, surveys the three-piece suits, the sport jackets with suede elbow patches, the potbellies, the bifocals, the balding crowns, the thumbs pressing tobacco into the bowls of pipes. He nods at several of the Institute's professors whom he knows from international symposiums. He notices Rebbe Nachman smiling encouragingly.

"I can say you—" Lemuel begins.

"Can you speak up, Professor?" someone calls from the back of the room.

Lemuel clears his throat. "I can say you, you may not want to hear it," he starts again in a stronger voice, "that I have arrived to Backwater armed with more questions than answers. I will not bore you with the easy ones—how is it possible to wear your heart on your sleeve? In what respect can a lady barber be compared to a number? What does 'Nonstops to the most Florida cities' really mean? How can one city be more Florida than another? Concerning which side is up, who gets to decide that in America? I will not occupy your time even with the tantalizing question Rebbe Nachman posed me last night, namely, if God really loved man, would He have created him? I will, with your permission, move right on to the question which keeps me awake nights. . . ."

Lemuel glances at the plate to make sure the seeded roll is still there, then looks up at the audience. "What is chaos? It has been variously defined—as order without periodicity, for instance; as seemingly random recurrent behavior in deterministic systems such as ocean tides and temperatures, stock-market prices, weather, fish populations in ponds, the dripping of a faucet. I would suggest you these definitions do not cut to the bone, I would like to offer another way of looking at chaos, here it is: that systems too complex for classical mathematics can be said to obey simple laws. Let me give you a for instance. Using the tools of classical mathematics, we can more or less calculate the long-term motion of the fifty or so bodies in the solar system. But trying to comprehend the short-term motion of the hundred trillion or so particles in a milligram of gas is beyond the competence of the most powerful computer, not to say the most brilliant programmer. Yet we can understand a great deal about the motion of the gas particles if we grasp that the incredibly complex world contained in this milligram of gas can be said to obey simple laws."

Lemuel's mouth is suddenly bone dry. He takes a sip of water. When he looks up he discovers the luncheon guests leaning forward, hanging on his words. Encouraged, he plunges on. "The science of chaos can accordingly be seen as an effort to come to grips with the essence of complexity. In my view the traditional sciences, which is to say physics, chemistry, biology, et cetera, have become 'tenders to.' They are the small boats servicing the yacht, which is the science of chaos." This elicits a titter from the audience, all of whom at one time or another have visited Rain's Tender To. "The only really original, and in some cases elegant, work around today is being done by chaoticists, who have demonstrated that complex systems obey simple laws, and in so doing act in seemingly random ways. Which permits us to conclude"—Lemuel is speaking slowly now, selecting his words warily—"that deterministic chaos is the explanation for most randomness. But . . . but is it the explanation for *all* randomness?"

Several people in the audience whisper excitedly to each other. "Vat is he telling us?" demands the visiting professor from Germany.

"He is suggesting chaos should play second fiddle to randomness," grumbles his neighbor, an astrophysicist on loan from the Massachusetts Institute of Technology. Several people within earshot nod in agreement.

Lemuel looks directly at the Rebbe. "Excuse me if I say you my question is more critical to our understanding of the universe, and our place in it, than the one you posed last night, Rebbe. Let me phrase my question another way. In paring away layers of seeming randomness we arrive at a terminus, which up to now has turned out to be chaos. But the real quest is only beginning. Is it not within the realm of possibility that this terminus, chaos, is really only a way station? Is it not equally within the realm of possibility that the *real* terminus, the theoretical horizon beyond which there is no other horizon, is pure, unadulterated, nonchaotic randomness?"

There is an angry buzz in the room. "You are not really a chaoticist," Sebastian Skarr exclaims from his seat. "You are a randomnist exploiting chaos—"

The Rebbe reluctantly agrees. "In your heart of hearts, you admitted it yourself last night, you do not love chaos—"

"Chaos is not God," Lemuel defends himself. "In any case, I am basically a randomnist who stumbled into chaos—"

"You admit to being ein reluctant chaoticist," the German professor blusters. "Conzider ze pozzibility zat you have stumbled into ze wrong institute."

The Rebbe throws up his arms. "Pure, unadulterated randomness does not exist. You are chasing rainbows."

Lemuel is startled by the storm he has stirred. "My approach to pure randomness," he defends himself, "is chaos-related."

Matilda Birtwhistle raises a finger. "Mind a question, Professor?"

"This is getting out of hand," the Director announces. "It's not supposed to be a working session."

"The chaoticists are waxing chaotic," Charlie Atwater notes wryly.

"If you please," Lemuel tells Matilda Birtwhistle.

"You are widely known for your assertion that all randomness is fool's randomness, and that this fool's randomness is a footprint of chaos."

"Up to now it has unfortunately always turned out that way," Lemuel agrees.

"If I understand you correctly," Birtwhistle continues, "you seem to be suggesting that chaos could turn out to be a footprint of randomness—"

"Of pure, unadulterated randomness," Lemuel corrects her.

"Of pure, unadulterated randomness, of course. But if this proves to be the case, where will it end? Perhaps the pure, unadulterated randomness that comes after chaos is, in its turn, merely a footprint of something else—"

"Maybe it'sh a footprint of pure, unadulterated chaosh," Charlie Atwater interjects.

The visiting professor from Germany scrapes back his chair in disgust. "You ask me, he iz looking for pure randomnezz—okay, vy not? Everyone haz eine ax to grind—but vat he found iz pure ridiculouznezz."

There is a ripple of nervous laughter, which quickly subsides. The luncheon guests gaze expectantly at the speaker at the head of the parenthesis.

Lemuel collects his thoughts. "When it was discovered, the molecule was, in a manner of speaking, a footprint of the atom. The atom turned out to be, among other things, a footprint of a nucleus, the nucleus a footprint of protons and neutrons, which we now think are footprints of mesons and quarks. But what are quarks a footprint of? Who can say you they are not a footprint of something buried deeper inside them?"

"Matilda is right," Sebastian Skarr calls from his seat. "If what you say is true, the voyage will never end. There is no terminus."

"We are not chaoticists," Matilda Birtwhistle informs her colleagues, "so much as space travelers condemned to spend eternity exploring an endless universe."

Lemuel shrugs. "We will reach a terminus when we discover a single example of pure, unadulterated randomness. At which point we will know that everything under the sun is not determined—that man, woman also, is the master of his fate."

"And if there is no such thing as pure, unadulterated randomness," Matilda Birtwhistle retorts, "what then?"

Lemuel, suddenly exhausted, mumbles, "You are all doorknobs."

"Speak up, Professor," someone calls.

Charlie Atwater belches into the back of his fist. "Thish is all very depreshing," he groans. "I badly need a drink."

The guests gaze silently into their coffee cups for a long while. Lemuel's head bobs uncertainly several times. He glances at the Director, who appears to be having a conversation with himself, then manages to sink into his seat so awkwardly he upsets the plate containing the seed roll. Scrambling under the chair, Lemuel slips the roll into his briefcase and surfaces with the empty plate.

A coed carrying a tray of after-dinner mints passes behind him and drops one onto his coffee saucer.

"I thank you," Lemuel says.

The girl smiles engagingly. "I welcome you," she shoots back with a giggle.

"You may be the only one here who does."

Staring out at his colleagues at the Institute for Chaos-Related Studies, watching them as they push back their chairs and drift away from the parenthesis, Lemuel wonders if this vision of a never-ending cycle of randomness and chaos is not simply another one of his convenient fictions, something that satisfies parts of himself he has not been to yet.

Dejected, he bumps into the Rebbe outside the Institute Center. "Where did I go wrong?" he asks him. "What do I do now?"

Rebbe Nachman dances on the ice to keep his toes from turning numb. "A smart-ass goy once offered to convert to Judaism if the famous Rebbe Hillel could teach him the entire Torah while the goy was standing on one foot. You have maybe heard the story? Rebbe Hillel agreed, the goy balanced on his one foot, Rebbe Hillel said to him, 'That which is hateful to you do not do to your friend. This is the whole Torah, the rest is commentary. Go and study.' "

Rebbe Nachman's smile seems more asymmetric than usual. "I don't believe you will ever find randomness, I'm talking pure, I'm talking unadulterated, for the simple reason it doesn't exist. On the other hand, you certainly won't find it if you don't look for it. Go and study."

Chapter Three

"I was wrist-cuffed to a lady movie reviewer who also signed the petition," Lemuel shouts over the noise he refuses to acknowledge as music. "I heard she spent three years in a Siberian gulag, sucking frozen sticks of milk over open fires at mealtimes."

"How did you worm out of it?" hollers a fraternity brother wearing a tie and jacket and football helmet.

"Hey, how did you?" Rain, sipping wine, smiling whimsically, wants to know.

"Lem here signed the petition, the fuzz picked him up and took him in for questioning," Dwayne, the E-Z Mart manager, recapitulates in a loud voice, "but they didn't charge him. He had to have a wrinkle."

"A wrinkle?"

"A gimmick," Dwayne's girlfriend, Shirley, explains.

"A stratagem," Dwayne adds. "A ruse."

Lemuel smiles sourly. "I had a wrinkle—it was two signatures," he shouts. "One I used to sign my internal passport or my pay book or my applications for exit visas. The other signature I used to sign documents I might want to deny I signed. When they finally got around to interrogating me, I said them someone had forged my signature. They verified it with a handwriting expert and let me go."

"Like it must have been goddamn dangerous, living in a Communist country and not being a Communist," observes Rain.

"In Russia we have a proverb: It is dangerous to be right when the government is wrong."

Lemuel turns to watch the couples in the next room. In the half light, they appear to be jumping up and down, their heads hanging off to one side as if their necks are broken. He leans closer to Rain and shouts into her ear, "Looks like—" The noise ends as suddenly as it began. "—communal hiccups," he hears himself shout. Heads swivel. Lemuel blushes.

The three musicians in a corner of the room strike up a slow fox-trot. Shirley sinks into Dwayne's arms and they start to shuffle around in time to the music.

"Hey, in Russia they must dance, right?" Rain tells Lemuel. He feels her breath warm his ear. "Let's you and me . . ." Her forefinger describes a circle.

"I do not know if I know—" Lemuel starts to protest, but Rain, polishing off the wine, dangling the empty glass by its stem, pulls him into the other room and melts into his arms. He feels the wineglass against the back of his neck, he feels her breasts against his chest, he feels her thighs against his legs, he smells her lipstick. He hears the Rebbe's "Oy" seep between his lips.

Rain presses her mouth against his ear. When she speaks, her words actually tickle. "The business with the two signatures—when did that happen?"

"Eight years ago."

"I remember something that happened twenty-three years ago," she says lazily. "I remember my birth."

"You are inventing this up? I do not even remember my childhood, mainly because I never had one."

"Honest to Christ, I'm not inventing. I was very young at birth, who isn't? but I remember every detail. I remember the dampness and the darkness and then the coldness and the blinding light. I remember being held upside down and whacked. You want me to give you the dirty details?"

"Another time maybe."

They shuffle around the floor in silence. After a while Rain's voice tickles his ear again. "So are you married?"

"I was married. I am divorced."

"How many times in your life have you been in love?"

Lemuel tries to shrug, but finds it difficult because Rain is hanging on his shoulders. "Perhaps once. Once, perhaps. Yes, once."

"You don't sound sure."

"I am sure. I was in love once."

"With your wife?"

"I showed up in the Leningrad Palace of Marriage to sign the book under the photograph of Lenin because my wife's father was the rector at the V. A. Steklov Institute of Mathematics, where I would have given my right arm to work. Also his daughter had a sixty-square-meter apartment all to herself."

"So who were you in love with if it wasn't your wife?"

"A girl . . . I never knew her name, I never spoke with her."

"You fucked with her, right?"

Lemuel tosses his head in embarrassment.

"I don't get it. If you never talked to her, if you never fucked with her, then even if she existed it's the same as if she didn't exist. She was a figment of your imagination."

"She was real," Lemuel insists, but Rain is following her own thoughts.

"I don't see how it's possible to be passionate about someone who doesn't exist?"

Lemuel tries to change the subject. "I suppose you have been in love many times."

Rain laughs. "More than many. I have been briefly in love dozens of times. Hundreds even."

"What does it mean, briefly in love?"

"Thirty seconds. Two minutes. Ten."

"How much time must pass before your love affairs become serious?"

Rain is insulted. "For the thirty seconds or two minutes or ten, they are very serious. While I am making love, I am in love." She crushes her miniskirt into Lemuel's crotch. "And when I am in love, I am usually making love."

"What about a love affair which lasts for a month or a year? What about marriage?"

"Tried marriage," Rain smugly informs him. "Didn't like it. Tried divorce."

"You were married how long?"

"It seemed like an ice age, but it was only two months."

"What was it about marriage you did not like?"

"My ex was good in bed, but not with me."

"He was unfaithful?"

"He was fucking his friends, if that's what you mean. So was I. Fucking my friends. But that wasn't why I quit him." She tells Lemuel the story of how her ex supplied rice instead of birdseed at her wedding. "I ought to have seen the handwriting on the wall," she adds. "I ought to have left him then and there."

"You did not divorce because of the rice," Lemuel insists.

Rain leans back and searches his face. "Like you think the birdseed story is for the birds, right?" He lifts his eyebrows in a shrug. She smiles anxiously as she drifts back into his arms. When she speaks again her voice is thicker. "I kept trying to figure out what Vernon wanted me to be, and then I tried to be it. After a few weeks on this merry-go-round I lost track of who I was. I lost track of me." A high-pitched laugh catches at her throat. "I don't program myself anymore. I don't try to be what some dude wants me to be." She takes a deep breath. "I am what I goddamn am."

Lemuel says very quietly, "You will be when and where you will be."

Rain is startled. "Yeah, that's it exactly. What you see is what you get."

Lemuel remembers the Rebbe's description of Eve in the garden of Yahweh. "What I see," he mumbles awkwardly, "is a saving grace—originality."

Rain stops in her tracks and scrutinizes his eyes. The freckles on her face burn. "Yo," she says quietly.

A barefoot young man wearing a djellaba comes hurtling into the room and whispers to the musicians. The music breaks off abruptly. The musicians stack their instruments and follow the young man out of the room. Dwayne tries to talk Shirley into going downstairs with the musicians. They have a whispered argument. Shirley shakes her head stubbornly. Lemuel hears her say, "I just don't feel in the mood tonight, angel." Annoyed, Dwayne stalks off by himself. Shirley, eyeing Lemuel across the room, slides a stick of gum into her mouth.

Rain folds herself back into Lemuel's arms and continues dancing.

"They must be starting the cassettes downstairs," she tells him. Still dancing, she presses her mouth against his ear and imitates the rat-a-tat-tat of a drumroll.

"What is that?"

"Drums."

"Drums?"

"The drums I hear in my head, right?"

"It is probably not serious."

"Can't you hear them?" She leans her head against Lemuel's ear. "Listen up. Rat-a-tat-tat, rat-a-tat-tat. I hear them. They're sending me a Morse code message. Right in my goddamn ear."

"What do they say?"

"They say, 'You're getting old.' They say, 'Pretty soon you'll wear see-through shirts and nobody'll wanna look.' They say, 'You haven't done anything with your life besides wheel and deal. You are so obsessed with safe sex,' they say, 'all you get is no sex.' Like some days I don't notice the goddamn drums, right? But they're always there. If I close my eyes and concentrate, I hear them. Rat-a-tat-tat. Rat-a-tat-tat."

"You seem a little young to worry about growing old."

Annoyed, Rain backs away from him. "Like you're never too young to worry about growing old. I'm taking D.J.'s Russian Lit 404, which is mostly L. Tolstoy, to fill a humanities requirement. So you've heard of L. Tolstoy, right? He once said something about how one thing in life was certain, namely, you live, therefore you are dying. The only time your body's not dying is when you're fucking. That's me talking, not L. Tolstoy. Don't smile that smug smile all men smile when they don't understand something—it happens to be a goddamn scientific fact. When you're fucking, time stops dead. When you're fucking, there is no such thing as time." Rain pitches the empty wineglass into a wastepaper basket. "That's a three pointer," she mutters. "I need to pee."

As Rain disappears through a door, Shirley meanders across the room toward Lemuel. She is wearing high heels and a flared miniskirt and shoulder padding under a sweater.

"Great party," she says.

Lemuel nods in vague agreement.

She holds out a stick of gum. Lemuel shakes his head. "I recognized you from the supermarket," Shirley says, adding the fresh stick to the one already in her mouth, chewing away, "but I don't remember seeing you around a Delta pour before."

"I have never attended a Delta pour before."

"You're a gate-crasher," Shirley exclaims. "I like men who aren't invited. Do you dance or anything?"

Backing against a wall, Lemuel clears his throat. "There is no music."

She pouts. "No music didn't stop you from dancing with the Tender To."

She collapses into Lemuel's arms, giving him no choice. "My name's Shirley," she announces. "I'm Dwayne's main squeeze. Pleased to make your acquaintance." She shifts her weight from one foot to the other in a lumbering dance. "That was some story you told before, about having two signatures. I can write my name backwards. Yel-rihs."

Lemuel, flustered, looks around. He sees the Rebbe, in the next room, rolling his head from side to side in mock admiration.

Hanging from Lemuel's neck, Shirley says, "Dwayne and me, we smoked some of the Tender To's dope before we got here. I'm so high I've had this pain for two hours, but I don't know where it is."

Lemuel gently pries Shirley's wrists loose from his neck. She grabs his sleeve. "You talk with an accent," she notes. "I like men who aren't invited and talk funny. I like men who have two signatures." When Lemuel jerks his arm free she says urgently, "I could teach you to write your name backwards. Oh, shit," she moans as Lemuel backs away. "I never seem to get it right like Rain."

Lemuel wanders over to the Rebbe, who is talking animatedly with D.J. but breaks off to greet Lemuel. "*Hekinah degul.* This is your idea of study? On the other hand, who can say there is nothing to be learned about chaos at a fraternity party?"

D.J., absorbed, aims a civil smile at Lemuel over the Rebbe's head. "Go on about Sodom," she prompts Nachman.

The Rebbe picks up the thread of their conversation. "I was reading into Genesis 18 this afternoon. That's where Abraham tries to argue Yahweh out of killing everyone in Sodom. 'Wilt thou also destroy the righteous with the wicked?' Abraham asks. Abraham's all for getting rid of sin, but not at the expense of throwing out the baby with the bathwater. Yahweh destroys Sodom anyhow. He kills the righteous along with the sinners. The riddle is, Why?"

"He's lazy," D.J. suggests. "He doesn't want to bother sorting."

Rain joins the group. "Who's lazy?" she asks D.J. "Your sideburns look fantastic," she tells the Rebbe. "When are you going to break down and give me the secret?"

"*Hekinah degul,*" says the Rebbe. "My sideburns are classified."

D.J. smiles coolly at Rain. "Good evening, dear."

"Why *does* Yahweh kill the righteous along with the sinners?" Lemuel wants to know.

"I'm glad you asked," says the Rebbe. "Because Yahweh is high on randomness. Randomness is in His blood, in His bones, in His head. Randomness is His modus operandi. When He punishes, He punishes randomly. Which is why we never really know until the end of the saga whether His chosen people are maybe going to wind up alive and well in the land of milk and honey, or dead as doornails in the desert. Take for instance the story of Yahweh hanging out on Mount Sinai, I'm talking Exodus 19. He instructs Moses to warn the Jews sweltering in the burning fiery furnace of a desert down below not to gaze on Him lest many of them perish. Okay, He was maybe having a bad day—a toothache, indigestion, diarrhea, you name it. Sinai wasn't your average Club Med. But is this a reason to make looking at you a capital crime? What we can deduce is that He's being capricious. He's being His old random Self. One day He threatens to kill Isaac, another time He dispatches an angel of death to do in Jacob, on still another occasion He personally tries to murder Moses, His anointed gofer. I'm talking Exodus 4:24–26. Ha! With Yahweh on our side, what do Jews need enemies for? He threatens as often as other people fart: Take one bite out of the fruit of the tree of knowledge and you've had it; look at Me and you meet your Maker; lay a finger on My ark and you get electrocuted—I'm talking 1 Chronicles 13." Angling his head, transported by his text, the Rebbe recites in a singsong voice. " 'And they carried the ark of God in a new cart out of the house of Abinadab: and Uzza and Ahio drave the cart. And David and all Israel played before God with all their might, and with singing, and with harps, and with psalteries, and with timbrels, and with cymbals, and with trumpets. And when they came unto the threshing floor of Chidon, Uzza'—the poor son of a bitch, that's me talking, not King James—'Uzza put forth his hand to hold the ark; for the oxen stumbled. And the anger of the Lord was kindled against Uzza, and he smote him, because he put his hand to the ark.' "

The Rebbe trembles in exasperation. "Consider, please, the possibility, I'm flirting with *probability* even, that this God of our fathers, this Yahweh, holy be His name, maybe has a flaw in His character. The flaw is that He can only relate to people who fear Him. 'Serve the Lord with fear,' the Psalmist advises us—I'm talking Psalm 2:11. And how does Yahweh instill the fear of God? By being unpredictable is how. Which is to say, by inflicting punishment at random."

"I dig what you're saying," Rain remarks. Three heads swivel slowly toward her. "Like if God didn't punish randomly, if He only killed certified sinners or blonds who stuttered or left-handed lesbians, everyone'd know where they stood. They'd know whether or not they were potential victims. And the ones who figured out they weren't potential victims wouldn't fear God. I mean, why bother? Fearing God? If you're not a potential victim? It's because God punishes at random that anyone could become an actual victim without even knowing she was a potential victim. So to be on the safe side"—Rain's voice starts to peter out—"everyone fears God, right?"

"I could have maybe phrased it better," the Rebbe declares, "but you hit the nail on the head." He turns back to D.J. and Lemuel. "Fear is His flaw, randomness is His vice, randomness is His middle name. Yahweh keeps the chosen people on their toes through randomness. He has decided that without *yir'ah*, which means fear of God, there will be no *emunah*, which means faith in God. And who can say He is wrong?" The Rebbe aims a lopsided grin at Lemuel. "Here you are, all hot under the collar to find randomness, and it's staring you in the face. Seek God! Selah."

"You put on a good show," Lemuel observes mildly. "Yahweh's randomness, assuming He exists, assuming it exists, is neither pure nor unadulterated. It looks like randomness to us because we do not know enough about Yahweh and what is going on in that head of His. In the end, Yahweh's randomness will turn out to be like all randomness—which is to say, fool's randomness and nothing more than a footprint of chaos."

The Rebbe shrugs, leans toward D.J. and starts to whisper something to her. She blushes, murmurs "Not now" under her breath.

The Rebbe is not put off. "You have maybe heard of Rebbe Hillel, an *illui*, which means genius, if there ever was one. He is remembered, among other things, for a second-century sound bite: 'If not now, when?' "

Rain tugs at Lemuel's elbow and draws him toward the door. "Where are you taking me?" he wants to know.

The Rebbe's taunting laugh follows them out of the room. "Remember what that archetypal goy Augustine once said," he calls after Lemuel. " 'Lord, make me chaste'—ha!—'but not yet.' "

"I'm taking you to the bowels of the earth," Rain confides gleefully, pulling Lemuel down the winding staircase toward the basement. They thread their way around boys and girls sitting on the stairs passing a cigarette from hand to hand.

"Yo, Rain," one of the boy says. "We're almost high and dry."

A handsome boy with hawklike features and pitch-black hair grips Rain's ankle. "We could use a refill."

Rain jerks her ankle free. "You need a refill, Izzat," she shoots back, "see me in my orifice."

Lemuel is struck by the total concentration of the boys and girls as they follow the cigarette with their eyes. A whiff of smoke reaches his nostrils. The odor seems vaguely familiar.

Passing an open door at the bottom of the staircase, he spots half a dozen boys wearing purple cardigans, each with a large yellow "BU" sewn on it, sitting around a bare wooden table with several pitchers in the middle. A girl with long hair falling across her pimply face is topping off tiny shot glasses from one of the pitchers. She glances at her wristwatch. "Okay—now," she says. The boys raise their shot glasses and drain off the liquid in one gulp.

"Kid stuff," Rain comments, steering Lemuel toward a room at the end of the corridor. "I'll show you what the consenting adults are into."

She pulls him into a room. Black-and-white images shimmer on a television screen. A haze drifts lazily through the flickering half-light. Lemuel sniffs at the haze. It reminds him of . . . ah! the rain cloud hovering over the Rebbe's stock-market pages. He inhales again, begins to feel giddy.

A voice comes out of the darkness. "Hey, Rain."

"Yo, Warren."

"I see you made it after all."

"Shhh."

"Shhhhhhhh," someone says to the person who said "Shhh."

"Like there's no sound track," says Rain. "So why can't we talk?"

"What'cha doing, Rain," someone else whispers, "robbing the grave?"

"Fuck you, Elliott," Rain whispers back. "In ways which are over your head, he's younger than both of us put together."

Elliott laughs. "Aren't you confusing youth with innocence?"

"You guys want to have an intellectual conversation, take it upstairs," Dwayne gripes.

"For crying out loud, knock it off," someone else calls.

The television screen is obscured by the smoke swirling in front of it. Guided by Rain, Lemuel settles heavily onto a cushion, his back to a wall. As his eyes gradually become accustomed to the darkness, he makes out a dozen or so boys and girls crowded onto low couches and cushions. Several of them seem to be joined together like Siamese twins. From the darkest corner of the room comes the throaty purring sound that a cat produces when it is being caressed.

Rain slips her arms through Lemuel's. "This may be one of the best fucking films I've ever seen," she breathes.

Lemuel pats his jacket pockets in desperate search of his eyeglasses, fumbles them onto his nose, rivets his eyes on the television screen. Thoroughly intoxicated by the haze, he feels as if he is peering through the wrong end of binoculars. Everything looks incredibly small. . . . He wipes perspiration off his forehead, blinks hard several times, concentrates on the tiny images on the television screen. Through the haze, he manages to distinguish three silvery figures who appear to be engaged in some sort of stylized, musicless ballet, alternately leaning over each other and impaling themselves on one another.

"Elliott, babe, why don't'cha dial back and run that part again on slow?" suggests Dwayne.

Someone sitting on the couch separates himself from his Siamese twin and points a small black box at the television set. The film skids backward. With a jerk the impaled figures disengage, causing everyone to laugh. The image freezes for an instant, then the ballet begins again in slow motion.

In the darkest corner of the room a boy moans, "For God's sake don't stop."

A girl giggles quietly. "I need to come up for air."

"Knock it off, huh?"

"Shhhhh."

"Oy!"

Walking Rain back to her apartment after the film, Lemuel is lost in a beguiling fiction. He is twenty-five years younger, a student at the mathematical faculty of Lomonosov University on the Lenin Hills overlooking Moscow. Medium shot of Lemuel, a wallflower at a Komsomol dance in a basement cultural center. Suddenly the lights dim and loud rock music blasts from the speakers. Tight on Lemuel as he glances to his left, discovers that he has a Siamese twin attached to his hip, a girl with a long, dirty-blond ponytail. Various shots of students moving in excruciatingly slow motion, lighting up hand-rolled cigarettes and impaling themselves on one another. Pan to Lemuel's Siamese twin as she leans toward him. On Lemuel's face as he feels one of her breasts brush against his arm, smells her lipstick. "Kid stuff!" she calls over the music. Her words seem to tickle his ear. Quick cut of the Siamese twin reaching for the night moth hiding inside his fly. "I'll show you what the consenting adults are into."

"Oy . . ."

Walking next to Lemuel, Rain notices the faraway look in his eyes. "A ruble for your thoughts?"

"There is no ruble anymore, at least not one that is worth anything."

Rain tries to keep the ember of conversation alive, but runs smack into his guttural "Uh-huh." They pass a twenty-four-hour laundromat, swing into an unpaved alleyway, stop at a narrow wooden staircase leading to a second-floor loft. Rain, breathing into her mittens to warm her fingers, turns to confront Lemuel. She looks at him, trying to make up her mind.

Lemuel holds out a hand. "I thank you for an interesting evening."

Rain ignores his hand, searches for an ironic tone. "I welcome you for an interesting evening. So what did you think of the flick?"

"The flick?"

She shuffles her feet nervously. "Flick, as in movie. Like they must have X-rated flicks in Russia, right? I'm curious how American pornography compares."

An agitated grunt escapes from the back of Lemuel's throat. "I was looking through the wrong end. . . . The figures were too small. . . ."

"You didn't see it?" She reads the answer on his face. "Get a life,
L. Falk. You're not only a doorknob, you're an earlobe. If I had an
ounce of sense I'd be out of here like Vladimir. Here I go and take
you to an X-rated flick and you don't goddamn see it! How is a girl
supposed to turn you on?"

"Turn me on?"

"Arouse. Stimulate. Stoke the fire for a major merge."

Lemuel says quietly, "You turned me on when you cut the hair sticking out of my nostrils. You turn me on when you walk into the room."

Rain's mouth falls open, then slowly closes as she comes to a decision. "Like I could talk subtext, right? I learned all about goddamn
subtexts in introductory psychology. You say one thing, but you mean
something else? 'I can't' means 'I won't.' 'I don't know' means 'I
don't want to think about it.' I could invite you up to Y-jack with me."
She spots the blank look in his eyes. "I keep forgetting you're from
another planet. Y-jacking is when you plug two sets of earphones into
the same jack on a Walkman. So if I asked you up to Y-jack, what I'd
really be saying, the subtext, right? is: I am totally stoked, I have decided you're nonviolent enough to collaborate with me in a violent
act. Are you reading me at all, L. Fucking Falk? Most dudes spend
their lives saying one thing and meaning another. Not yours truly.
Which is why I don't beat around the goddamn bush." Rain takes a
deep breath. "Hey, would you or wouldn't you? Like to fuck? R.S.V.P."

"You are asking me," Lemuel repeats the question to be sure he has
decoded it correctly, "if I want to . . . fuck?"

Rain blows air through her lips in exasperation. "Like do you or
don't you? Will you or won't you?"

"Fuck is a . . . brutal way . . . of putting it."

"What would you say, 'make love'?"

" 'Make love,' yes."

" 'Make love' misses the point, L. Falk. It misses the violence. It
misses the orgasm."

"I can understand how you would not want to miss the orgasm."

"Listen up, L. Falk: I steal sardines from the E-Z Mart, I steal money
from church baskets, I cheat at strip poker and midterm exams and
I don't declare the tips I get cutting hair to the IRS. But I don't cheat
at words, right? I call things like fucking by their real name. And I
never fake an orgasm."

At a loss for words, Lemuel pulls off a glove and, reaching out, touches the side of Rain's face with the back of his callused fingers. "You are a young girl," he says huskily. "Also a beautiful girl. Boys would kill to make love to you. Only smile to them, you can have all the lovers your heart desires. Only cross your legs wearing that short skirt, you will have to call in the police to keep order. You do not want to take an old man like me into your bed. If you please, take a good look at me. I am a doorknob, I am an earlobe, I am forty-six going on a hundred and six, my back aches when I walk uphill, my knees ache when I walk downhill. I am on the lam from terrestrial chaos, but I seem to take my chaos with me wherever I go." Lemuel elevates his chin a notch. "I can honestly say you I am not a great lover. I can even say you I am not a good lover. After a certain age sex is spoiled for men by the worry over whether you will perform . . . each orgasm is a triumph. I am a run-down battery—you push the starter button, you hear a grinding noise, the motor turns over, you hold your breath hoping it will catch, praying even, then nothing." He shrugs. "Nothing at all."

Rain struggles with a lump in her throat, a pain in her chest. "Hey, I could jump-start you," she whispers, "like when you roll a car downhill and it picks up speed, right? and the motor cranks over even if the battery is low. And the next thing you know, whooooosh, you're pushing the speed limit on the interstate." She leans toward him and brushes her lips against his so lightly he catches his breath. "I've had it with the uphill crowd," she says. "What I need is someone who's downwardly mobile." She angles her head, bats her eyelashes, stares at him with the seaweed green eyes that he is sure he has seen before. "Like what do you say we check out your battery, L. Falk? Yo?"

Slipping into a delectable fiction, Lemuel imagines that what is happening to him is really happening to him. He watches her closely to see if she is suffering from second thoughts before he finally clears his throat.

What he coughs up is a timid "Yo."

Once again Rain, unsmiling, holds out her hand. Once again Lemuel, unsmiling, takes it. They shake.

Like I could see right off L. Falk was walking wounded, I'm talking sexually, not physically, right? My instincts told me he'd have trouble getting it out, forget up, so for once

I decided it wouldn't hurt to beat around the goddamn bush. I switched off the overhead and put on the projector with the piece of mauve silk over it, I poured him a shot of one-star cooking cognac, I burned some incense, I tried to make small talk. "So what is it you actually do for a living?"

For furniture I have a low couch I once liberated from a Salvation Army truck and some folding kitchen chairs, some of which still fold, some of which don't, time takes its toll on everything, right? The apartment was a riot; it was not that things were out of place, it was more a matter, I openly admit it, that nothing had a place. I stashed my French horn in the bathtub, kicked the dirty laundry under the dresser, collected the magazines scattered around into a pile, buried the loose Tampaxes under Mayday's blanket and tugged the blanket, with Mayday clinging to it, into the spare bedroom. I didn't want my arthritic rat of a dog spoiling the atmosphere with one of her silent farts. The vet attributes her farting to age: Mayday's fifteen dog years and two dog months old—which, talk about coincidences, is the same as 106 human years. I kicked off my shoes and sprawled on the couch, my mini riding up my green tights, my arms back so that my nipples were pressing against the inside of my shirt. This last is a little trick I picked up when I was working summers as a parole officer in Atlantic City. (It's a lousy lie that the paroler, yours truly, was fired for sleeping with the parolees; I was fired for pleading no contest to shoplifting a pair of seventy-nine-cent earrings from Woolworth's.) I patted the couch next to me, but L. Falk pulled over a folding chair, turned it so the back was to the front and straddled it.

"I dabble in chaos," he said, as if what I was waiting for with bated breath was an answer to my question, "but my life's passion is pure randomness, which probably does not exist."

"I like randomness, I like things that happen out of order," I told him. "But I still don't see how it's possible to be passionate about something that doesn't exist."

"I can say you it is not easy."

I told him to put on some music while I slipped into something less comfortable. I have this Arab-type robe, the good news is it plunges to my belly button, the bad news is it itches, but I figured I'd better pull out all the stops. I could see L. Falk's nuts were going to be tough to crack.

I was in the bedroom spritzing rose-scented toilet water on the sheets when some music I didn't recognize came on. "Where'd you find that?" I called through the partly open door.

"On the pile of records."

I remembered D.J. had converted the Rebbe to CDs, which is how come he gave me some of his old LPs the night he told me about the oral tradition in the O.T. and the birth-control pioneer named Onan. The Rebbe could have scored, too. I mean, he talked a nonviolent game and he was convincing enough for me to collaborate, except I was menstruating.

Remember *averted*? *Menstruating*'s in the same goddamn league.

Where was I? When the Rebbe saw red, his eyes bulged more than usual, he mumbled something about me being impure and packed it in.

Me.

Impure.

Go figure.

I opened the door of the bedroom and positioned myself so I was in a frame. I picked this one up from a Lauren Bacall flick. When I spoke, I purred like a kitten. "So what's the record you went and put on?"

"It is a quintet . . ." He turned toward me, he took in the Arab-type robe, he followed the V down to my belly button, he swallowed hard.

The secret to good sex can be summed up in one word, which is *foreplay*, right? though to be really effective, foreplay, contrary to the conventional wisdom, should take place after as well as before the dirty deed. Which is another way of saying that good sex should not start or stop, it should go on forever. Obviously different people mean different things by *foreplay*. My freshman year at Backwater I roomed with a girl from Corning who used a Water Pik as a vaginal spray—she described it as the longest ejaculation in the history of the universe. My roommate loaned me her Water Pik once, but it was too wet for my taste, so I stuck with my trusty Hitachi Magic Wand.

I'm wandering. Foreplay.

Like it was only natural, right? when I tried to jump-start L. Falk's battery, for me to concentrate on foreplay. After what seemed like an eternity of small talk, I got him to stretch out on the bed, though his idea of making himself comfortable bore a curious resemblance to the fetal position. He wanted me to turn out the bed lamps, but we negotiated and compromised on turning one out and putting the other on the floor. I had a hell of a time untying his goddamn shoelaces, would you believe he had double-knotted them? and straightening out his legs.

"Hey, relaaaax," I said in my sexiest voice as I began to unbutton the buttons on his shirt. Sitting up, I reached for the hem of my Arab-type robe and pulled it over my head, I was still wearing my green tights, I leaned over him, letting my tits graze his chest. Then I started sucking his nipples.

Nipples, in my humble opinion, are the most neglected part of a man's body, dudes tend to melt with gratitude when you pay the slightest attention to them. After a while L. Falk's became erect, which I took as an auspicious, even positive, sign. I began to escalate. I undid his belt buckle and the top button of his trousers and slowly unzipped the zipper on his fly and snaked my hand down along his belly, which was surprisingly smooth, I had expected steel wool—to discover this soft, wilted Willie of a cock cringing in a tangle of underbrush.

My *Homo chaoticus* had a long way to go to become a *Homo erectus*.

L. Falk became very agitated, clutching his trousers, tugging at the zipper. "Oy . . . I said you I was a run-down battery."

I stretched out alongside him, one thigh draped over him, I kept my hand on his cock, nothing aggressive, just holding on to it the way you hang on to a strap in a subway, and I started whispering in his ear. "I don't know how things are in Russia," I remember saying something like this, "but you have an awful lot to learn about we Americans. There's nothing that turns a girl on more than a dude who has trouble performing. We get fed up with all those hard-ons men get at the drop of a hat. Some stud asks you to dance and, whoops, he's got to advertise his goddamn erection by pushing it into you. What we really like, what we lust after, is a dude whose sexuality is more subtle. You'll get it up, L. Falk, and when you do it'll be me who did it, it'll be me who gets the credit."

The funny part was I had never thought these thoughts before, but when I heard myself say them, I knew I believed them. L. Falk must have believed I believed them too, because I could feel his body, which had been to say the least strung like a bow, relax under mine, I could feel his cock begin to stiffen in the palm of my hand.

Weird how the body can grow soft while part of it grows hard.

I won't bore you with dirty details, I'll only give you highlights. At one point, when we were kissing, I came up for air long enough to tell L. Falk, "Hey, I like your music."

Thinking I was talking about the Rebbe's LP, he said breathlessly, "Schubert ... it is his quintet ... in C major."

"C major, wow! Rock 'n' roll. Like what can you do that I haven't done before?"

In the other room the phonograph needle began scratching around in the end grooves. "I can put the record on again," he said.

If I am ever nominated for sainthood, don't smile, the idea may not be as far out as you think, if I'm nominated, for sainthood, right? it will go on the credit side of my ledger that I went to Mass every single Sunday I was in Italy and I was impatient with my *Homo chaoticus,* L. Falk, only once that night. "I don't want to hear What's-His-Face's C major," I coolly informed him. "I want to hear *your* C major."

It must have been about then he rolled over on top of me and began paying attention to my boobs, which is when he spotted the tattoo, which is located in a field of freckles under my right tit. I got the tattoo on sale in Atlantic City in a moment of madness. L. Falk must have been a butterfly in a previous incarnation, because the tattoo made a big impression on him. He reached for the lamp on the floor and held it up to get a better look.

"A Siberian night moth!" he cried, touching it with his fingertips.

"It's a goddamn butterfly," I corrected him, but I don't think he heard me.

"Imagine coming across a Siberian night moth in Backwater, America," he whispered in surprise. Then he said some strange things I didn't really understand, things about how turbulence is created when a moth's wings flail the air, how the turbulence sets off ripples, how the ripples, I'm not sure I got this right, right? could paralyze the east coast of America the Beautiful. Something like that.

You need to have a weird imagination to blame a butterfly for the weather.

Like different folks have different strokes. So the sight of the tattoo really turned him on and the next thing you know we were doing it, the wild thang, the major merge. He was sweating and grunting and panting and looking down every now and then to make sure the butterfly hadn't flown the coop, and then he seemed to freeze in midair, his bloodshot eyes wide open and unblinking and startled. And then he collapsed on me.

No, I didn't actually feel him come off, but I didn't want to embarrass him by asking.

I'll answer the question before you ask it. How it was was . . . different. In ways I haven't really figured out yet, how it was was . . . satisfying. His performance, also the time it lasted, also the actual size of his equipment, excuse me for putting it so crudely, left something to be desired. On the other hand I could feel that L. Falk . . .

Just give me a sec. . . .

I could feel that L. Falk wanted . . . me, which is an impression I must have had before, I just couldn't remember when.

Naturally L. Falk needed to know how he'd done, what is it with dudes that they always have to hear what fantastic lovers they are? I didn't want to hit him with the truth—that for sheer physical sensation I couldn't see there was much of a difference between safe sex and no sex. So I hit him with a joke. "Like I've always imagined what I call the phenomenal fuck—a fuck so totally awesome that it's the mother of all fucks. In my imagination, it's so out of sight that the two or three or four who participate decide to never fuck again. So the bad news is that screwing you wasn't the phenomenal fuck. Which means the good news is we can fuck again."

I laughed. He smiled that razor-thin smile of his, which comes across as one-third faintly amused, two-thirds intensely thoughtful, as if he was trying to read between the lines.

"Hey, you asked."

"And you answered."

Later on I let Mayday back into the living room and went and warmed up some frozen pizza in the clothes drier, my stove has no oven, pizza is one of the few things I can do in a kitchen besides sunny-side-ups. I had slipped back into my Arab-type robe, but L. Falk kept parting the V with a fingertip to get a look at the butterfly. We were sitting around the table staring at the dirty dishes when he spotted this piece of chalk hanging from a string next to the blackboard where I list what I need to buy or who I need to call or when I had my last period. Suddenly L. Falk lunged for the chalk, he was a man possessed, and scribbled like a madman on the blackboard, I never erased it, it's still there if you want to check it out, y.y.a.y.t.f.h.r.m.c.o.m.a.a.t.i.o.h.f.m. Naturally I asked him what it meant, but all he said was it'd been written by L. Tolstoy, that every Russian schoolchild knew the story, that I needed to decode it for myself.

Coming back to the table he sat down so hard the folding chair folded and L. Falk landed flat on the floor.

Like I cracked up, right?

So did L. Falk. We cracked up together. I don't know why, I started laughing and he started smiling a smile that was two-thirds amused and pretty soon he was also laughing, and suddenly I was laughing so hard at him laughing I was crying. And then, I swear to Christ, he started crying too. You should have seen us, L. Falk on the floor, me kneeling next to him, doubled over with laughter, tears streaming down our faces. When we finally wiped away the tears we started in laughing all over again. Somewhere in all the laughing and crying and laughing he blurted out something else I couldn't get a handle on—something about him understanding how it was possible to wear a heart on a sleeve.

The next thing you know we were into the foreplay that comes after.

L. Fucking Falk.

Go figure.

The morning after they have their first quarrel. On the surface, at least, it seems to be about nothing.

Rain cracks two eggs into a frying pan. "Sunny-side-ups over easy, with a side order of recently swiped smoked clams, are a specialty of the house," she boasts.

"What does it mean, 'over easy'?"

"At the last second I flip the sunny-side-ups over and cook the yolk. That way the sun doesn't run into the clams."

"If you please, skip the over easy. I prefer yolks that run."

"The specialty of the house isn't sunny-side-ups," Rain announces stiffly. "It's sunny-side-downs."

Lemuel scrutinizes her. He is smiling the thin smile that is mostly thoughtful. "Who gets to decide which side is up?"

"Like it's my kitchen, right? It's my eggs. It's my frying pan. I get to decide."

"You do not give a centimeter."

Rain turns on him. "My dad, who was the hangar boss of a B-52 bomber ground crew, brought me up to defend my territory at the goddamn frontier. Sometimes it means making a big deal out of a small deal."

"We come at this dilemma from opposite ends of the spectrum," Lemuel tells her. "My father raised me to give ground, to live and fight another day, to make my stand at major rivers or cities. The Russians who stopped Napoleon, who stopped the Fascists in the Great Patriotic War, followed this formula with some success."

"Hey, do I look like a fascist?" Mayday, curled up under the table, follows the argument with her eyes. "Does this look like a major river or city? Do me a personal favor, eat the eggs over easy."

Rain flips the eggs in the frying pan. Lemuel shrugs philosophically. "When we come to a major river, a city," he says quietly, "you will discover another L. Falk."

Chapter Four

Lemuel starts off the day with a brisk walk through the aisles of the E-Z Mart. On his way out he drops off a note in Dwayne's in box pointing out which items are in dangerously short supply. "There were many more low-calorie yogurts yesterday than today," he writes. "Ditto for the Kellogg's Corn Flakes, also Mrs. Foster's crumble-proof chocolate-chipped cookies."

As the bell in the steeple of the freshly whitewashed Seventh-Day Baptist church on North Main strikes nine, Lemuel turns up at the Institute, flirts for a moment with his girl Friday, a large-bodied woman named Mrs. Shipp, who blushes when he grazes the back of her hand with his lips. Inside his office, he adjusts the venetian blinds until he gets the lighting right, paces off the distance between the walls to confirm what he already knows, that the space allotted to him is twice as big as his old office in Petersburg. From a shelf he plucks one of the books he brought with him, thumbs through it to check out variables dealing with the slow wheeling of galaxies and the wild flight of electrons, then calls in Mrs. Shipp to take dictation.

"The paper should begin," Lemuel intones, his head tilted back, his eyes closed, his ear tuned to the scratching of the fountain pen on her pad, which reminds him of the needle going round and round in the end grooves of Schubert's Quintet in C Major, "with the definition of principal eigenvalue and eigenfunction in the classical case, then should go on to discuss what I mean by the Max principle. Here I ought to insert a footnote saying that in the classical or smooth case, I am using Krein-Rutman theory for the principal eigenvalue."

"Excuse me," Mrs. Shipp interrupts. "How is the professor spelling 'eigenvalue'?"

"K, V, A, double S."

"I'm sorry . . ."

Lemuel comes up with the idiom Rain used when she was trying to explain the G-spot. "I was . . . pulling your leg, Mrs. Shipp." He spells "eigenvalue" for her, resumes dictating. "I must remember to specify that the smooth domain requires the Hopf lemma at the boundary—"

"Excuse me . . ."

Lemuel opens his eyes.

"How is the professor spelling 'Hopf lemma'?"

"D, O, O, R, followed by a new word, K, N, O, B."

Mrs. Shipp scratches it on her pad, then looks up. "That's another witticism, isn't it?"

Lemuel swivels in his chair and gazes out through the venetian blinds. He can make out students at the foot of the carillon tower riding garbage-can covers down the icy slope into the library parking lot. If he strains, he can hear their shrieks. He longs to drop what he is doing and climb the hill to the tower and ride a garbage-can cover down the slope. He wonders if it is possible, given the weight and configuration of the garbage-can cover, given the coefficient of friction of ice, given the topography of the slope, to predict the trajectory of the cover on any given run. He wonders what keeps him from joining the students howling deliriously on the hill.

He wonders what is wrong with him that he turns every earthly pleasure into food for chaos.

"I can say you it is a poor example of Russian humor," Lemuel finally tells Mrs. Shipp over his shoulder.

Later, while his secretary is typing up her notes, he copies some software from his personal floppy disks into his office workstation, then networks with the Institute's Cray Y-MP C-90 supercomputer. At the Institute, there is stiff competition for supercomputer time; Lemuel has been asked to limit himself to four hours a day so the resident scholars and visiting fellows can also access the Cray. Working quickly, he types in some variables and a few lines of computer code, runs a program, paces the room while the Cray plays with the numbers, darts to the printer when the results start to come though. He studies the paper as it runs through his fingers, shakes his head in frustration. He is convinced there is a missing variable, but where is it? How is it possible to find a variable when it is missing because it is variable? How is it possible to be passionate about something that does not exist?

"Oy"—he hears the Rebbe's refrain in his ear—"my head is spinning from all these questions without answers."

At mid-morning Lemuel joins the Rebbe for a tea break in his vast office, which is diagonally across the corridor from Lemuel's. The Rebbe's desk, at one end of the room, is awash with magazines and unanswered letters and unfinished essays and pages of *The Jewish Daily Forward* in which sandwiches have been wrapped. There are two telephones and a jar of mustard and Elmer's Glue-All and several spare light bulbs and an old portable Underwood and a box of tea bags and a Scotch tape dispenser without tape in it and a pair of opera glasses and a mug filled with sharpened pencils and a tin of Petrossian caviar filled (Lemuel learns when he gets to know his housemate better) with Procurator coins and pottery shards the Rebbe himself scavenged from the dunes of Caesarea on his first trip to the Promised Land a lifetime ago. Waist-high stacks of books are propped against the walls and the sides of chairs. Towers of books rise above the windowsills, partially blocking out the light. On the far end of the Rebbe's office, the stacked books form alleyways, the alleyways form a labyrinth. More books are piled on a table in a corner or jammed into the bookshelves on the wall facing the window.

The Rebbe reads Lemuel's mind. "You are overwhelmed by the disorder. You are asking yourself how I can find anything." He holds two cubes of sugar over his cup and, squinting, releases them one by one like bombs, splashing his desk with tea. He stirs the contents of the cup with a letter opener. "Disorder," he says, blowing loudly across the surface of the tea, taking a first noisy sip, "is the ultimate luxury of those who live in order. We create a chaos. We go slumming in disorder."

For a moment Lemuel is sucked against his will into a sinister fiction. Out-of-focus images of disorder press like a migraine against the backs of his eyeballs; a tidal wave of faceless men spills out of doors and windows; thick-soled, steel-toed shoes kick at figures on the ground.

"In St. Petersburg," he tells the Rebbe, shivering like a dog emerging from water, shedding the fiction, "we lived in a kind of permanent chaos and went slumming in order when we could find any." He adds moodily: "Which was not often."

The Rebbe nods reflectively. Lemuel shrugs. After a while he gestures with his teacup toward the stacks of books. "How many?"

"At home, here, I maybe have twelve, fifteen thousand."

"You have read them all?"

"I haven't read any of them," the Rebbe says with pride. "Jews have been depositing books on my doorstep like a Moses in swaddling for years. I take them in because they refer to God—it is against Jewish law to destroy a book containing the sacred name of God."

"Some day you will have so many books they will bury you alive."

"What a way to maybe die ... the Eastern Parkway Or Hachaim Hakadosh, crushed to death under an avalanche of books containing the sacred name of God. From such a death Christian saints are made."

"I did not know Jews could become Christian saints."

The Rebbe's face lights up in a lopsided smile. "And Simon called Peter was what?"

Lemuel takes a gulp of tea and blurts out the question he has up to now not dared ask. "If you please, how does a Jewish rabbi, a holy man from the heart of the heart of Brooklyn, wind up at an institute devoted to chaos?"

The Rebbe regards Lemuel. "Which version do you want?"

"How many versions are there?"

"There is the official version, which is available in the Institute's glossy, three-color catalogue. Then there is the more or less genuine story."

Lemuel grunts, indicating a preference for the genuine story.

"I will begin in the middle," the Rebbe announces. "I was teaching at a yeshiva in St. Louis, but was obliged to resign when my students got it into their thick skulls I maybe was Messiah. I tried laughing it off the way Jesus of Nazareth laughed it off, i.e. by telling them, 'You say that I am.' Ha! Being a Messiah is like being a spy. People keep asking you: 'So are you or aren't you?' When you point out the obvious—'If I am, would I tell you?'—it only convinces them you are.

Which I am not, though if I were I'd still say I wasn't. Anyhow, I went and bought a brownstone on Eastern Parkway in the Crown Heights section of Brooklyn and founded my own yeshiva. Things went well for the first few years, but who could have predicted the neighborhood would turn into a *shvartzer* ghetto? You are probably not aware of it, but there is a lot of competition in the yeshiva business. I began having difficulty attracting students. The hardy few who were willing to brave streets filled with unemployed Negroes were not, to say the least, the cream of the crop. Some of them could barely read and write Hebrew, much less Aramaic. I gave remedial reading and writing courses, it was like spitting on a fire. Pretty soon I was having trouble meeting the mortgage payments. I made ends meet by selling kosher wine out of the yeshiva's basement and held off the Nazi-bastard bankers—some of whom were Jewish—by accusing them of being anti-Semites. But then I brought the world down on my head with the talk-show interview. . . ."

"I thought in America you could say whatever came into your head."

"In America you can *think* whatever comes into your head. Some things you don't say out loud. What I said out loud was: We had to face the music even if we did not like the melody, the music being that in a million years goys would not forgive Jews for the Holocaust. Ha! If I had a dollar for every time my phone rang I could have paid off the mortgage. The Jewish organizations howled like wolves at my door. *The Jewish Daily Forward* castrated me in an editorial. The lending institutions smelled blood, assumed a wound and foreclosed. I lost my beloved yeshiva."

"Which brings us to the Institute . . ."

"Which brings us to the Institute. I remembered reading, maybe it was in *Scientific American*, a story about the Institute for Chaos-Related Studies. On an impulse I wrote a proposition—what did I have to lose?—pretending a lifelong passion for the traces of chaos in Torah. Since physicists and chemists and mathematicians dominated the Institute's selection board, I calculated they would not know enough Torah to refute a Rebbe, not to mention the Brooklyn Or Hachaim Hakadosh. Just as I thought, they accepted my candidacy."

The Rebbe unscrews the cover on the jar of mustard, takes a whiff of the contents, screws the cover back on again. "To tell you the honest-to-God truth, I did not at first swallow my own blah-blah-blah.

But as I went through the motions I came to see there really were traces of chaos in Torah. Ha! I have been a Torah junkie since I was a child, prying open oysters of wisdom in search of the Pearl with a capital P, which I took to be God with a capital G. And what did I find? I found a curio with a small c that turned out to be chaos!"

The Rebbe sinks back into his chair. His lids closed tiredly over his bulging eyes. "As your friend Rain says, go figure."

Just before the lunch break, Charlie Atwater shows up in Lemuel's office carrying several pages filled with measurements of the surface tension of teardrops. He doesn't specify how he got the raw data, but it is common gossip at the Institute that he is having an affair with his secretary and giving her a hard time. As it is before noon, he has not yet taken his first drink, so he talks without slurring his consonants. He is very excited.

"I've never put teardrops through the hoop before," he says. He points a slightly trembling finger at neat columns filled with figures that, to the naked eye, appear to have no order, no repetitiveness. "The numbers start out exactly as they do with room-temperature water dripping from a faucet, but then"—Atwater flips to the second page—"they go wild. I went fishing in teardrops, but I'm not sure whether I caught fool's randomness or pure randomness."

Lemuel, for the first time patrolling his Pale on this side of the Atlantic, networks with the Institute's Cray Y-MP C-90 supercomputer from his office workstation. Using a software program he devised back in the former Soviet Union, he runs Atwater's numbers through the computer looking for the telltale traces of order. The initial results are inconclusive, so he extrapolates—he extends Atwater's experiment by nine to the ninth power. Before the hour is out he stumbles across a faint trail and heads down it. By early afternoon he discerns on a horizon the almost imperceptible shadow of a pattern, the mathematical portrait of the order at the heart of a chaotic system, which chaoticists call a strange attractor. Lemuel points out the pattern, by then clearly distinguishable, to Atwater, who slurs his words. "Sho tear dropsh are chaosh-related after all. I badly need a drink."

A brittle darkness is blanketing Backwater by the time Lemuel calls it a day. "Have you heard the latest?" Mrs. Shipp asks him as he strides past her desk on the way out. "Everyone's talking about it. The random killer has struck again."

Rain, her bare feet resting on Mayday, is listening to the news on the clock radio in her kitchen when Lemuel turns up. The body of a graduate student at a nearby state university has been discovered chained to a pipe in a subbasement, a plastic bag over her head, a .38 caliber bullet hole in her ear. Rain is so terrified she forgets she has put a slice of whole wheat bread in the old-fashioned toaster with the sides that come down like flaps. She remembers when the bread bursts into flame. Mayday staggers to her feet and watches the smoke billowing from the toaster.

"I can't even do goddamn toast anymore," Rain wails. "From now on," she vows, beating at the flames with a kitchen towel, "anybody I don't know comes into Tender To, he gets a shot of laughing gas in the kisser."

Suddenly the towel in Rain's hands is ablaze. With a shriek, she flings it across the kitchen. It lands on a carton filled with paper towels and napkins. In an instant the carton is aflame. Rain grabs the container of milk on the table and tries to pour milk on the fire, but the container is almost empty. She darts to the sink, fills a glass with water and in her panic flings both the glass and the water in it at the carton, but the fire only spreads to some newspapers piled nearby. The kitchen begins to fill with smoke.

"Jesus Christ, do something!" Rain cries.

Lemuel opens his fly, takes out his penis and urinates on the fire. The flames subside, then sputter out. Rain throws open the window. Cold air invades the kitchen, which smells of smoke, urine and burned paper. She hugs herself and regards Lemuel with something akin to admiration.

"On second thought," she remarks, "your equipment leaves nothing to be desired."

Lemuel mops the kitchen floor with ammonia while Rain douses the walls with rose-scented toilet water. Later, they both collapse on the couch. Lemuel mentions an advertisement he saw in the *Backwater Sentinel* for a Nikita Mikhailkov film being shown that night in the original Russian, with English subtitles. He remarks that he longs to hear the sound of Russian again, but Rain says she absolutely has to attend a meeting at the Seventh-Day Baptist Church, there is no question of not going; likewise there is no question, with a random killer stalking the county, of her strolling down North Main Street without an armed guard.

Lemuel dryly points out that he is not armed.

Rain's face is drawn and serious as she tells him, "Hey, I know you don't actually go around with a goddamn pistol in your pocket. When I was a parole officer I hung around cops a lot, which is how I discovered that dudes who are armed look at dudes who aren't in a peculiar way. The first time I saw your wild head of hair pushing through the curtain into Tender To, I knew right off you weren't armed, right?"

Her eyes open wide in discovery. She is thinking about how he put out the fire. "With the usual weapons," she adds thoughtfully.

D.J. Starbuck removes a shoe and pounds the high heel on the lectern, but nobody pays attention.

"We've signed petitions until they're coming out of our ears," Matilda Birtwhistle shouts over the din. "We owe it to the next generation to escalate."

"Here's the deal," Rain yells, clutching Mayday under an arm. "We need to draw the line."

"This far and no farther," the Rebbe cries into one of the remote microphones. His voice booms from the two loudspeakers attached to the wall on either side of the wooden Jesus Christ crucified.

Shirley, sitting on Dwayne's shoulders, shrieks, "If they come sucking around Backwater looking for trouble with a capital T, let's give 'em trouble with a capital T!"

Lemuel shouts into Rain's ear, "Who is coming to Backwater? And what kind of trouble with a capital T are they looking for?"

An elderly professor of art history with a neatly trimmed gray goatee snatches the microphone from the Rebbe. Brandishing his cane, he shouts in a frail voice, "We must declare war. We must transform Backwater into the front line."

"Carpe diem, Professor Holloway," cries one of the football players standing under the stained-glass window. The other football players pick up the chant: "Car-pe di-em, car-pe di-em."

Half a dozen cheerleaders, fresh from a practice session and still wearing purple tights and short, pleated, gold-and-crimson skirts, scramble onto benches at the back of the church and begin chanting, "Roll 'em back, roll 'em back, roll 'em waaaaay back!" The hundred and fifty people jammed into the Seventh-Day Baptist Church take up the cry. "Roll 'em back, roll 'em back, roll 'em waaaaay back!"

"Roll who waaaaay back?" Lemuel demands plaintively.

"The bulldozers," Rain shouts into his ear.

"Can we pleeeease have some order here," D.J. cries shrilly into the lectern microphone.

"Simmer down, for Chrissake," bellows Jedediah Macy, the balding Baptist minister sitting on the organ stool to the right of the altar.

Gradually the bedlam subsides. The cheerleaders climb down from the benches. People settle into their seats.

"I move we put the question to a vote," D.J. shouts into the microphone.

"I second the motion," the Rebbe, his eyes bulging dangerously, calls into the remote microphone.

Word Perkins, the Institute's factotum, leaps to his feet. "I third the motion, huh?"

"All those in favor of militant action indicate same by saying aye."

A babble of delirious "Ayes" echoes from the rafters.

"All those against?"

D.J. surveys the suddenly still church. A leer overpowers her usual sardonic expression. "The ayes have it," she announces jubilantly.

"I say we draw lots and the loser immolates himself under the first bulldozer," Word Perkins cries excitedly.

"We voted for militant action, not a suicide raid," D.J. notes in alarm. She leans closer to the microphone. "I'll accept motions on militant action."

The Baptist minister vaults off the organ stool and thrusts a fist into the air. "Let's knock off this parliamentary crap, break up into committees and put the show on the road."

The crowd, with a bewildered Lemuel lost in its heart, roars approval.

Science says us the core of our planet is molten iron and nickel, millions of degrees hot if not hotter. Empirical evidence contradicts this. Crouching behind a low fence at the edge of the field with what Rain called the B Team, with sunrise a good half hour off, I felt through the thick soles of my new Timberland boots (which cost the equivalent, I must have been out of my mind to buy them, of 79,990 rubles at the Village Store) a bone-numbing iciness emanating from the bowels of the earth. If there was molten anything between my feet and China, I could not feel a hint of it.

Rain had warned me to dress warmly, which is how come I was wearing almost everything I owned: I had on long underwear over my short underwear, I had on two shirts, I wore the sleeveless sweater my mother knitted me after she was released from prison over my store-bought sweater with sleeves, I wore my khaki scarf wound around the lower half of my face, I had on my faded brown overcoat which fell to my ankles, I had on Rain's ski cap with something called a pom-pom at the crown.

I could have been wearing nothing for all the good it did.

We had gotten there at four in the morning in order to "take up positions" before the state troopers blocked the highway. That was how the Baptist minister had phrased it. He had been an Army chaplain in Vietnam during the imperialist war waged by America the Beautiful to dominate southeast Asia. He spoke in military terminology and made taking up positions sound like the kind of maneuver a Roman legion might execute.

I remember looking to my right and left to see if anyone in the B Team beside the Rebbe, who had not stopped whispering since we arrived, was still alive. In the silvery stillness of a waning moon, I spotted vapor seeping from the lips of Rain and Mayday and Dwayne and Shirley and Word Perkins, I heard muffled coughs and grunts farther down the line. These faint signs reassured me there was life on earth.

"In classical Hindu mythology," the Rebbe was lecturing me, he was frightened, it was his way of keeping the devils at bay, "the cosmos passes through three phases: creation, symbolized by Brahma; order, symbolized by Vishnu; and a return to disorder, symbolized by Shiva. This mirrors Creation, Eden and the Great Flood in Torah. The order of Vishnu and the disorder of Shiva, like the order of Eden and the disorder of the Flood, should maybe be seen as two sides of the same coin, two faces of the same God, two visions of the same reality. The way I read Torah, these visions coexist as they coexist in the theory of chaos,

demonstrating, you want an unbiased opinion, once
more—"

Rain's tight voice interrupted the Rebbe. "So here they
come."

Her words were picked up down the line. "Here they
come, angel," Shirley echoed in a tense undertone.

"Here they come," said Word Perkins, and snorted.

"Here who comes?" I asked Rain, but she was too busy
peering over the top of the fence we were crouching behind to pay attention to me. Willing my joints to defrost, I
rose to my knees and looked over the top of the fence. I
could see the headlights of cars creeping slowly around a
curve about a kilometer down the highway. Rain started
counting out loud in a voice that indicated her jaw muscles
were frozen. "One, two, three, four, Jesus, five, six, holy
Christ, seven, eight, nine. Seven carloads full of goddamn
cops! The big headlights behind must be the flatbeds with
the bulldozers. Who do they think they're going up against,
Saddam Hussein?"

The A Team was positioned between us and the headlights. The dozen or so kamikazes, the Baptist minister's
code name for the volunteers on the A Team, had chained
themselves together, with the ones on either end chained to
the stanchions of the bridge that straddled a frozen stream.
We could make out the kamikazes silhouetted in the headlights as the police cars drew up, three abreast, on the far
end of the bridge. We could hear car doors slam, we could
hear the kamikazes shouting the slogans they had rehearsed in the church: "Backwater has no taste for nuclear
waste," or words to that effect.

Suddenly a brilliant light flashed on, bathing the bridge
in daylight. "That means the TV cameras are filming," Rain
announced excitedly.

We could see old Professor Holloway striding back and
forth in front of the human chain, his cane flailing over his
head, as a phalanx of state troopers, some of them armed
with what looked like shotguns, approached. Then a voice
brayed over a battery-powered bullhorn, "I'm holdin' here
in my hand uh court injunction prohibitin' you from
interferin' with the 'dozers scheduled to break ground for
the nuclear-waste dump. I'm orderin' you to circulate. If

you refuse to circulate, I'm gonna hafta go an' arrest you for obstruction uh—"

The rest of the warning was lost in wailing, sirenlike feedback.

Rain pressed her lips against my ear. "Dudes who are armed also *talk* to dudes who aren't in a peculiar way, right?"

The state police made short work of the A Team. Troopers carrying enormous wirecutters moved in and severed the locks on the chains, and the kamikazes, gallantly chanting their slogan, were hauled off to a bus that had pulled up behind the flatbed trucks.

I remember wondering if the bus would be heated; I remember thinking the sooner we were arrested, the greater our chances would be of living through the night.

Our master plan, devised by the Baptist minister, the only one among us besides me (I spent my two years in the army picking cotton in Uzbekistan) with any serious military experience, was the same as Wellington's at Waterloo. As the Baptist minister explained it, our strategy was one against ten, our tactic ten against one. The A Team was the key to success. As their chains were being clipped, the kamikazes were supposed to mislead the police into thinking the other members of the anti-nuclear-waste-dump movement (are you ready for this one, Raymond Chandler?) had chickened out.

The state troopers apparently fell for the ruse, because they waved the two flatbed trucks on without inspecting the dump site. The first faint smudge of light gray mixed with streaks of ocher appeared in the east as the trucks pulled up parallel to the field, not fifty meters from where we were huddled behind the fence. Thinking that if more demonstrators turned up they would come from the direction of Backwater, the police parked their cars on the bridge, blocking it to traffic. The drivers of the two giant bulldozers, along with four men wearing plastic helmets over ski hoods, started winching down the ramps fitted onto the tailgates of the trucks.

The winches squealed. The four steel ramps clanged onto the pavement.

As if this was a prearranged signal, the Baptist minister stood up and bellowed "Onward, Christian soldiers!" With that, he leaped through a gap in the fence. D.J., a tentlike cape swirling around her ankles, plunged after him. Off to my right several football players started a flanking movement. I caught a glimpse of some nice asses as the cheerleaders, still wearing short skirts and tights, scrambled over the fence. I caught a glimpse of the Rebbe, in a coal-black overcoat and a coal-black fedora, rising with great dignity to his feet, carefully dusting the dirt from his knees before striding off toward the flatbed trucks.

"*Chazak,*" he exclaimed more to himself than to those around him, so it seemed to me. "Be strong."

"Come on," Rain yelled, pulling Mayday and me after her. Dwayne led Shirley through another gap in the fence. The next thing you know a wave of about fifty of us were dancing like American Indians around the six workmen and the two flatbed trucks.

Our tactic—ten of us to one of them—had succeeded.

One of the workers climbed up on a running board, reached into the cabin and leaned on the Klaxon. From the bridge, a siren on one of the police cars answered. We could see the state troopers scrambling into their cars. Two started up simultaneously and collided. With a screech of tires, the other cars bore down on us. Close by, the motor of one of the mammoth bulldozers spurted into life; then the engine was gunned and the bulldozer started to crawl on its giant tank treads toward the tailgate ramp.

"Kamikazes needed to block the ramps with their bodies," roared the Baptist minister.

"The kamikazes have all been arrested," shouted Dwayne.

"Oh, dear," moaned the Baptist minister.

Then state troopers in brown uniforms and brown Stetsons were spilling out of police cruisers and charging the cheerleaders, who bravely defended themselves with their batons. A blinding white light sputtered on, bathing the scene in daylight. I could make out two men with long, thin cameras mounted on their shoulders right behind the state troopers.

Rain pulled Mayday and me around to the back of the first flatbed truck, the one with the enormous bulldozer inching toward the ramp. "Lie down on the ramp," she shouted in my ear. "They won't have the guts to squash anyone."

She was holding on to Mayday's leash with one hand and my scarf with the other hand, as if the last thing in the world she wanted me to do was follow her instructions. Her voice said go, her hand on my leash said stay. Her seaweed eyes, as big as eyes get and brimming with fear, stared at me as if I was a potential victim.

Suddenly I knew where I had seen those eyes before.

Under the circumstances, lying down on the ramp was effortless. The fact is I was disappointed when I realized that this was all she expected me to do for her. I would have done anything. I would have leaped from a cliff with one of those long hemp cords that brings you up short centimeters from the ground tied to my ankle. It was a way of paying a debt.

Here I ought to insert a footnote, I ought to put the story into time. I saw a demonstration in Leningrad once, it took place in 1968 the day the state television interrupted its programs to announce that Soviet troops had liberated Prague from the counterrevolutionaries. I happened to be driving in my Skoda past the Smolny Institute, which was the Communist party headquarters when there was still a Communist party and it had a headquarters, when six valiant souls unfurled banners denouncing the Soviet invasion of Czechoslovakia. They had barely raised the banners over their innocent heads when they were engulfed by a tidal wave of KGB agents spilling out of the doors and ground-floor windows of the building, as if they had been bottled up inside for just such an eventuality. The KGB agents were not gentle with the four young men and two young women: They tore the banners from their hands and flung the demonstrators to the ground and kicked at them with the thick-soled, steel-toed shoes that KGB men always wore. I saw one of the young women being dragged by her hair toward an unmarked truck. As she was pulled across the cobblestones past my car she gazed up at me, her seaweed-green eyes fixed on mine with an intensity only a lover can bring to the act of looking. She stared at me, I realized this later, as if I were a potential victim. In the time it takes a heart to beat, an eye to blink, a lung to suck in a thimbleful of air, I fell wildly, eternally, achingly in love with her. I am humiliated to say you this, but watching her being dragged away by her hair, dear God, this is a true detail, I did not go to the aid of my beloved. I did not get out of my Czechoslovak-made Skoda and walk up to the officer in charge and identify myself as the youngest candidate member in the history of the Soviet Academy of Sciences and lodge a protest. Here were the Fascists, here was a major river, yet I did not make a stand. I still had two signatures, you see, one for internal passports and pay books and visa applications, one for documents I might want to deny having signed.

I wish to God it would be otherwise, but in my case what you see is not what you get. To my dying day I will never forgive myself for this cowardliness—which, I suppose, is why, when Rain said me lie on the ramp, I thought: What besides my life do I have to lose, since everything else I have already lost?

Which is how I came to stretch out my hundred-and-six-year-old body on the ramp while the world went crazy around me. Shadowy figures were running in every direction, people were screaming, a tear-gas canister landed at Dwayne's feet, rolled a short way, exploded under the short skirt of one of the cheerleaders, releasing a thin white cloud, the state troopers were fumbling with the gas masks, the Baptist minister was cursing and choking, D.J. was vomiting, the Rebbe, hatless, was holding her head. Out of the corner of my eye I could see Dwayne's main squeeze Shirley being dragged away by two state troopers twice her size, I could not see their shoes but I knew they had to be thick-soled, steel-toed, I could see Mayday calmly urinating in the middle of this madness, I could see Word Perkins, a crazy grin frozen on his face, letting the air out of a giant tire, I could see Rain dancing up and down under the cab of the enormous bulldozer rubbing her eyes and shrieking to the driver, "There is a human being lying on the ramp. So do you hear me, you goddamn motherfucker? You're gonna murder a *Homo chaoticus* if you're not careful."

It is hard to know whether the driver heard her over the chaos of the moment, or if he did, whether he simply did not believe her. Whatever the explanation, he continued backing the bulldozer toward the ramp. Twisting my neck, I looked up and saw the giant tread jut out over the end of the flatbed truck and begin to tilt down toward the ramp on which I was lying. I turned my head away. I was not going to move, but I certainly did not have the stomach to watch either. I felt my body grow hot and thought there might be molten iron and nickel between me and China after all until I found myself squinting into an incredibly brilliant light and heard someone yelling for everyone to get out of his way so he could shoot. It occurred to me that the state troopers were going to put a bullet through my heart before the bulldozer crushed the body it was beating in, which I interpreted as the American way of preventing cruelty to *Homo sapiens.*

I heard an unearthly Mayday-like howl from Rain. "Get off the goddamn ramp!"

I heard myself tell myself this was a major river, I was lucky to have found another one in my lifetime.

Then suddenly the pandemonium gave way to a silence so profound the planet Earth seemed to me to have abruptly stopped rotating. I wondered if such a thing was possible, I wondered if this could be the pure, unadulterated random event in the history of the universe that I was looking for. Then I noticed the Rebbe's eyes bulging out of his skull and I distinctly heard the words *oy* and *vey* spatter on the pavement like two swollen drops from a faucet and it dawned on me that I was able to hear the Eastern Parkway Or Hachaim Hakadosh because I could no longer hear the motor of the bulldozer. I turned my head to look back up the ramp but I could not see anything and then I understood why I could not see anything, it was because the tank tread was centimeters from my face and blocking my view, and I saw in my mind's eye the girl being dragged by her hair across the landscape of my uncrushed heart and I thought, Whoever you are, I have paid my debt to you, I have been passionate about someone who did not exist, and then Rain was pulling at my feet and helping me squirm out from under the tread and climb off the ramp and clinging to me and sobbing hysterically.

And then I fainted.

Chapter Five

The doors on the three large wire-mesh holding cages have been left ajar so that the sixty-eight people being detained for trial can use the toilets without bothering the sheriff, who can be heard through the open door that leads to the front office. He is trying to figure out where Jerusalem is.

"When there's sun, which isn't uh everyday occurrence, it rises through that window," the sheriff, Chester Combes, is saying, "which means by rights east oughta be somewhere over there."

"You got to take into account this here is a winter sun, sheriff," cautions Norman, the rail-thin deputy sheriff who deftly fingerprinted the demonstrators when they were bused in by the state troopers. "Which means a hair south of east oughta be just about where the water cooler is."

"You went'n asked my opinion, I'm givin' you my opinion," the sheriff tells the Rebbe with a hint of irritation. "Jerusalem looks to be to the lefta the water cooler, more near the middle row uh wanted posters on the bulletin board. You can take it, you can leave it, either way. I got other things to think about asides tryin' to figure out where Jerusalem is, like findin' uh serial killer."

"Uh-huh," Norman agrees.

"To be on the safe side," Rebbe Nachman says diplomatically, "I'll split the difference."

The Rebbe meanders back into his holding pen, converts a scarf into a prayer shawl, covers his head with an enormous handkerchief knotted at the four corners and, facing a putative Jerusalem, begins his evening prayers. Bowing and straightening and glancing over his left shoulder now and then to check for Cossacks, he intones in a singsong voice, *Borukh atoh adoynoy, eloyheynu melekh ha'oylom, asher bidvoroy ma'ariv arovim uvekhokhmoh poyseyakh she'orim uvisvunoh makhalif es hazemanim . . ."*

The football players and cheerleaders, camping on mattresses supplied by the county from its stock of disaster supplies, fill the air with a slightly jazzed-up version of "We shall overcome," but quickly get bored with it and drift into bawdy limericks. "There once was a cockney from Boston . . ." they intone in voices that become inaudible at the X-rated parts. Each limerick is capped by a burst of raucous laughter.

Sitting on a bench outside the holding pens, the Baptist minister is reading Saint Mark from a small leather-bound Bible: "They came unto the sepulchre at the rising of the sun. And they said among themselves, Who shall roll us away the stone from the door of the sepulchre?"

In a corner of the middle holding pen, a dozen graduate students, along with Backwater U's three librarians, D.J. and half a dozen teachers from the university sit in a circle around Professor Holloway, who is conducting a seminar on Etruscan votive art.

Word Perkins, half-dozing on a nearby mattress, props himself up on an elbow, smothers a yawn, adjusts his hearing aid and listens to the lecture for a while. "Can anyone ask a question, huh, Professor?" Perkins interrupts. "It's interestin', what yaw sayin', I don't mean to infer otherwise, but I don't follow how these trashcans was able to vote whit art."

"America is a country where anyone can ask a question," D.J. murmurs dryly. "Anyone has."

In the holding pen nearest Jerusalem, not far from where the Rebbe is praying, Lemuel and four fellows of the Institute for Advanced Interdisciplinary Chaos-Related Studies discuss chaos theory in low, animated tones. "Every time I read an article tracing the origins of chaos to the origins of the universe," one of the fellows complains,

"I am left with the queasy feeling that the exercise is pointless. What's the difference whether chaos came into existence before or after the Big Bang? Surely the point is that it's here."

"Shema yisro'eyl, adoynoy eloheynu, adoynoy ekh-o-o-o-d . . ." the Rebbe intones, covering his eyes with a hand, drawing out the last syllable of the word "one."

"There once was an orphan from Killarney . . ."

"And when they looked," the Baptist minister mumbles, "they saw that the stone was rolled away."

In the middle holding pen, Word Perkins sits up and addresses D.J. directly. "The trouble whit eggheads is they think once they know something, they own the thing they know."

"The *origins* of chaos," Lemuel tells the Institute fellows, "can tell us a great deal about the *nature* of chaos. Did the Big Bang, in a microsecond of quirkiness, beget chaos? Or was the Big Bang itself determined but unpredictable, and hence chaotic from the start? What was the sequence?"

"Adoynoy eloheynu emes . . ."

"There once was a wrestler from Baltimore . . ."

"Ye seek Jesus of Nazareth, which was crucified: he is risen; he is not here: behold the place where they laid him."

Word Perkins snatches the hearing aid out of his ear in disgust. "I hate folks who own what they know. . . ."

"Sequence can be elusive," one of the Institute fellows remarks to Lemuel. "Which came first, the chicken or the egg?"

"I tend to agree," says the fellow who raised the original question. He nods toward the Baptist minister. "Some things *appear* to come before other things. But do they really? Did Jesus disappear from the sepulchre before the stone was rolled away from the mouth of the cave, in which case we could conclude He was resurrected? Or did He disappear afterward, in which case we could conclude He somehow survived the crucifixion and walked off on His own two feet?"

Lemuel turns to look at Rain, who is sitting on a nearby mattress cradling Mayday in her lap, deep in whispered conversation with Dwayne. Shirley squats behind Rain, braiding her ponytail. Rain's face is drawn, her eyes dark and damaged, as if she is seeing what might have been. Her sucked-in cheeks still bear the traces of a river of tears, so it seems to Lemuel.

He turns back to the fellows. "It is true that choices made now, today, have a way of projecting themselves backward in time," he says, massaging his brow with his thumb and third finger to keep a migraine at bay. With a self-conscious grunt he paraphrases Einstein: "It is the theory which decides what we observed."

"*Mi khomoykho bo'eylim adoynoy, mi khomoykho ne'edor bakoydesh, noyroh sehiloys oysey feleh . . .*"

"There once was a lady from Tulsa . . ."

"And he said unto them, Go ye into all the world, and preach the gospel to every creature. He that believeth and is baptized shall be saved; but he that believeth not shall be damned."

"Do you consider it possible to observe something independent of all theory?" one of the fellows asks Lemuel.

"I can say you the fact that you consider observation a useful technique," Lemuel tells the fellow, "*is* a theory."

"We are the prisoners of theory," another fellow says dejectedly.

"Hey, what we're the prisoners of," Rain calls, scratching Mayday's ragged ears, gesturing with her chin toward the deputy sheriff who has appeared at the door, "is the military-industrial dudes who think they can palm off their goddamn radioactive garbage on us."

"Right on, babe," says Dwayne.

"*Borukh atoh adoynoy, goy'eyl yisro'eyl . . .*"

"There once was a scout from Milwaukee . . ."

"As I was saying," Professor Holloway tries to pick up where he left off, "the Etruscans, and most especially the early Etruscans of the 900-to-800-B.C. period, considered votive pieces—"

Carrying a clipboard, the deputy sheriff comes into the cage area. The prayers, limericks and discussions break off. "This is the last call for McDonald's," he announces. "To recapitulate, I got thirty-seven burgers, sixteen with cheese, twenty-one without. I got fourteen medium fries—"

Shirley raises a hand. "Hey, Norman, can I still switch from medium to large fries?"

"Uh-huh," the deputy sheriff acknowledges the change. With infinite patience, he scratches out one medium and adds one more to his column of large fries.

After dinner, Lemuel goes around collecting the garbage in a plastic sack, then wanders into the front office to have a word with the sheriff.

"I was just now asking myself if you got my message the other night," he says.

The sheriff, a balding, middle-aged man with a potbelly spilling over a wide, tooled-leather belt, is writing in his logbook. "What message are we talkin' about?"

"It concerned the serial killer."

The sheriff turns back a page, verifies an entry, flips the page, starts writing again. "What do you know about the serial killer that I don't know?" he asks without looking up.

"I telephoned a radio talk-show host to say him the serial murders were not random. He said me he would pass the information on to the sheriff's office."

The sheriff slowly raises his eyes. "How would you know the murders wasn't random?"

"These crimes may look random, but this seeming randomness is nothing more than the name we give to our ignorance."

The sheriff purses his lips. "What are you, some kind uh criminologist?"

"I am a randomologist who has never found pure randomness, for the simple reason it probably does not exist. I can say you there is a pattern to the crimes, you only have to find it."

Sheriff Combes, who is nobody's fool, closes his logbook and sizes up Lemuel. In the trade he has a reputation for being able to reckon a man's height and weight within one inch and two pounds. "I figure you for five nine 'n' uh half, uh hundred seventy."

Lemuel quickly converts inches to centimeters, pounds to kilos. "How did you know that?"

The sheriff ignores the question. "You gotta be from that Institute over at Backwater . . . the Advanced Confusion-Related Studies, whichever." When Lemuel nods, he adds, "I happen to be old-school law enforcement, which means unlike some uh the hotshots workin' for the State Bureau uh Criminal Investigation, I don't rule nothin' out when it comes to solvin' crimes. I wouldn't want this to get around— the state police would laugh me outa the county—but I got me uh gypsy in Schenectady who reads entrails, I got me uh stone-blind Rumanian lady in Long Branch who reads tarot cards, I got me uh defrocked Catholic priest in Buffalo who dangles uh silver ring over uh map. They're all workin' on the case, so why not uh randomologist? Tell me something, Mr. . . . ."

"Falk, Lemuel."

The sheriff cocks his head. "So you're the Falk everybody's talkin' about. I ain't personally had uh opportunity to catch you on the tube yet. So tell me, Mister Falk, what makes uh random event random?"

"An event is random," Lemuel explains, "if it is not determined and not predictable."

The sheriff's eyes stretch into a professional squint. "Let's say you was to find uh pattern to the crimes, it might lead to uh motive, uh motive might lead to uh perpetrator. Hnnn. If I was to fix you up with photocopies uh the files, would you be willin' to comb through 'em with an eye to ascertainin' whether or not the crimes in question was genuinely random?"

Lemuel says, "I have never done anything like this before. It could be an interesting exercise."

Later, before putting out the lights for the night, Norman, the deputy sheriff, threads his way around the mattresses in the holding pens and distributes plastic cups and thermoses of scalding herb tea brought over by the wives of several of the professors.

"Hey, thanks, Norman."

"Yeah, man, thanks a lot."

"Why, how thoughtful of you, Norman."

"Uh-huh."

Sitting cross-legged on a mattress in the third holding pen, Rain fills two plastic cups and passes one to Lemuel, who is on the mattress next to hers, his back against the mesh of the cage, a blanket pulled up to his neck.

"D.J. told me what all those letters you wrote on my blackboard meant," Rain remarks. "I scored points for asking the question." She takes a sip of herb tea, finds it too hot, rolls it around in her mouth before swallowing.

"I'm gonna hafta turn out the lights now," Norman calls from the doorway. "I'm leaving the lights on in the cans and the doors open, okay? Breakfast will be at eight. The trial starts at nine. On behalf of the sheriff and the other deputies, I want to say we're as much against putting nuclear-waste dumps in the county as you are. We hope you don't hold it against us, getting arrested. We was only following orders. Anyways, we want to wish you all good night and sweet dreams."

" 'Night, Norman."

" 'Night, Norman."

" 'Night, Norman."

"Uh-huh."

In the darkness, Rain reaches under Lemuel's blanket and caresses his knuckles. "Hey, you don't really believe L. Tolstoy's coded message to Sonya, right?" Touching her lips to his ear, she quotes: " 'Your youth and your thirst for happiness remind me cruelly of my age and the impossibility of happiness for me.' "

"I believe it," Lemuel mutters after a moment. "You are a figment of my fictions."

Rain leans her head against his shoulder. "Like how did L. Tolstoy and Sonya finish up?"

"Badly. They fought like wildcats for most of their married lives."

"Oh."

"In the end he ran away to die in a train station in the middle of nowhere."

Rain's voice is pitched higher than usual; she is conscious of having the first intellectual discussion of her life. "From what D.J. says, this Tolstoy dude was a phony, he liked to play at poverty, he liked wearing peasant shirts but he changed them every day, the ones he'd worn were washed and ironed by servants. You're no phony, L. Falk. A girl'd be auspicious to latch onto someone as straight as you."

"You do not know me," Lemuel groans. "What you see is not what you get. There are parts of me you have not been to yet. . . . There are parts of me I have not been to yet."

"Hey, I have nothing against the occasional side trip."

"Everyone likes the going," Lemuel shoots back angrily, though the person he is annoyed with is himself. He discovers that his thumb and middle finger are massaging his eyes again. "It is the getting there that gives you migraines."

Lemuel, insomniac, is too distracted to use the night. Dark shapes stir restlessly on the mattresses, reminding him of the reformatory he was sent to after his parents ran afoul of the KGB. He wishes he could remember where and when he lost his *Royal Canadian Air Force Exercise Manual.* He wishes he could remember why he cannot remember something as simple as the fate of a book. If only he could, a weight might lift from his shoulders. . . ."

If . . .

If . . . His entire life seems to be constructed on pilings of ifs that have been driven into a quicksand of shifting memories.

His thoughts drift to the girl Rain. Trying to reconstruct the love-making, to figure out what came before what, he feels himself being sucked into an erotic fiction. A hand slips under the blanket, discovers his hand and begins stroking his thumb as if it is something that can be coaxed into becoming longer, thicker.

A voice breathes into his ear. "Yo! You were totally hype this morning. Lying down on the ramp. . . . You could have been killed. . . . Now you're going to get your just desserts."

Lemuel, talking food, not sex, hears himself say, "I have not yet had the main course."

The voice, talking sex, not food, murmurs, "We'll begin the meal with the dessert anyhow. Think of it as the foreplay that comes after."

Lemuel hears someone fumbling with a thermos. He hears herb tea spilling into a cup. He hears someone drink. Then a body leans against him, a hand finds his hand, a warmed mouth closes over his thumb and begins to caress it with tongue and lips.

After what seems like a lifetime the warmth wanes, the mouth pulls back. More herb tea is poured into a cup and drunk. In the still darkness Lemuel thinks he can hear the liquid being rolled around in a mouth. A hand slips down to his fly and works the zipper. A voice breathes into his ear. "Like here comes the main course," it says.

It dawns on Lemuel, as the warmed mouth closes over a part of him it has not been to yet, that he is not in a fiction after all.

The court clerk is calling the roll and checking off the names on his clipboard.

"Starbuck, D. J."

"Present."

"Perkins, Word."

"Present, huh?"

"Holloway, Lawrence R."

"Present."

On a wooden bench in the back row of the county court, Rain inches closer to Lemuel, who is thumbing through file folders in a plastic shopping bag. Fondling the dog on her lap, she talks to him without looking at him. "Sometimes I think, Why bother?" she says out of the corner of her mouth. "With wheeling and dealing, I mean. With safe sex, I mean. Sometimes I think I ought to buy a boat and sail off to the goddamn horizon."

"When you reach the horizon," Lemuel tells her, "there is another horizon on the horizon."

"Fargo, Elliott."

"Present."

"Afshar, Izzat."

"Present."

"Hey, it's a lousy idea. Anyhow, boats make me nervous. They're usually on water. I can't swim."

"Woodbridge, Warren."

"Present."

"Jedzhorskinski, Zbigniew."

"Present."

"About last night." Lemuel broaches the subject warily. "Where did you learn that trick?"

Rain, coy, scratches Mayday's ear. "You mean drinking tea to warm my mouth?"

Lemuel, embarrassed, grunts.

"Nachman, Asher ben."

"Present."

"Macy, Jedediah."

"Present."

"Dearborn, Dwayne."

"Present."

"Stifter, Shirley."

"Also present."

The court clerk removes his eyeglasses, breathes onto the lenses and starts to clean them with his handkerchief.

"I learned it in junior high school," Rain says. "I must have been twelve going on thirteen. They caught me in the boys' locker room sucking face with my cousin Bobby, the basketball player I told you about? and packed me off to the school shrink, who packed me off to my mother, who packed me off to the parish priest. The priest must have suspected I was holding out on him because he asked if Bobby had touched my tits. He asked if Bobby had slipped a hand inside my underwear. He asked if I had touched Bobby's pecker. He asked if I had indulged in oral intercourse. Later I found a dictionary and looked up *indulged* and *oral* and *intercourse*. Which was when the priest's next question started to make sense. He was leaning right up against the grille, I could hear him inhaling and exhaling to beat the band when he asked me if I went and warmed my mouth beforehand. Here I was, right behind the Virgin Mary in the innocence department, right? exploring the frontiers of forbidden sex. I got the message. Thanks to the priest, I understood there was more to sex than kissing my first cousin Bobby on the lips."

"Morgan, Rain."

Rain looks up. "Yo."

The court clerk peers over the tops of his reading glasses. "The traditional response is 'Present.' "

Rain flashes a defiant smile. "Yo," she says again fiercely.

The football players and cheerleaders snicker at Rain's insolence. Dwayne whispers encouragement. "Right on, babe."

The court clerk sucks in his cheeks.

"Falk, Lemuel."

Lemuel raises a paw. "Yo."

This time there is a wild burst of applause from everyone on the benches.

"Darling, Christine," the bailiff calls over the noise.

One of the cheerleaders leaps into the aisle. "Give me a yo!" she yells.

All sixty-eight defendants respond in joyous chorus, "YO!"

"I can't hear you," the cheerleader calls.

The defendants crank the decibel count up a notch. "YOOO!"

"I still can't hear you."

"YOOOOOOOO!"

Rain leans toward Lemuel again. "When I was twelve going on thirteen, I was thin as a nail file and flat as an ironing board. I had buck teeth and knobby knees. For a while I stuffed cotton into my bra to break even. I was all arms and legs, I used to trip over myself getting out of bed. I even came down with terminal acne, I thought I'd caught it from my cousin Bobby. You can bet I was depressed, right? That's when I decided to give myself ten years to become beautiful." With a nervous toss of her head, she flicks her hair away from her eye. "This is my first year of being beautiful. I am enjoying it. A lot."

Lemuel turns to look at her. "I can say you, me too, I am enjoying it. A lot."

A door at the back of the court opens. "Everyone rise," the bailiff cries as a lady judge makes her way, heels tapping on the wooden floor, to the high bench. "County court is convened," the bailiff announces. "Honorable Henrietta Parslow presiding."

Settling into a leather swivel chair, the judge fixes her eyeglasses on her nose and summons the lawyers and prosecutors with a curt wave. Four men dressed in three-piece suits step forward. There is a whispered conference. One of the lawyers raises his voice.

"Trespassing is the most my people will plead to."

The judge taps her gavel once. The lawyers return to their seats. The judge, mumbling, starts to read the charge sheet: ". . . on or about . . . did knowingly . . . county trespass ordinance . . ." She looks up. "I'll take the defendants' pleas now."

The bailiff calls the roll again.

"Starbuck, D. J."

"Guilty."

"Perkins, Word."

"Guilty, huh?"

"Holloway, Lawrence R."

"Guilty."

Lemuel turns to Rain in panic. "Why is everyone admitting guilty?" he whispers.

"Our lawyers got them to reduce the charge to simple trespass in return for a guilty plea," Rain whispers back.

On the high bench, the lady judge is touching up her lipstick.

"Nachman, Asher ben."

"Guilty."

"Macy, Jedediah."

"Guilty."

"Dearborn, Dwayne."

"Guilty."

"Stifter, Shirley."

"Also guilty."

"Morgan, Rain."

"Yo. Guilty."

"Falk, Lemuel."

The judge stops applying lipstick and surveys the courtroom. The bailiff, the lawyers, the court stenographer twist in their seats to get a good look at the man who answers to the name of Falk, Lemuel.

"Falk, Lemuel," the bailiff calls again.

Rain elbows Lemuel in the ribs. "The fix is in," she whispers. "You cough up thirty dollars for the fine and you'll be out of here like Vladimir."

Lemuel climbs to his feet. He clears his throat. He raises his chin. "In a civilized country the man driving the tractor would be on trial," he tells the court. "He almost killed me."

The judge handles Falk with kid gloves. "The court notes you signed a charge sheet acknowledging trespass."

Lemuel shakes his head. "That is not my signature."

"He signed it in front of me, Your Honor," the bailiff asserts.

"I saw you sign too," Rain whispers. "How'd you pull it off?"

"I wrote it from right to left," Lemuel whispers back. " 'klaF leumeL.' It still says Lemuel Falk, but the handwriting comes out different."

The judge addresses the county prosecutor. "Does the defendant have a prior record?"

The prosecutor, a nearsighted political appointee sporting a bow tie, holds a yellow file card up in front of his nose. "When he was booked, Your Honor, he admitted to a previous arrest, but he claimed there was no conviction."

"I had tribulation but no trial," Lemuel says.

"As this allegedly occurred in the former Soviet Union," the prosecutor continues, casting dark looks in Lemuel's direction, "we are unable to verify the facts in the case at this moment in time."

The judge speaks directly to Lemuel. "What were you arrested for, Mr. Falk?"

"The Komitet Gosudarstvennoi Bezopasnosti discovered that someone named Falk, L. had signed a petition criticizing Soviet imperialism in Afghanistan."

"What is this Komitet whatever?"

"It was the official name of the KGB."

"And did you sign the said petition?"

"My name was on it, but I was able to convince them it was not me who did the signing. I had two signatures, one for my internal passport or my pay book or my applications for exit visas. The other signature I used to sign documents I might want to deny I signed."

"And which of these two signatures is on the charge sheet admitting trespass?" the judge wants to know.

"The one that a handwriting expert will swear you is not mine."

Somewhat testily, the judge turns to the two defense attorneys. "I don't see how I can accept guilty pleas from sixty-seven defendants if the sixty-eighth pleads not guilty. If he is found not guilty of trespass, which we have to treat as a theoretic possibility, it would mean the other sixty-seven were likewise not guilty."

The defendants in the front rows hold a hasty conference with their two lawyers, then break out of the huddle and try to talk Lemuel into pleading guilty.

"If you don't cop a plea, there'll be a trial," D.J. warns. "Who's going to feed my pussycats?"

"Another trial maybe means another night or two in jail," the Rebbe adds. "And I'm not even sure which way's Jerusalem."

"How am I gonna pay the rent on Tender To if I don't cut hair?" Rain asks.

"I've already missed two graduate seminars," Professor Holloway complains.

"I've already missed two gridiron scrimmages," one of the football players says. "Hobart is gonna swamp us Saturday night if we don't come up with a credible zone defense."

"That's Zbig," Rain informs Lemuel in a whisper. "He's a Polish-origin nose tackle with an unpronounceable last name."

"We'll have to rent lawyers," Word Perkins says, angrily eyeing the three-piece suits. "They make more an hour than I make a week."

"Does the defendant wish to enter a plea?" the lady judge prompts from the bench.

"You *were* trespassing," Rain whispers.

"Who gets to decide which side is up?" Lemuel asks Rain.

"Hey, they own the dump site," Rain says quietly. "They own the state police. They own the courthouse. *They* get to decide."

"Falk, Lemuel?" calls the bailiff.

Lemuel shrugs. "Guilty," he mumbles.

The judge brings down her gavel as if an item has been sold at auction. When the last guilty plea has been recorded, she sentences everyone to thirty dollars or thirty days, gathers her papers and scuttles like a crab from the courtroom before anyone can change his mind.

Spilling out of the county courthouse, the defendants, each thirty dollars lighter, are momentarily blinded by the dazzling sunlight. Flanked by Rain and the Rebbe, Lemuel—carrying the plastic shopping bag filled with the sheriff's file folders—hears a shy cheer float up from the street. Shading his eyes with one of the file folders, squinting, he makes out a hundred or so students milling behind police barriers in a small park across the street. An enormous spinnakerlike banner, billowing in the sunlight, floats over their heads. Printed in large letters across it is

L FALK

"What language is 'Klaf L'?" Lemuel asks the Rebbe.

"It is definitely not Hebrew, it is definitely not Yiddish. Sounds maybe Lilliputian to me."

Rain waves excitedly. "They're so stoked they're holding the goddamn banner outside in," she exclaims. "Don't you get it? It's like the 'oT redneT' on the window of my barbershop."

The students catch sight of something or someone and break into a roar that sounds like surf pounding a shore. They seem to repeat two words over and over:

"Ell fauk! Ell fauk! Ell fauk!"

"L. Fucking Falk!" breathes Rain in awe.

Two buses pull up at the curb in front of the courthouse, and the defendants begin boarding them for the fifteen-mile ride to the Backwater campus. On the street, near a white truck with "ABC" painted on its side, someone shouts, "There he is—the one in the faded brown overcoat and the ski cap with the pom-pom!"

Disoriented, Lemuel stumbles down the steps toward the buses, only to find himself confronted by two dozen grown men aiming an assortment of cameras at him. Other men holding long booms dangle microphones over his head. Flashbulbs explode in his face. Lemuel, who knows a lynching party, as opposed to a reception committee, when he sees one, backpedals; traces of alarm appear in the sudden whiteness of his normally bloodshot eyes, in the delicate lift of his brows, in the slight flaring of his nostrils.

"What made you risk your life for a garbage dump?" someone shouts.

"How do you feel about the governor suspending work on the dump site pending a new feasibility study?"

Rain grabs Lemuel's wrist and thrusts his arm over his head as if he has just won a heavyweight championship. "How he feels is totally stellar," she cries. "He comes from the country that gave the world Chernobyl. He knows what it means to drink milk from cows raised on goddamn radioactive grass."

"He is against poisoning the garden of God with nuclear waste," the Rebbe puts in.

The cameras, the microphones zoom in on Lemuel.

"Is it true you're a visiting professor at the Institute for Chaos-Related Studies?"

"What can you tell us about the relationship between chaos and death?"

"I can say you . . ." Lemuel starts to respond, but his voice is drowned out by journalists shouting questions. The hook on the question mark at the end of each question snags another question. Caught up in a feeding frenzy, the journalists don't seem to notice the absence of answers.

"Is that a designer overcoat you're wearing, Professor?"

"Have you ever attempted suicide before?"

"If they bring the bulldozers back, will you lie down on the ramp again?"

"He knows which side is up," yells Rain. At her feet, Mayday senses her mistress's excitement and responds with a nervous fart. "If they come back," Rain adds, "so will the visiting professor."

"Were you aware you were being televised while you were lying on the ramp?"

"Did you realize the shot would appear on prime-time TV?"

"Eighty million Americans saw you defy death. How does it feel to be an instant hero?"

"How does it feel to attract crowds?"

"I am allegoric to crowds," Lemuel mumbles.

"What did he say?"

"Could you repeat that?"

Before Lemuel can open his mouth, someone calls, "Can you comment on how it feels to be alive?"

"Is it true you were a leading dissident in the Soviet Union?"

Lemuel tries to slip a word in. "There is no Soviet Union anymore—"

"Can you confirm the rumor that you once lay in the path of Brezhnev's limousine to block it from leaving the Kremlin?"

"Is it true you were arrested in Red Square for demonstrating against the Soviet invasion of Afghanistan?"

"Is it true you signed petitions calling on the KGB to publicly apologize for seventy years of terror?"

"I signed petitions, but I did not use my real signature—" Lemuel tries to explain, but the questions continue to drown out his answers.

"Is there anything to the rumor that you left Russia to avoid military service?"

"What do you think of American women?"

"What do you think of American food?"

"What do you think of America?"

"Your towns, your citizens are smaller than in Russia," Lemuel starts to reply, "though maybe they only seem smaller because I was expecting—"

"Are you married?"

"Have you ever been unfaithful to your wife?"

"If you were to meet the President of the United States, what would you ask him?"

In a sudden lull Lemuel can clearly be heard to say, "I would ask him how one city can be more Florida than another."

"Are you for or against the fifty-five-mile-an-hour speed limit?"

"Are you for or against women's liberation?"

"Are you for or against capital punishment?"

"The socialists had their chance," Lemuel says, "now the capitalists must be given the opportunity to—"

A television reporter turns and speaks into the camera. "The Russian immigrant who risked his life to defend the county against nuclear pollution is definitely in favor of capital punishment."

"Would you share your views on acid rain with us?"

"What is your opinion on busing as a way of solving racial imbalances?"

"If you buy a car, will you buy American or Japanese?"

"Do you have an opinion on the budget deficit?"

"Are you now or have you ever been a member of the Communist party?"

Lemuel murmurs, "There is no Communist party anymore," but he might as well not be there.

"Are you now or have you ever been a homosexual?"

"Is there any truth to the rumor about your testing HIV-positive?"

"If you had it to do all over again, would you do it all over again?"

"If you could re-live your life, what would you do differently?"

"If you could undo something you've done, what would it be?"

"If you could do something you left undone, what would it be?"

Without thinking, Lemuel blurts out words that make no sense to him. "I would say them it was me who hid the exercise manual." But nobody pays attention.

"How do you feel about abortion?"

"Do you plan to apply for political asylum?"

"Do you plan to apply for American citizenship?"

"Do you have any plans to run for Congress in the next election?"

"What are your academic ambitions?"

Rain pulls one of the dangling microphones down to her mouth. "He has no ambition," she shouts into the microphone—it is a sound bite that will make the national six o'clock news programs. "L. Falk is downwardly mobile. He wants to live and let live in a county without radioactive garbage dumps, without serial murders, without birds choking to death on bloated rice."

"What's *your* name?" a reporter demands.

"R. Morgan," Rain shouts back, "as in J. P. Morgan. In case you are not familiar with him, he had something to do with money, which is what I want to have something to do with."

"Would you look this way, Mr. Falk."

"Could you gaze up at the American flag over the courthouse, Mr. Falk."

"Can you raise his hand over his head again, Miss."

"What is your position on legalizing drugs?"

"On protecting the ozone layer?"

"On using fossil fuels?"

"What is your position on abortion?"

"He's already fielded that question," a well-known anchorwoman notes.

"How do you feel about distributing free condoms in high schools?"

"I am too busy looking for pure, unadulterated—" Lemuel starts to say.

"How do you feel about doing away with the Electoral College?"

"I am *for* educa—" Lemuel starts to say.

"Thank you for the interview, Mr. Falk," one of the journalists shouts up from the street.

"You are—" Lemuel starts to reply, but the journalists are already racing off to meet deadlines. Muttering under his breath, he completes the sentence: "—a pack of earlobes."

Part Two

AMBULANCE

Chapter One

A whisper of something other than winter finds its way into Lemuel's ear: a breeze grazing ground that is no longer frozen, water gushing through the throat of a creek that is no longer choked with ice, the knell of the carillon reverberating through air that no longer stings the nostrils. Confirming the beginning of the end of winter, Lemuel discovers the single hand on Rain's Swiss watch that tells the phase of the moon and the season leaning against the "S" of "Spring."

In a wistful fiction, he sees himself leaning against the "R" of "Randomness."

Something of a celebrity now, Lemuel holds out in the apartment over the Rebbe's for three full weeks after the trespassing trial before packing his enormous cardboard valise, his Red Army knapsack and his duty-free shopping bag and spiriting them into Rain's loft. The official explanation for this change of venue is that he is on the lam from the television reporters who besiege the Rebbe's house day and night, who set up klieg lights outside in the hope that he will crack a window and holler answers to their hollered questions. The real reason for the move is that he has grown accustomed to Y-jacking in the bathtub with a female whose nakedness is more than skin-deep, to sleeping in the same bed with a Siberian night moth, to being roused mornings by Occasional Rain murmuring "Yo!" in his ear as she coaxes exploitable erections from his drowsy flesh.

From long experience with tribulation, he wonders when the bubble will burst and the trial will begin.

The telephone in the apartment over the Rebbe's head never stops ringing after Lemuel moves out. The Rebbe bounds up the stairs, toppling several waist-high towers of books in his eagerness to answer the phone. Introducing himself to each caller as Lemuel's business agent, he jots down offers to endorse ecological laundry detergents or non-polluting oven cleaners.

"You are letting yet another lucrative opportunity slip through your callused fingers," he scolds Lemuel when he phones in with the day's messages.

Lemuel pays scant attention to the Rebbe. There have been five more murders in the three weeks he has been working with the dossiers the sheriff gave him, bringing the total number of victims to eighteen. He is obsessed with quantifying the information in the sheriff's files, feeding bytes into his computer and devising software to test the material for randomness. Has he, at long last, stumbled across an example of pure, albeit macabre, randomness? His heart says, Why not? His head tells him that this seeming randomness is nothing more than the name he gives to his ignorance.

But what doesn't he know?

"What would I do with the money?" he asks when the Rebbe nags him about the latest phone call, an offer to endorse biodegradable underwear. "I am already rich beyond my wildest dreams. The Institute pays me two thousand U.S. dollars a month. In Petersburg, this is worth two million rubles. When I left Russia, my monthly salary at Steklov was seven thousand, five hundred rubles."

"In your wanderings, haven't you stumbled across something called capitalism? With money you make more money," cries the Rebbe. "With more money you can serve God, you can build a yeshiva, you can spend your waking hours, your sleeping hours too, unraveling strands of chaos in Torah." He adds in exasperation: "I don't understand your attitude. It is not American."

"I am not American," Lemuel reminds the Rebbe.

"That's no excuse."

With the temperature running above freezing for the third day in a row, Rain can be heard in the garage under the apartment tuning up an antique Harley-Davidson. Come Sunday, she revs the motor and takes Lemuel for a spin on the narrow, winding unpaved road that meanders around the lake and through a forest of pines west of Backwater. Glued to the jump seat behind Rain, hanging onto her with his thighs and arms, the side of his head flat against the back of her worn leather aviator's jacket, the wind whistling past his ears, the clouds flitting through the bare branches overhead, he experiences a curious elation . . . a letting go. He feels he is moving for the first time beyond the world of chaos toward . . . what?

Toward something he has had no experience with, cannot quantify, much less identify.

Skirting the lake on the way back to Backwater, Rain pulls the Harley off the road, cuts the motor, strolls down to the edge of the lake to study her reflection in the still water. "I really did get beautiful," she observes as Lemuel comes up beside her.

"You did not get modest," he comments dryly.

"Hey, don't rag on me," Rain fires back. "A girl needs to know what she's got going for her."

They stretch out in the sun, which projects warmth as well as light for the first time since Lemuel's arrival in the Promised Land. The sound of Rain's voice droning in his ear makes him drowsy, and he drifts into a fitful sleep. The little boy is cringing in a corner . . . the faceless men wearing thick-soled, steel-toed shoes are taking apart an armoire. . . .

Rain shakes him awake. "You're not going to go to sleep on me!"

"I was resting my eyes."

"Where was I? Like when they cremate people, right? the fillings in teeth disintegrate and eat away at the layer of ozone protecting us from the sun. The fancy name for this is the greenhouse effect." Rain turns her head and spots a smug grin on Lemuel's face. "So I don't see how you can smile about something as serious as the end of the world. I read where in ten years' time there'll be no more ozone, which means no more winter. The polar ice caps are already melting. If it keeps up, every coastal city in the world will be under water."

"How do you know so much about the greenhouse effect?"

"My ex-husband, the bird killer, grew marijuana in a greenhouse. You want some free financial advice, L. Falk—invest in companies making rowboats, canoes, inflatable rafts, things like that. I used to live in Atlantic City, but being a nonswimmer, I moved inland to Back-water."

On the way home Rain stops off at the E-Z Mart and scores two jars of imported gefilte fish. Passing the checkout counters, she gets into a long discussion with Dwayne and Shirley, her best friends in Backwater. Dwayne argues that the basic division in the world is between the haves and the have-nots and, by extension, between the largely white, industrialized countries in the Northern Hemisphere and the largely black, agrarian countries in the Southern Hemisphere. Shirley claims Dwayne has never recovered from his Harvard education. The world is divided, any idiot ought to be able to see it, she says, between males and females. Rain cracks everyone up by insisting the world is really divided into anal and oral camps. "Anyone who thinks different is out to lunch," she says.

"Which one are you, babe?" Dwayne asks with a leer. "Anal or oral?"

"I'll give you an educated guess," Rain retorts.

On the spur of the moment Rain invites them up for a pot luck supper. Shirley, chewing gum intently as she eyes Lemuel sitting on the Harley's jump seat in the parking lot, asks, "Is your Russian squeeze gonna hang around to party?"

"Your hard-on is showing, babe," Dwayne taunts.

Shirley actually blushes. "Only boys get hards-on."

"The plural of hard-on," Dwayne informs her with a raunchy smirk, "happens to be hard-ons."

"There he goes again," Shirley tells Rain, "opening his fly and exposing his Harvard education."

Rain told me you dudes were tight," Lemuel says as they pull folding chairs up to the kitchen table.

"We go back a long way," Dwayne says. "Isn't that a fact, babe?"

Rummaging in a drawer for a church key, Rain smiles at Dwayne. "I worked as a cashier at the Mart my freshman year," she explains to Lemuel. "It was Dwayne here who bankrolled me when I came up with the idea of opening Tender To and cutting hair."

"And dealing drugs," Shirley adds mischievously.

"You go with the flow," Rain says. "Dwayne saved my butt—he cosigned the lease and loaned me the money to buy the barber's chair Shirley found in the junk shop in Rochester."

Dreaming away on her blanket, Mayday twitches in her sleep.

"She's chasing butterflies," Rain explains.

Lemuel says moodily, "Me also, I chase small winged creatures in my sleep. Along with pure, unadulterated rainbows."

Shirley pushes the jars of gefilte fish across the table to Lemuel. "I bet you thought she was swiping this stuff from the Mart," she tells him. "Dwayne's the last of the bleeding hearts—he lets all his friends score."

Lemuel remarks, "A bleeding heart can also be worn on the sleeve."

Shirley looks puzzled. "A *what* can be worn *where?*"

Lemuel turns to Dwayne. "So you knew all along Rain was scoring things from the store."

"No skin off my nose," Dwayne says. "I mark up everything to make up for what I lose to shoplifters."

Rain tosses the church key to Dwayne, who opens the beers. "Hey, I told you they padded the prices," she says.

Shirley says, "Rain likes to say we have got to shoplift every now and then to make sure supermarkets don't profit from people not shoplifting." She flings an arm around Rain's ass and gives it a squeeze. "You are something else."

"I like you to death," Rain laughs. She leans down and kisses Shirley lightly on the lips.

"Oh God, me too," Shirley says with an awkward giggle.

Lemuel serves the gefilte fish. Rain deals matzos as if they were cards. "You being of Jewish persuasion," she tells Lemuel, "I thought you'd dig this."

"It comes from Israel," Shirley puts in brightly.

"As long as you were scoring gefilte fish, you could have scored horseradish," Dwayne complains.

After supper Lemuel excuses himself to go into the spare bedroom and feed more bytes from the sheriff's files into his desktop work-station. The others drift into the living room. Shirley drapes herself over the back of the couch and asks Rain for a hit. Rain pulls a hollowed-out copy of *The Hite Report* from a shelf, opens it on the table, pushes aside the LSD tabs and packets of hash, helps herself to a joint, curls up in front of the television set, which has a Humphrey Bogart movie on without the sound. She lights up, takes a long drag, hands the joint to Shirley, who takes a drag and passes it on to Dwayne.

"I don't get it, babe," Dwayne says to Rain in an undertone.

"What don't he get?" Shirley asks Rain. "What don't you get, angel?" Shirley asks Dwayne.

Dwayne toys with the silver ring in his ear. "I don't get Lem and her. I see what's in it for him, you'd need to be blind not to. But what's in it for Rain?"

"Lem's a cutie-pie," Shirley says. "I'll take sloppy seconds any time."

"He comes from a country where there's practically no Black Plague," Rain explains with a defiant half smile. "Also he's innocent—when's the last time one of you dudes wore a bleeding heart on your sleeve? Also, he's smarter than the three of us put together."

"Right as Rain," Shirley says dreamily.

"I have a last-but-not-least," Rain adds. "Since I've been rooming with him, I don't hear drums in my ear."

"But does he like yogurt?" Dwayne asks suggestively.

"Dwayne here sure likes yogurt," Shirley notes. "Don't you like yogurt, angel?"

"Rain is aware I like yogurt. Isn't that the case, babe?"

Rain watches Lemuel, hunched over his computer, through the open doorway of the bedroom. Halfway through the second joint, she jumps up, snaps off the television and motions for Dwayne and Shirley to put the show on the road.

Shirley pouts. "You're not gonna go and kick us out, are you? It's still today."

"I was sorta hoping we could crash, babe," Dwayne announces.

"I was hoping to check out the merchandise," Shirley, by now pleasantly high, admits.

"Take a rain check," Rain says.

"We get off on Rain's checks, don't we, angel?" Shirley coos.

"Rain's checks don't bounce," Dwayne says with a knowing smile.

Rain supplies them with a couple of joints for the road. Collapsing onto the couch, she kicks off a shoe and caresses Mayday with her toes. After a while she calls out, "Like being around you makes me feel inadequate, right? Can you hear me, L. Fucking Falk? I mean, I know beans compared to you. You know so much you even know what you don't know. Where'd you learn all that stuff about chaos and randomness?"

Lemuel ambles into the room, raises his brows when he notices the hollowed-out book filled with capsules and packets and joints. "What happened to Dwayne and Shirley?"

"They packed it in." She regards Lemuel suspiciously. "So like how does someone become a *Homo chaoticus*?"

Lemuel sinks onto the couch next to her and rubs his eyes, which are redder than usual. "I picked up everything I know on the subway," he explains. "I had a professor, his name was Litzky, he was an innovator, he lived, he breathed chaos before the rest of the world knew it was a science. He was expelled from Moscow University for antiparty tendencies after someone found a copy of Solzhenitsyn's *First Circle* in his desk drawer. That happened in mid-term. Professor Litzky continued giving his lectures on the subway. He would phone up his students, name a Metro stop, specify a time. We all crowded into the car, the doors closed, Litzky would start talking about fractals as a way of seeing infinity, about the infinite cascades of bifurcations, about intermittencies, about periodicities. He would lecture for twelve or fifteen stops, some of us scribbling drunken notes as the subway lurched down the tracks. We would slip envelopes filled with rubles into the enormous pockets of his overcoat while he lectured. Scholarly articles written by Litzky were never published, books were out of the realm of possibility, but even today he is thought of as the father of Soviet chaos."

Lemuel shakes his head in despair. His voice thickens. "You should have seen us, hanging out on the subway, holding on for dear life to the straps, leaning toward him so as not to miss a word, a syllable, him in his two-sizes-too-big overcoat, pausing at each stop when the recorded announcement came on to say us the name of the station, then plunging back into chaos. Folded-towel diffeomorphisms I learned about between Aeroport and Rechnoi Vokzal. Smooth-noodle maps, between Komsomolskaya and Marx Prospekt. We relished the voyage, we dreaded the getting there. We never knew at what station the lecture would end. Litzky always waited until the last instant, leaping out of the train as the doors closed, once his coat got pinched in the door, we had to pull the emergency cord to free him. He would stalk off and disappear in the crowd, his head pulled in like a turtle's, lost in his coat, lost in his thoughts. We would look at each other, bewildered by things he had not explained, had assumed we would understand, bewildered by a world where chaos was passed from hand to hand, like an old shirt, to passengers on a subway. Later, when we sat for orals we were asked to cite our sources, but no one had the courage to mention Litzky, so we lied and named papers by obscure Transylvanians or Magyars." Lemuel shakes his head, trying to digest his own story. "In *Crime and Punishment*, Dostoevsky has a character named Razumikhin say us how it is possible to lie your way to truth." His voice chokes up, his eyes focus on something in his past. "I have, all my life, God help me, lied my way to truth."

Walking with one shoe on, one shoe off, Rain comes up behind Lemuel, pulls his head back onto her chest and massages his brow. "Russia," she hears him mutter, "is an inner eyelid."

"Compared to America," Rain says, following her own thoughts, "Russia is totally hype. The only interesting thing that ever happened to me on a subway was when this dude exposed himself. Go figure."

Insomniac, Lemuel patrols the cluttered living room into the early hours of the morning, contemplating the lack of whiteness to the night, scribbling differential equations on the backs of envelopes, trying to unravel the mystery of the serial murders, which keep coming up random no matter how many times he tosses the coin.

Sometime after midnight Rain wanders through in search of a glass of water. She is wearing furry bedroom slippers with no backs and a T-shirt that has shrunk in the wash and barely covers her navel. The faded letters across the chest read: "Women who seek to be equal to men lack ambition." Under the message is the name "T. Leary."

"Who is T. Leary?" Lemuel asks as Rain shuffles back from the kitchen.

"I think he was a contemporary of L. Tolstoy." She flops into the only easy chair in the room, her legs dangling over the arm. On her blanket, Mayday stirs, yawns, then closes one eye and watches Rain with the other. Glancing back through the open kitchen door, Rain notices the "y.y.a.y.t.f.h.r.m.c.o.m.a.a.t.i.o.h.f.m." on the blackboard. "So I've been meaning to ask you," she says with elaborate casualness, "how long are you signed up for at that chaos institute of yours."

"The visiting-professorship contract is for one semester."

The silence between question and answer is suddenly alive with electricity.

"What happens then?"

Lemuel shrugs.

"Like did you ever think of staying? At the Institute? In America?"

"What do I have to do to become American?"

Rain manages a strained smile. "Hey, buy a gun."

Lemuel laughs, but his heart obviously isn't in it. "Me staying on at the Institute depends on whether there is an opening as a resident scholar."

"So if you decided to stay in America, there might be other ways, right?"

He grunts.

"I mean," continues Rain, annoyed, "do you *want* to stay in America?"

"I have not given it much thought," Lemuel says vaguely.

"Maybe you ought to give it much thought," she says. When he does not respond, she shrugs irritably. Her bare arm reaches out to flick on the radio. She catches the end of the WHIM news break:

". . . weather in the tri-county on this third day of March looks to be partly cloudy, which means partly not cloudy, with occasional showers in the afternoon and temperatures rising into the high forties or low fifties. If you're staying indoors, you want to wear as little as possible. Are you taking notes, Charlene, honey? Ha ha! Okay, we'll go and take some more calls now."

The host chats for a few minutes with a woman who is against abortion, then talks with a Catholic priest who is against contraceptive devices. "What justifies carnal knowledge," the priest says, "is the possibility of procreation."

Incensed, Rain grabs the phone and punches in a number, which she seems to know by heart. "I have enough credits to get a goddamn bachelor's degree in carnal knowledge," she remarks. "Hello," she shouts into the phone. "So it's me again."

A staticky voice echoes back at her from the radio. "It's me again."

"You're up kinda early, Rain. Or maybe you're up kinda late."

"I got woken up . . ." "I got woken up by the previous caller shooting off his mouth about carnal knowledge. Like is he out to lunch. He knows so little he doesn't know what he doesn't know."

"Can you play that back for me slow like."

"Like what do priests know . . ." "Like what do priests know about screwing? The reason I'm a practicing Catholic but Catholicism is not what I'm practicing, right? is because organized religion is a conspiracy against women."

"Pay attention, Charlene, honey. Rain's coming up with a new conspiracy theory."

"Fucking A. You want my opinion ..." "Fucking A. You want my opinion, religion is a male plot to deny women multiple orgasms, which men can't have, by making us feel guilty if we take pleasure from sex. And let's not beat around the goddamn bush. Everyone knows good orgasms come in twos."

"I take it you're speaking from experience."

"Hey, I've had my share ..." "Hey, I've had my share of experiences. The best ones were with people of the Jewish persuasion."

"What's so great about Jewish lovers? What with me being a practicing Seventh-Avenue Adventurist, maybe it'd be better if you don't listen in to this part, Charlene, honey."

"Like I'll tell you ..." "Like I'll tell you what's so great about Jewish lovers. First off, you stand less chance of getting cervical cancer, right? if your partner's circumcised."

"Where'd you shop that pearl of wisdom from?"

"I read it ..." "I read it, it was either in *The Hite Report* or *The Backwater Sentinel* or *National Geographic*. The reason I know it was one of these three is because they're the only things I read extracurricular."

"I always heard men who were circumcised had less feeling."

"I never had ..." "I never had complaints along those lines."

"I'll bet you haven't. You want to leave your phone number with the operator before you hang up. Ha! Only kidding, Charlene, honey. Nice talking to you, Rain. For anyone just joining us, you're listening to WHIM Elmira, where the elite meet to beat the meat. I'll take another call."

"Hey, I could tell you a thing or two about priests," Rain forges on. "Like the time I had to confess to kissing my cousin Bobby on the lips ..." She notices her voice is no longer echoing from the radio. "How do you like that? The earlobe went and hung down on me."

Lemuel stops by the E-Z Mart on his way to the Institute, takes a quick turn around the aisles with Dwayne trailing after him, a stub of a pencil poised over his pad. He has discovered in Lemuel a natural talent for supermarket management. The visiting professor has figured out that a supermarket has a lot in common with a ship: both are perfect metaphors for the science of chaos in the sense that order is thought to be lurking behind the appearance of disorder. On more than one occasion, searching for traces of order amid the chaos of the shelves, Lemuel has alerted Dwayne to flaws in the Mart's computer program, which tailors the inventory to meet the projected needs of the community.

"I have a sinking feeling you are low on iceberged lettuce," Lemuel observes as they pass the vegetable counter. "Ditto for Dijon mustard, Mrs. Hammersmith's low-calorie doughnuts, the imported French dressing, economy size Stay Free." Lemuel stops in front of an item he has not noticed before. "Yo! Like what is a Roach Motel, Dwayne? If someone checks in what would prevent him from checking out?"

Making his way past the checkout counters, Lemuel is saluted by Shirley. She runs her fingers through her naturally wavy hair. "Z'up?" she asks.

"Nuch," Lemuel tells her.

Shirley arches her body, pushing tiny pointed breasts into her white smock. "So I still got this soft spot for gate crashers."

"Don't have a cow," Lemuel laughs.

A scrawny cashier, ringing up the purchases of a squat Oriental man at the next counter, interrupts her work to shyly ask Lemuel for an autograph.

The Oriental man, dressed in a pin-striped suit and speaking with a clipped British accent, asks the cashier, "I say, is he a celebrity?"

Shirley giggles happily. "Is he a celebrity or is he a celebrity?"

The scrawny cashier bats enormous false eyelashes. "I seen you on the tube," she tells Lemuel with great solemnity. "I think you was fly."

The Oriental man grimaces. "Fly?"

Lemuel snickers, "Like your customer needs a clue or two, right?" He turns to the Oriental man. "I can say you 'fly' is the same thing as 'beautimous,' which is a kissing cousin to 'volumptuous.' The King's English," he adds with a wink. "Go figure."

Lemuel's girl Friday flags him down as he is entering his office. "J. Alfred wants a word with you," Mrs. Shipp confides.

"I am delighted to see you," the Director tells Lemuel, drawing him into his corner office a few minutes later. He steers his visitor to a leather couch, hovers over him wringing his hands. "Coffee, tea, slivovitz with or without mineral water?"

Goodacre nods in eager agreement when Lemuel suggests that it is too late in the morning for coffee, too early in the day for alcohol. The director settles onto an Eames chair, swivels 360 degrees as if he is winding himself up, gnaws thoughtfully on his lower lip, clears a throat that doesn't need clearing.

"Is your work going well?" he inquires solicitously. "Have you been made to feel at home in the Institute for Advanced Interdisciplinary Chaos-Related Studies?"

Lemuel blinks slowly. "Like being here is opening my eyes to a lot of things."

"I'm relieved to hear it," says Goodacre. "You convey the impression of someone who knows which side his bread is buttered on, who is not offended by a discreet word to the wise. The day you arrived I remember dropping a hint about grooming. No sooner said than done." He fires off a jovial burst of conspiratorial laughter in Lemuel's direction. "I can tell you the Institute is not insensitive to the distinction of having someone of your caliber on the faculty. We like to think we are giving the Institute for Advanced Studies at Princeton a run for its money. Having the likes of you around certainly helps make us competitive. Which brings me to the kernel of the corn, the eye of the storm. Even though we are located in an out-of-the-way valley in an out-of-the-way corner of Puritan America, we like to think of ourselves as a citadel of liberalism, a tolerant community composed of consenting intellectuals. What you do, whom you do it with, is your affair."

Lemuel grunts.

"Still," Goodacre goes on, his voice barely distinguishable from the sound emitted by a rusty hinge, "there is a threshold to pain. . . . There are limits to liberalism. . . ."

Lemuel reads between the lines. "You are talking about Rain."

"You moved out of the apartment over the Rebbe. You moved in with her."

"The goddamn phone was all the time ringing off the hook, right? The nights were artificially white—there were klieg lights on the street. I could no longer use the night to—"

"I was confident I would be able to get through to you—"

"Rain offered to teach me American English—"

"There is a chair opening up . . . a resident scholar's contract . . ."

"I can say you our relationship, Rain and me, is purely oral—"

"The Rebbe has made it known he wants to return to Eastern Parkway and set up a yeshiva that teaches chaos in the O.T. . . ."

Both men take deep breaths.

"To dot the i's and cross the t's," Goodacre begins again, "a high-profile liaison between one of the Institute's visiting professors and an undergraduate barber half his age strains our liberal tradition. You are here, Lemuel—you don't mind if I call you Lemuel?—on a one-semester contract. It was our hope, and, given what is happening in the former Soviet Union, I suspect yours, too, that this would lead to an offer of a permanent chair."

Lemuel stirs uneasily on the couch. His heart tells him the Russians who fought Napoleon were wrong to give ground, Rain's dad was right: Territory has got to be defended at the goddamn frontier. I am going to make a big deal out of a big deal, he thinks, I am going to say something for the first time in my life without a subtext. Can I reasonably expect to survive the experience? Do I really want to survive the experience? He closes his eyes, kneads a lurking migraine with his thumb and third finger, sees himself, in an aching fiction, stride up to the officer in charge, identify himself as the youngest candidate member in history of the Soviet Academy of Sciences and begin to protest against police brutality.

"I am probably missing something, J. Alfred," he hears himself mutter in a voice he can not quite place; like the second of his two signatures it is certainly not his. "You do not mind if I call you J. Alfred? Is who I fuck chaos-related?"

Goodacre's mouth falls open. For a moment Lemuel has the impression that the director is suffering from cardiac arrest. He wonders if you can be convicted for manslaughter in America the Beautiful for saying something without a subtext.

Eventually Goodacre's jaw snaps shut. He pushes himself to his feet. "Thank you for stopping by," he tells his visitor. He does not offer to shake hands.

Lemuel hikes a shoulder. "Nuch," he mumbles. "Fly."

"You said what?" Rain explodes when Lemuel phones up Tender To to tell her about his conversation with J. Alfred Goodacre. "You think there was no subtext, right? but there was."

Lemuel hears heartache where he expected happiness. "So what was the subtext?"

"Like you don't want to stay on in Backwater, that's the subtext. Like you don't want to live with an undergraduate barber half your age." Lemuel starts to protest, but she cuts him off. "You relate to my butterfly tattoo, but you don't much like the female *Homo sapien* that goes with it."

"You are reading this wrong," Lemuel protests. "He wanted me to stop the bus and get off our relationship. I said him not. I said him to fuck off."

"Hey, terrific. What *are* you going to do when the visiting professorship expires? Who else in America is going to employ a *Homo chaoticus* who's passionate about something that doesn't exist? Boy, are you out to lunch!"

"*Give her time,* she'll maybe calm down," the Rebbe tells a depressed Lemuel when he turns up in Nachman's office for tea and sympathy.

"Is it true what Goodacre said about you going back to Eastern Parkway when the school year is up?"

"It happened very suddenly. I sold IBM, I sold General Dynamics, I raised some seed money from a third party for whom I occasionally do free-lance work, I used the money to buy into a cooperative yeshiva opening on the corner of Kingston Avenue and Eastern Parkway in the heart of the heart of Brooklyn. The object is to create a parochial school that is not parochial. There are two other Rebbes besides me, one will teach anti-anti-Semitism, a positive approach to the New Testament that will stress the Jewishness of Jesus and the Apostles. The other Rebbe will teach a survey course on martyrology from the serpent in Eden, condemned to crawl on the surface of the earth for the capital crime of recommending fruit, to Jesus of Nazareth, condemned to crucifixion for the capital crime of claiming to be King of the Jews. Me, I will offer a course called "Chaos and Yahweh: Two Sides of the Same Coin." I came across a delectable quote for the course description in the yeshiva's three-color catalogue, maybe you know it, maybe you don't, it's George Russell warning the young James Joyce, 'You have not enough chaos in you to make a world.' What do you think?"

Before Lemuel can respond, the Rebbe has hurtled off on another tack. "My predicament, I was agonizing over it last night, I am agonizing over it this morning, is that I love Yahweh, how could it be otherwise? but I don't really *like* Him, blessed be His name. There are days when I am sick to my gut. Why, I ask myself, is the Eastern Parkway Or Hachaim Hakadosh, who lusts among other things after order, sucking up to a God whose middle name is Randomness? There are days, I will admit it to you, when I am tempted to follow the advice of Job's wife—I'm talking Job 2:9. When she finds her poor bastard of a husband scraping away at his boils, she tells him, 'Dost thou still retain thine integrity? curse God, and die.' "

"Hey, what stops you?"

The Rebbe flings his arms into the air in a gesture of resignation. "I love life," he admits, "especially when you consider the alternative. Also, there's an old Jewish proverb which I am about to invent. It holds you should live as long as possible so that you'll be dead as short a time as possible."

One of the two phones on the Rebbe's desk purrs. He snatches it off the hook, mumbles *"Hekinah degul,"* listens, raises an eyebrow, passes the phone to Lemuel. "It's your amanuensis," he says. "That's Lilliputian for girl Friday."

Over the phone, Mrs. Shipp sounds as if she is broadcasting from an airport control tower. "Another one of those journalist creatures has requested permission to land on your runway," she informs Lemuel. "This one is a she who speaks with an accent which reminds me of yours, only thicker. When I asked her where she hailed from, she said something about other people's chaos being greener. Is that a country? I put her into a holding pattern in the conference room at the end of the hall."

"I do not trust journalists," Lemuel tells the Rebbe. "Marx, Lenin, Trotsky were all, at one time, journalists, and look what they did to Mother Russia."

Lemuel barrels through the door into the conference room, prepared to send the journalist packing, he only gives interviews by appointment, he never gives apppointments, but comes to a skidding stop when he spots the lady journalist in question.

"Zdrastvui, Lemuel Melorovich."

"Yo! Axinya! *Shto ti delaesh v'Amerike?"*

"Horoshi vopros," she says excitedly.

Chapter Two

If you cannot believe your own eyes, whose eyes can you believe? Yet there she was, large as life, larger even, flashing an uptight smile that had no relation to humor, her tits sagging into a brassiere that had been washed so often it looked like a dust rag, the dust rag of a brassiere clearly visible through a rayon shirt that had turned yellow with age, her eyebrows plucked to the bone and arched in anxiety. My mistress from St. Petersburg, Axinya Petrovna Volkova, come to coax God knows what from my reluctant flesh.

"*Zdrastvui*, Lemuel Melorovich."

"Yo! Axinya! *Shto ti delaesh v'Amerike?*"

"*Horoshi vopros,*" she said excitedly. "Where can we talk?"

Speaking Russian felt awkward. I racked my brain in vain for the equivalent of "Z'up?" or "Don't have a cow." "It depends on what you have to say," I finally told her.

"Your Russian has grown rusty," she remarked. "You speak with an accent."

I could see she was tense. She kept glancing at Mrs. Shipp through the open door, she kept ironing nonexistent wrinkles out of her skirt with the palm of her hand, a gesture which brought back to me an image of Axinya in Petersburg—after making love, she would spread a towel on my desk and meticulously iron each of her garments before putting it on. Once I accused her of trying to erase the traces of passion, but she vehemently denied it. "Wrinkles, even in clothing, make you look older than you are," is what she answered.

"My editors at *Petersburg Pravda,*" she was saying now, "subscribe to the Associated Press. They saw the story about the crazy Russian lying down on the ramp to stop the bulldozers from breaking ground for a nuclear-garbage dump. They sent me to interview you."

"That happened more than three weeks ago. You took your sweet time getting here."

"I came by train and cargo boat and bus," she said. "Plane fares are too expensive for *Petersburg Pravda.*"

Something told me I should have been out of there like Vladimir. "You did not come all this way to ask me my opinion about abortion or the ozone layer," I guessed.

She leaned closer. Her breasts fell into their washed-out safety net. "Has someone else's chaos turned out to be greener? Come home to the chaos you know, Lemuel Melorovich. I made discreet inquiries; your tenure at the Steklov Institute of Mathematics has not been revoked." She let her fingertips drift onto my thigh. I noticed that her nails were bitten to the quick. "Things have changed in Russia," she went on. "The Americans have established a fund to keep Russian scientists from going to work for Libya or Iraq; now they pay everyone except the cleaning women at Steklov in United States of America dollars. I have been told that someone with your seniority would get sixteen dollars a week. That comes to almost sixteen thousand rubles a week, sixty-four thousand rubles a month."

"There is no such thing as a ruble anymore," I started to say, but Axinya forged ahead with her pitch.

"That's not counting a year-end bonus of fifty dollars, that's not counting what you can pilfer from faculty luncheons—"

"I am toast," I told her in English.

"What language is 'I am toast'?" Axinya asked in Russian.

"It is Lilliputian," I informed her. "It means I am tired," I added tiredly.

Axinya got up and shut the door and came back and pulled her chair around so that we were sitting side by side. She leaned to her right, she talked to me out of the side of her mouth, her eyes fixed straight ahead, I leaned to my left, I listened to her with my eyes closed.

"The truth is they sent me because they thought the message would be more congenial if you had screwed the messenger."

"Who sent you?"

Her lips barely moved. "They. Them. The people you did the cipher work for. They also subscribe to the Associated Press."

I was alarmed to hear her refer to my work in ciphers, I myself had never breathed a word of it to anyone back in Petersburg. In situations like this I almost always clear my throat, so I suppose that is what I must have done.

"They are not angry at you, Lemuel Melorovich," she rushed on. "They will not hold your leaving against you as long as there is a coming back to balance the scales. The way they see it, you panicked when your request for a visa was not turned down."

It occurred to me that her little speech had the wooden ring words acquire when they have been rehearsed. In front of a mirror? In front of the *they* who would not hold my leaving against me as long as there was a coming back?

"You decided chaos had infected the rotting core of the bureaucracy," Axinya was saying. "Those were your words. You decided the situation was worse than you had imagined. They want you back, Lemuel Melorovich, which means the situation is better than you imagined. Which also means things are not as chaotic as they appear to be. You decided the time had come to go because they gave you permission to leave. Now the time has come to return because they want you back."

I raised a finger, a student requesting permission to get a word in edgewise. "I would like to ask you a delicate question."

Out of the corner of an eye I saw her hesitate.

"Do you have something called a G-spot?"

She turned to stare at me. "A what spot?"

I admitted her that I was enormously relieved to hear it, and every syllable of every word came from the heart.

Please understand, after a certain amount of instruction from Rain I more or less knew *where* the G-spot was, but I was still not absolutely sure *what* it was. There are only so many questions you can ask without looking like the idiot you are.

I decided to change the subject. "Where are you staying?"

"In the motel at the edge of town," Axinya replied. "It costs forty thousand rubles a day. Thank God it's not me who's paying. I only earn four thousand, eight hundred rubles a month." She burst into tears. "For the love of God," she blurted out, her breasts heaving in time to her sobs, "come home."

I opened the door and called down the hall for Mrs. Shipp to get Rain on the phone for me.

A moment later the telephone in the conference room buzzed. I snatched up the receiver and heard Rain's voice in my ear.

"Z'up?" she said.

"Hey, you are not still pissed?"

"Not," she replied in a tone that made it clear she was.

I turned my back on Axinya and cupped my hand around the phone. "I relate to your body," I said quickly. "I think it is fly. I relate to your Siberian night moth—"

"Like I don't need this. . . ."

"You take getting used to," I insisted with some urgency.

"Yo." She sounded reluctant to be gotten used to.

"I need you."

"What you need is a clue or two."

"I am seriously weighing the pros and cons of becoming passionate about someone who exists."

There was a long pause.

"Did you hear what I said you?"

"I'm not deaf."

"A Russian friend from Petersburg has turned up in Backwater. . . ."

"Hype for him."

"Him is a she."

Rain hesitated an instant, then casually dropped an invitation into the conversation. "Hey, bring her home for supper."

I explained the situation to Axinya. The person I shared an apartment with, a barber, right? a senior at the university specializing in the economics of the home, had invited her for supper. Axinya, to whom communal apartments were the rule, not the exception, anything else would have caused her to become suspicious, shrugged. "I don't mind," she told me with a distant look in her eyes, "as long as the going involves a getting there."

She let me work her arms into the sleeves of her leather overcoat lined with an old cloth overcoat, she let me lead her out of the building, down the street past the laundromat to the block of flats in the alleyway off North Main, up the narrow flight of wooden steps. She never uttered a word the whole way. I was running my fingers over the cement lintel, feeling for the hidden key, when Rain threw open the door. Angling her head, smiling an iceberg-lettuce smile, she sized up the Russian competition.

"Axinya, Rain. Rain, Axinya."

"I am pleased to make your acquaintance, I'm sure," Rain announced in a strangely masculine voice. She took Axinya's coat and flung it over the back of the couch, which was piled high with coats and sweaters and mini-skirts. "Like where does she go for her glad rags?" she asked me out of the corner of her mouth.

Axinya eyed the room with distaste. Left to herself, she would have rolled up her sleeves and put it in order. *"Shto ona gavorit?"* she wanted to know.

"She is asking where you bought your shirt. She has a weakness for transparent clothing."

"Hey, the two of you must be talking Russian, right?" Rain decided. "Like I'd actually forgotten L. Falk was a foreigner."

At supper Rain pulled out all the stops, serving sunny-side-downs on cold toast, serving Italian wine from a bottle covered with plastic straw, serving whole wheat bread and thin slices of cheese so badly made it had holes in it. She set a plate in front of Axinya, offered her the bottle of catsup, smothered her own eggs with catsup when Axinya warily declined.

To her credit, Rain tried to strike up a conversation with the extraterrestrial who had landed on her doorstep, which was how she saw the Russian lady with the see-through blouse and the washed-out brassiere. "So what do you do when you're not visiting Backwater?" she asked Axinya.

"I khad a gooood voyage, tank you so much," Axinya replied.

Rain was not put off by the failure of the answers to have any immediately apparent relation to her questions. "Is this your first visit to America?"

Axinya looked at me. "Isn't she on the young side for you?" she inquired in Russian.

"Our relationship is platonic," I informed Axinya in Russian. "She cracks eggs, she makes sunny-side-downs, I wash up afterward."

Axinya hung out a smile to dry on her face, a sure sign that she had not swallowed a word I had said. She turned back to Rain. "I vas borned"—she asked me in Russian how to say *after* in English—"affta de death of Iosif Stalin, so I am not k-nowing vat it vas like." Having gotten this off her chest, Axinya for some reason breathed a sigh of relief.

"Hey, I want you to know I'm really sorry," Rain, her face longer, grimmer than I had ever seen it, told her.

"She says you she is sorry," I translated when Axinya looked blank.

"She talks like a machine gun," Axinya remarked in Russian. "For what is she sorry?"

I batted the question on to Rain.

"I am sorry about Stalin. Dying."

Mayday picked that moment to stagger into the kitchen and sniff at the patterns on Axinya's stockings. Wagging an obscenely hairless stump of a tail, peering through cataract-studded eyes, the dog must have thought she was getting a whiff of an exotic skin disease.

Jerking her knees away from the snorting pink nose, Axinya shrieked in Russian, "What is it?"

"A dog. She is very old," I added, as if it explained everything—the folds of gray skin hanging from the neck, the black tongue trailing from the drooling mouth, the runny eyes, the pink pig's nose.

"Age is no excuse." Axinya detected a noxious odor and screwed up her nose in disgust.

Rain, always alert to Mayday's social failings, coaxed the dog away from Axinya's feet. "Chill out, Mayday. Go fart into your blanket."

Axinya said smugly, "She called the *thing* Mayday."

"That happens to be its name."

"Could it be you fled Soviet chaos only to wind up sharing a flat with an American Communist?"

I laughed under my breath. "The only Marx she ever heard of is Groucho."

Axinya was not convinced. "She named that grotesque animal after the proletariat's high holy day, the first of May."

When I passed this tidbit on to Rain, she giggled nervously. "Hey, Mayday's not named after a holiday. She's named after my dad's last words. He was a sergeant in the air force, right? He was heading back to the air base late one night in January when his Volkswagen Beetle skidded into a telephone pole. I was mostly living alone at the time, my dad's squeeze was hanging out with this chief petty officer from the *Forrestal,* so when he dialed the only number he knew by heart, it was me that picked up the phone. He was calling from a booth which turned out to be down the road from the scene of the accident. All he said was *Mayday.* Over and over. Again and again. *Mayday. Mayday.* I decided he was drunk and hung down on him. To this day I don't know what Mayday means, assuming it means anything. The next morning the military cops came by to say they'd gone and found my dad's body in this telephone booth. They said he'd bled to death."

Rain's story, or more exactly the matter-of-fact way she told it, took my breath away.

"If you're going to faint," Axinya said anxiously, "put your head between your knees."

In my skull I could hear a child's voice whine, over and over, again and again, *It was not me who hid the code book.* For the first time in my life I recognized the voice. It was mine, though God knows why I was denying hiding a code book.

I turned on Rain. "What are you telling me?" I demanded in the fierce whisper Russians employ when they argue in communal apartments.

She freaked out. "If he'd gone and used the King's English like any normal human being, maybe I would've understood he was in some kind of difficulty."

"Your father was bleeding to death in a phone booth and you call that some kind of difficulty?"

"The last thing I need is for you to lay a guilt trip on me." She kicked at the plastic garbage sack in exasperation.

"All this happened before I gave my first blow job to Bobby Moran, I wasn't even a consenting adolescent, forget adult. Get off my case."

Axinya was thumbing through the M's in her English-Russian phrase book. "Mayhem. Mayonnaise. Maypole. But no Mayday." She looked up, hoping to pour oil on our fire. "It's probably some kind of American Indian religious rite. It sounds like the kind of thing a primitive person would say before dying."

Rain insisted I translate. "My dad was definitely not a primitive person," she icily informed Axinya.

It went on that way for an epic half hour or so. Giving a workmanlike imitation of a housewife, Rain cleared away the dirty dishes, stacked them on top of the mountain of dirty dishes already piled next to the sink, served decaf and doughnuts. Axinya asked if there was a toilet in the apartment and disappeared into it when I flicked on the light. When I returned to the kitchen, Rain looked at me in what I thought was a peculiar way.

"She has to be the lady friend you told me about, right? The one you saw on Monday afternoons and Thursday evenings? The one who straightened your room beforehand and ironed the sex out of her glad rags afterhand? So do you want to make it with her?"

"Yo?"

"Here's the deal: you want to fuck her, go with the flow, it's cool with me. Like I could watch, right? Or I could participate. Or I could pull a disappearing act. Whichever."

"You want to par-ti-ci-pate?"

"Join in. Take part. Co-lab-o-rate." One of her eyes twitched suggestively. "Hey, check it out. Rock 'n' roll."

I took a deep breath, I squared my drooping shoulders, I threaded my fingers through my tangled hair. "I do not want to fuck her," I announced with what I took to be grim dignity. "I do not want you to participate or disappear."

"So there's no reason to get pissed."

"I am not pissed," I insisted, but I was lying through my badly repaired, tarnished teeth. I was pissed at Rain for not feeling responsible for the death of her father. I was pissed at Axinya for turning up in Backwater. I was pissed that Rain was being so cool about it. I was pissed that she could think I would want her to collaborate with me collaborating with Axinya. (I had heard about such things, I had even fantasized about such things, but I considered them to be manifestations of the decadence of the West.) Most of all, I was pissed at myself for being frightened because the earlobes I had done cipher work for back in Russia had noticed my departure and wanted me back.

Down the hallway, the toilet flushed. Axinya took her sweet time returning. Rain and I exchanged looks. I shrugged. Rain shrugged back. When she reached up to put the decaf back on the shelf, her T-shirt drifted away from her body, exposing for a fraction of a second the soft undercurve of a breast and the Siberian night moth lost in a sea of freckles.

As we say in Russian, I rinsed my eye. Also my heart.

Axinya wandered into the kitchen. She had a diabolical expression on her face. "I saw the Swedish safety razor I gave you for your name day in the medicine chest next to her sanitary napkins," she informed me frostily in Russian.

"Hey, I don't mind your talking to each other in a secret language," Rain said snappily.

"There is only one bathroom," I explained to Axinya in Russian. "In the one bathroom there is only one medicine chest."

"There is only one bedroom," Axinya shot back. "In the one bedroom there is only one bed."

"There is a couch in the room with my computer which opens into a bed."

"It is currently closed. If you ever bothered to open it you would see it has no sheets."

"I was wondering what took you so long," I said under my breath.

"Act as if I'm not here," Rain muttered. "I'm cool."

Axinya fumbled in her handbag for an embroidered handkerchief, delicately blew her nose into the part of it that was not embroidered. "When is your contract here up?" she asked. "What can I do to convince you to return with me to Russia?"

Suddenly, I do not know why, I wanted to hurt her. "What is in it for you if I go back?"

Tears welled in Axinya's eyes, causing her mascara to run. "How can you ask me such a thing?" She tucked a stray tuft of silver hair back into place. "You are in it for me."

Observing Axinya's tears brim, observing one of them trickle down her cheek, I made a mental note to talk to Charlie Atwater. He had already taken a look at the surface tension of teardrops, but there was another chaos-related angle to explore. Given the weight, configuration and surface tension of a teardrop, given the coefficient of friction of skin, given the topography of the cheek down which the tear would flow, I wondered if it would be possible to predict the trajectory of the teardrop on any given run.

I wondered how I could be so detached about Axinya's distress.

What was it with me when I should have been feeling emotion, I wound up thinking chaos?

Did I have enough chaos in me to make a world? Or too much chaos in me to live in the world I make?

Rock or roll, right?

Walking wounded, right?

My head was spinning from all these questions with painful answers.

Axinya must have noticed how distracted I was. "There was a time when the sight of me in tears moved you to tears," she said, turning her back on Rain to hide her emotions, dabbing at her eyes with a corner of the handkerchief. "When my mother died it was me who had to comfort you, it didn't matter that you had never met her. America has put its mark on you, Lemuel Melorovich. Even your English sounds strange—not like English, really."

Yawning noisily, Rain scraped back her chair and padded over to the sink and started washing her underwear in a basin, splashing water everywhere. "Your Russian lady friend is beginning to rub me the wrong way," she announced over the sound of the running faucet. "I don't think I'd collaborate even if you begged me."

"What does she say?"

"You are the second live Russian she has ever met," I explained tiredly. "Her basin runneth over."

Axinya slowly turned her head and sized up Rain the way only a woman can inspect another woman. "Her ass is too small," she said in Russian, "her mouth is too large, her earlobes have a peculiar shape, she does not come equipped with hips or breasts. Seen from certain angles, she looks like a boy. What's in it for you, sleeping with her?"

I thought, She is in it for me. But the urge to hurt Axinya had passed and I did not say it out loud.

Axinya folded her arms across her chest, or more accurately, rested her arms on her chest. "I'll bet she has a G-spot," she declared in a sudden flash of inspiration.

"If I did a major merge with someone whose breasts drooped as much as hers," Rain commented from the sink, her lips drawn into a tight smile, "I'd pass the Cadillac."

"She talks a great deal," Axinya commented nastily. "Does she say more than listening to can explain?"

"It is her kitchen. It is her eggs. It is also her frying pan."

"Does she really own a Cadillac?" Axinya, impressed despite herself, asked in Russian.

"She is not feeling well," I explained to Axinya. " 'Pass the Cadillac' is Lilliputian for 'throw up.' "

"That's the second time you have mentioned Lilliputian," Axinya noted irritably. "What is it, a local upstate New York dialect?"

God knows how I would have explained Lilliputian if we had not been distracted by the siren. Its pitch changed as it turned into the alleyway, a result, as any schoolchild knows, of the Doppler effect on sound waves. Axinya, who happened to be standing next to the kitchen window, stared at the flashing light on top of the police car as it skidded to a stop in front of the wooden staircase. I remember Raymond Chandler using the expression "The blood drained from her face," but I had never seen the phenomenon with my own eyes until then. Suddenly as gray as sidewalk, Axinya put a hand on the windowsill to keep from crumpling to the floor. "It's the militia," she gasped in Russian. "They have come to arrest me as a Russian spy."

I went over to the window as the car door slammed and recognized Norman, the deputy sheriff who knows where Jerusalem is. He looked up and waved. I raised a paw and saluted him through the window. He started up the stairs.

"Not to worry," I told Axinya. "It is only Norman."

Rain went through the living room to open the front door and returned with Norman in tow. He came striding into the kitchen. The metal taps on the soles of his shoes clicking on the linoleum sent an electric current up my spine. Dropping two file folders onto the kitchen table, he noticed Axinya cringing in the corner and nodded amiably in her direction.

"Explain him, for God's sake, that I am a journalist, not a spy," she hissed at me in Russian. She turned toward Norman and bared her teeth in a tense smile. "So good day to you, Police Officer."

"She is an old friend from St. Petersburg," I informed Norman, "here to interview me about the nuclear-dump affair."

Norman touched the broad brim of his sheriff's hat with his fingertips. "Any friend of Lem's."

"What does it mean, 'Any friend of Lem's'?" Axinya demanded in Russian.

"Americans have this habit of saying you half a sentence and letting you figure out the other half for yourself," I explained her. "That is why the political situation in the country is so confused. What I think he is saying you is, Any friend of Lemuel's is a friend of his."

My explanation only added to Axinya's bewilderment. "How could I be a friend of his when I only just now met him?"

Still wearing his hat, Norman adjusted his holster and testicles and straddled a folding chair as if it was a saddle. Rain placed a cup of lukewarm coffee on the table in front of him. Rocking back and balancing the chair on its hind legs, Norman announced, "The sheriff sent me over." He started to say something else, but his eyes went blank as he forgot what it was. To cover the lapse, he tilted the chair forward and spooned sugar into his cup until the coffee spilled over the rim into the saucer. He looked up at us looking at him. A light came into his eyes as he remembered what he wanted to say.

"It ain't been announced on the radio yet, but there's gone and been two more serial murders—one upcounty, a seventy-seven-year-old Caucasian male working as a night watchman at a shoe factory, the other in Wellsville two hours later. The second victim was a forty-four-year-old Japanese male working at an all-night gas station. Both the victims was shot in the ear with a garlic-coated dumdum bullet fired at point-blank range from the same .38 caliber pistol. First time we've had us two murders so close apart in time and place."

"Oh, Jesus," Rain gasped from the sink. "The goddamn random killer has struck again."

"Do you think I should contact the Soviet embassy?" Axinya anxiously asked in Russian from the window.

"There is no Soviet embassy anymore," I muttered in Russian.

"Like they are speaking a foreign language," Rain explained to Norman.

"Uh-huh," Norman said. He turned toward me. "Sheriff'd like to know where you're at. The gypsy in Schenectady who reads entrails, the blind Romanian lady in Long Branch who reads tarot cards, they've both thrown in the sponge. You and the defrocked Catholic priest who dangles a ring over a map are the only two still looking for the perpetrator." Norman flashed a boyish grin. "Asides the police."

I made a mental note of "throw in the sponge," the meaning was clear from the context, and started to leaf through the two file folders Norman had brought over. "When you see the sheriff," I told him, "say him I am getting warmer."

Norman took a gulp of lukewarm coffee, decided to add more sugar, as if sweetness could compensate for coldness, then took another gulp.

"You're getting warmer," he repeated.

"Warmer to knowing whether the killings are random or not."

"Uh-huh."

After Norman left I borrowed Rain's Harley, kicked the motor over and ran Axinya back to the motel across the Backwater town line.

"Welcome to the cockroach motel," I told her as we pulled up in front of her cabin. "You check in, you do not check out."

"You've changed," Axinya said. "You used to act dirty, but you never talked dirty." She leaned forward and fitted her lips against mine. In Russia this had passed for kissing. "Come home," she whispered breathlessly. "Here you are a fish out of water."

I disengaged her arms as gently as I could and backed

toward the Harley. "I will swim when and where I will swim."

"What keeps you here?" she wanted to know. Her voice had the plaintive quality the Russian language tends to take on when you ask questions to which you know the answers.

Two cabins down a porch light snapped on and the Oriental man I had run into at the E-Z Mart stuck his head out a door. "If you absolutely must quarrel," he called in his clipped British accent, "might I be so bold as to suggest you save it for the A.M. when you will both be fresher."

I kicked the Harley until it jumped under me and gunned the motor. Axinya must have repeated her question, I could see her lips mouthing the words "What keeps you here?" With the Harley roaring in my ears, I mouthed words back at her. In Russia, I tried to tell her, I used to stand around waiting for good news. Then I stood around waiting for news. Then I stood around waiting for death. Over the years my ankles had swelled. My heart, too.

The last memory I have of Axinya, as I drove off on the Harley, was the perplexed expression on her face, which led me to suspect that my message had been garbled in transmission.

Hey, lip reading is not easy. Heart reading neither.

When he gets back to the apartment, Lemuel finds the projector covered with mauve silk turned on and Rain sitting stark naked in a yoga position on the only bed in the only bedroom. He takes a long look at her hips, her breasts, decides they look perfectly female to him. Rain has switched off one of the two bed lamps and set the other on the floor, a signal she is expecting sexual activity.

"Like what's your position on yogurt?" she asks.

"In Russia, everyone thinks people who eat yogurt live longer."

Rain seems relieved. "I once read in this women's magazine where you don't get something called a yeast infection if you douche with yogurt, so from time to time that's what I go and do."

In the shadowy light of the bed lamp on the floor, Lemuel slips into a mouth-watering fiction. The Siberian night moth under Rain's right breast is fluttering its wings, almost as if it is beating off a swarm of freckles. . . .

"About the yogurt," Rain says with that half-defiant, half-defensive smile that Lemuel has come to recognize as her badge of insecurity, "you could think of it as a midnight snack."

Which is how Lemuel finally comes face to face with a part of the female body he has not been to before. Which is also how he comes to savor, he is sure it must have happened before, he only cannot remember when, a getting there as well as a going.

Occasional Fucking Rain!

Freshly shaven, the usual patch of toilet paper clinging to the usual coagulated cut on his chin, his cheeks reeking from a few dabs of Rain's rose-scented toilet water, Lemuel drifts at midmorning down South Main Street, past the post office, the drugstore, the pool hall, the bookstore. Overnight their façades have been whitewashed and splashed with psychedelic graffiti depicting in lurid detail the invasion of Backwater by Martians, the theme of this year's Spring Fest. Bands of Martians, their faces grease-painted the color of grass, their ears pasted back and pointed, their heads aflutter with rubber antennas glued to the bones above their eyes, scramble along the narrow paths of the long hill that dominates the village, shrieking unintelligible syllables of an invented language as they storm dormitories and leap out of ground-floor windows brandishing the spoils of interplanetary war: panties, brassieres, crinoline slips once the personal property of coed earthlings.

On the lawn in front of the bank across the street from Lemuel, the electronic billboard, instead of time and temperature, is flashing an inspirational communiqué: "It's never too late to have a happy childhood."

Lemuel has no illusions about the universality of the message. As far back as he can remember, it has been too late to have a childhood, forget happy. Beyond that point, events are veiled in a shifting haze that occasionally dissipates long enough for him to catch a glimpse of something he does not want to see . . .

"*Golbasto momaren evlame gurdilo shefin mully ully gue!*" a fraternity brother Lemuel remembers seeing at the Delta Delta Phi bash yells to a Martian friend as the two trot past the billboard.

"*Tolgo phonac,*" the boy shouts back.

"*Tolgo phonac,*" the first Martian agrees with a horselaugh.

From the carillon tower on the wood line of the hill comes a raucous peal of bells. Beating the air with their wings, dozens of pigeons nesting in the top of the tower swarm into the sky. Martians have occupied the carillon tower and are belting out what the *Backwater Sentinel* identified as the Spring Fest's official anthem, a melody that sounds suspiciously familiar to Lemuel. It hits him where he has heard it before: Rain has played it on her French horn. "Oh, when the saints, come marching in," Lemuel sings in time to the carillon bells, "Oh when the saints come march-ing in, da da da, da da da da-da, when the saints come march-ing in."

Farther down the street there is a commotion as a cavalcade of convertibles, their horns drowning out the carillon bells, turns off Sycamore onto South Main. The cars, packed with Martians, proceed in a slow cortege down the white line of the wide street. A pickup truck with a television crew from a Rochester TV station filming from the back drives parallel to the cortege. Lining the sidewalks on either side of South Main, Martians cheer on two streakers sandwiched between the cars of the motorcade. As they jog past, wearing only sneakers, Dwayne, the E-Z Mart manager, and Shirley, his main squeeze, who turns out to have naturally wavy pubic hair, salute the crowd.

Dwayne, his testicles and enormous penis flapping, catches sight of Lemuel. "Lem, babe, z'up?"

"Yo. Nuch." Lemuel tries to act as if chatting with a naked man jogging down South Main is an everyday occurrence. "Like I did not know you went in for jogging."

"Yeah, babe, I also do t'ai chi. A sound mind in a sound body, that's my philosophy."

"It would be mine too," Lemuel mutters, "if I still had my *Royal Canadian Air Force Exercise Manual.*"

"So I hear I'll be seeing you later," Dwayne calls over his shoulder.

"Rain went and invited us up again for supper," Shirley shouts in a high-pitched voice.

The TV cameraman calls to her from the back of the pickup truck, "How about a big hello for the folks back home."

Laughing hysterically, covering her small pointed breasts with one arm, Shirley twists and waves to the television camera with her free hand. She shouts back at Lemuel, "Whatcha say after supper I teach you how to write your name backwards?"

"Rock 'nnnnn' roll," Dwayne yells into the television camera, raising his fist.

An echo comes from the Martians in the open cars. "Rock 'nnnnn' roll."

Lemuel meanders into the Kampus Kave. The waitress, whose name is Molly, looks up from her comic book. "Well, if it ain't Mr. One With, One Without," she says. "With ya in a jiffy."

Lemuel notices the Rebbe in a booth near the back, slides onto the bench across from him. The Rebbe, looking like death warmed over, is carving יהוה into the tabletop with a small bone-handled penknife.

"So what are you writing?" Lemuel wants to know.

"Yod, he, waw, he. Which spells 'Yahweh.'" The Rebbe raises his bulging eyes heavenward, focuses on the three-blade ventilation fan hanging from the ceiling directly above him, daring God to strike him dead for pronouncing His sacred name out loud.

Molly sets two cups of coffee in front of Lemuel. "One with, one without," she says with a straight face. (It has become their little joke.) She angles her head to get a better look at the Rebbe's handiwork. "I don't mind folks carving initials in my tables, everyone does it, it's more or less traditional," she says, "but given the fact we're in the U.S. of A., it seems to me it ought to be in English."

"You'll maybe make an exception for the name of God?"

"Jesus, born in a manger in Bethlehem, is the name of God."

"Jesus, who almost certainly wasn't born in Bethlehem, that story had the rug pulled out from under it by biblical scholars, is the name of the son of God. I'm carving the name of His Father who art in heaven."

Molly watches the Rebbe etching the unfamiliar letters into the wood. "My first husband, may he rest in peace, all of a sudden started in writing backwards after his stroke. I had to hold the paper up to a mirror to see what he wanted."

"In Hebrew," the Rebbe says, "right to left is frontward."

"You're having me on."

The Rebbe squints up at her. "Stop me if you've heard the old Jewish proverb I am about to invent. It's the story of a man who's agnostic, insomniac and dyslexic. He lies awake nights wondering if there is such a thing as a dog."

"If that there's a joke, Rabbi Nachman, I sure don't get it," Molly admits.

" 'Dog' spelled backwards is 'God.' "

Molly purses her lips. "I don't see what a dog has to do with God."

Shaking her head, she pushes through the swinging doors to the kitchen. Lemuel adds sugar to both cups of coffee, absently stirs the without as he sips the with. "You look very depressed, Asher. Hey, I hope your yeshiva deal did not fall through."

The Rebbe, contemplating a tragedy worse than the Holocaust, shakes his head. "It's much more serious. There's this passage in Torah where Yahweh pulls Abraham outside the tent and points to the night sky. 'Count the stars,' He tells him. 'So shall thy seed be.' I'm talking Genesis 15:5. I was re-reading it yesterday when the tragic news hit me over the head like a ton of books." The Rebbe, wringing his oversized pink paws in agony, glances up. Lemuel spots tears glistening in his eyes. "Don't you see it? The number of stars in the sky is fixed, not endless. Which means Yahweh is telling Abraham he'll have a fixed, not an endless, number of descendants. What Yahweh is saying—my God, I could kick myself I didn't see it before, I could kick myself harder for seeing it now, who needs this kind of information rattling around in his brain?—is that the Jewish people will come to an end one day."

"New stars are forming from primordial gases all the time," Lemuel says.

The Rebbe perks up. "Are you sure of your information?"

"Sure I am sure. Only last week astronomers published photographs of fifteen embryonic stars in the Orion Nebula. Out in the infinite reaches of space, stars are dying and being born every day of the week, every hour of the day."

A sigh of relief bursts from the Rebbe's lips. "Oy, that was a close call. I feel like a condemned man who just got a last-minute reprieve."

The Rebbe folds away his pocketknife, irons the wrinkles out of a dollar bill with his palm, weighs the bill down with the small metal container filled with toothpicks, swipes some sugar cubes from the bowl. "Lucky for the Jews I ran into you today," he tells Lemuel as he slides off the bench and slumps toward the street.

Lemuel has finished the with and is taking his first sip of the lukewarm without when the squat Oriental man who berated him for arguing with Axinya at the cockroach motel approaches the booth. He is wearing a three-piece pin-striped suit and carrying an umbrella in one hand and an attaché case in the other.

"Do you mind?" he asks, speaking with a clipped, upper-class British accent.

Lemuel peers up into his Buddha face. "Do I mind what?"

"Do you mind if I join you?"

"Like it depends on what you are selling."

The Oriental man sits down in the Rebbe's place, touches the freshly etched Hebrew letters with his fingertips as if he is reading Braille. "Yah-weh," he says, sounding them out.

"You speak Hebrew," Lemuel notes in surprise.

"I read languages at Oxford," the Oriental man explains. "I speak seven Middle Eastern and Far Eastern tongues and twelve dialects. You are Lemuel Falk, the celebrated ramdomnist, are you not?"

"Hey, celebrated, I do not know."

"You are unduly modest," the Oriental man says in a soothing voice. "I would like to talk to you about the Data Encryption Standard used by the various agencies and organs of the United States government when they want to communicate with each other without having someone reading over their shoulders."

Lemuel starts to squirm out of the booth, but the Oriental man reaches across the table and clamps an iron grip on his wrist. "The Data Encryption Standard is based on a secret number, called the key, which is used to perform mathematical operations that scramble the message. Using the same key, the person receiving the message can unscramble it."

It dawns on Lemuel that the Oriental man has been shadowing him for days. He remembers seeing him at the checkout counter in the supermarket, he remembers seeing him again in the crowd watching Dwayne and Shirley streak down South Main, and he rented the cockroach motel room next to Axinya.

"So I do not see what all this has to do with yours truly."

"Bear with me. To break a cipher, one must run a computer program designed to test every possible key until one of them turns in the lock and the door clicks open. My masters have been led to believe that you developed for your former employers a near-random system of enciphering that makes it practically impossible for a computer to stumble across the key. My masters also believe that having achieved this miracle of near randomness, you could certainly work backward and develop a computer program that could map intricate statistical variations in large samples of data, which is the weak link in even near randomness, and thus break any cipher being used in the world today."

With some effort Lemuel extracts his wrist from the grip of the Oriental man and offers one of his noncommittal grunts.

"To make a long story only slightly shorter," the Oriental man says, "I am authorized to offer you permanent employment."

"I have a job."

"When does your contract at the Institute for Advanced Interdisciplinary Chaos-Related Studies expire?"

"Funny how everyone wants to know when my contract expires. End of May."

"What will you do then? Return to the saintly city of Petersburg and queue five hours a day in order to eat sausages fabricated out of dead dog?"

"Is there an alternative?"

Buddha's eyes narrow as he feels the tug on his line and begins to reel it in. "You could live in the lap of luxury not far from London in a small rural community devoted to theoretical mathematics. You could continue your quest for pure unadulterated randomness on our supercomputer. In your spare time you could give us the occasional helping hand in making or breaking ciphers. You could draw on a bank balance that has already been deposited in your name."

"What bank balance?"

The Oriental man's lips stretch into a guileless smile. He dials a number on the combination lock, snaps open the attaché case, removes a passport and a bank book from it and sets them down on the table. Lemuel riffles through the passport, British, filled with entry and exit stamps from various countries. The passport contains a mug shot of him taken years before, and is made out in the name of Quinbus Flestrin. It occurs to Lemuel that if he owned this passport he would have not only two signatures, he would have two names. He sets the passport aside and opens the bank book, notices that someone with the unlikely name of Quinbus Flestrin appears to have £100,000 to his credit in a bank called Lloyds. He makes a quick calculation, realizes that £100,000 is the equivalent of roughly one hundred and fifty million rubles. Set for life, set for the next one too,

Lemuel, flustered, blows across the surface of his lukewarm coffee to cool it, then to mask his confusion polishes it off in one long gulp.

"Lest you doubt that our intentions are, as they say, honorable, I also have in my possession a first-class Rochester–New York–London airplane ticket made out in the name of Quinbus Flestrin," the Oriental man adds.

Lemuel clears his throat. "I am curious about something."

"You would be acting out of character if it were otherwise," the Oriental man says with a Buddha-like flutter of his eyelids.

"How did you discover I was in Backwater?"

"I don't suppose I would be treading on anyone's toes if I were to tell you. My masters have been keeping track of a woman journalist who is free-lancing for the reconstituted Russian KGB. Her name is Axinya Petrovna Volkova. Nowadays, due to a severe shortage of foreign currency, Russian intelligence agents tend to cultivate fields close to home; they devote a great deal of time and energy to operations in the Ukraine, for instance, or Uzbekistan. So when one of their agents took a train across Europe, a boat across the Atlantic, then a bus to an out-of-the-way town in upstate New York, we naturally wanted to know what there could be in the backwater called Backwater to justify the expenditure of scarce hard currency. Which is how we stumbled across Lemuel Melorovich Falk, winner of the Lenin Prize for his work in the realm of pure randomness and theoretical chaos."

Molly passes by on her way to the kitchen. "Everything hunky-dory?"

"You have a delightful establishment," the Oriental man tells her.

"Well, aren't you a sweetheart? We sure as heck give it our best shot." She smiles prettily at the Oriental man. "Feel free to carve your initials in the table as long as they're in English."

"You mentioned that in my spare time I would give you a helping hand with ciphers," Lemuel says. "Is this optional, or a requirement?"

"It is what our Roman friends would have thought of as a quid pro quo," the Oriental man acknowledges.

Chapter Three

Undergraduates drift into the lecture hall with the aimlessness of debris wash-ing up on a shore after a shipwreck. They sink wearily into chairs, their limbs angling off in all directions, their eyes glazed over, their mouths sagging open in what appear to be permanent yawns. The minute hand of the large wall clock clicks loudly onto two minutes to the hour. The hour is eleven A.M.

"I mark on a curve," Professor Bellwether is explaining to Lemuel in front of the blackboard. She gestures toward the students scattered around the sloping lecture hall. "Take this class, which is listed in the catalogue as 'Introductory Chaos.' Out of eighteen students, I give two A's, ten B's, six C's."

"No D's, no F's?" Lemuel asks.

Miss Bellwether snickers. "You would need a good reason to flunk a student. As our dean of admissions is fond of saying, you don't want to forget who pays your salary." She nods toward the students, several of whom seem to have fallen asleep in their chairs. "If we flunked ev-eryone who catnapped in class, there would be no students left in Backwater. We'd wind up lecturing to empty rooms. I don't know what it was like back in Russia, Mr. Falk, but our undergraduates come to college to party and smoke dope and, excuse the expression, screw around. It's bad enough we interrupt this orgy with classes. Let's not lose our heads and insist the students stay awake in them."

Surveying the class, Lemuel mutters under his breath, "In America the Beautiful, education is chaos-related."

"You can say that again."

"Education is chaos-related."

Miss Bellwether eyes her guest lecturer with misgivings. The minute hand settles onto the twelve. She strolls over to the door and lets three more students wander in before she shuts it. Returning to stage center, she winds a tiny watch on her wrist as she counts heads. "My goodness gracious, thirteen out of eighteen isn't half bad for the morning after Spring Fest. Is it the fame of the guest lecturer that rouses you out of bed at the crack of eleven, or my reputation for giving a C to any Martian who regularly brings his or her warm body to class? No matter. Here, straight from St. Petersburg, Russia, is Lemuel Falk, currently a visiting professor at our very own Institute for Advanced Interdisciplinary Chaos-Related Studies. Mr. Falk is a world-class expert on pure randomness, which those of you who remained awake last week may remember we talked about. Today Mr. Falk will discuss the transcendental number represented by the Greek letter pi, and its relation to pure randomness. They're all yours, Mr. Falk."

Lemuel thrusts his hands deep into the pockets of the corduroy trousers Rain found for him in a used-clothing store in Hornell.

"Yo."

Two of the boys sleeping in the rear row rearrange their limbs. The girls in the front row exchange looks. Nobody has ever begun a guest lecture with "Yo" before.

"About pi, you probably need a clue or two. Pi expresses the relationship between the circumference and the diameter of a circle. Any circle. Every circle. A pinhole. Or the sun. Or the path of a spaceship orbiting the universe. You divide the circumference of a circle by its diameter and you get pi, which is roughly three point one four."

In the back row, a boy's head nods onto his chest.

"Three point one four," Lemuel repeats. "Those of you who are not getting some much-needed shuteye may recall Miss Bellwether referring to pi as a transcendental number. Pi is a transcendental number in the sense that it transcends our ability to pin it down; if you begin to work out the decimal expansion of pi, no matter how small your handwriting, you will fill the paper with numbers. In fact you will fill all the paper in the world and still not scratch the surface of pi. That is because the decimal expansion of pi goes on forever. It is infinitely long. I can say you infinity is something like the horizon seen from a ship; no matter how much you advance toward it, it is always beyond your reach. Trying to calculate pi"—Lemuel is suddenly alert to an aspect of the problem he never noticed before—"is a going without a getting there."

In the second row, a handsome, swarthy boy with hawklike features and pitch-black hair bends over an open notebook, writing as rapidly as Lemuel talks. He looks up when Lemuel pauses. Their eyes meet. The boy nods at Lemuel, as if inviting him to go on.

"Where was I?"

"Sir, you were saying that trying to calculate pi is a going without a getting there," prompts the swarthy boy.

"Yo. Like each time you add a digit to the decimal expansion of pi, you improve its accuracy ten times. Thus 3.141592—pi worked out to six places—zeros in on pi with ten times the precision of pi worked out to five places."

One of the coeds in the front row slips a note to the girl behind her. She reads it and starts to giggle. Miss Bellwether flashes a cranky look in her direction, and the girl stops.

"Five places. The first person to exploit pi, even though he did not call it by that name, was an Egyptian mathematician who used a very rough pi to calculate the area of a circle some 3,650 years ago. In the last century, mathematicians worked pi out to two decimal places, three point one four. With the invention of the electronic digital computer after what you in the West refer to as the Second World War, mathematicians were able to work pi out to two thousand decimal places. At the time this seemed awesome. Using the latest generation of parallel supercomputer, I myself have calculated pi out to more than three billion decimal places."

The swarthy boy in the second row raises a pencil, eraser end up. "Sir?"

"Yo."

"Why?"

"Why what?"

"Sir, why bother to calculate the decimal expansion when pi, worked out to a mere forty-seven decimal places, is accurate enough to plot the path of a spaceship orbiting the universe with almost perfect circularity, give or take the diameter of a proton?"

"Izzat Afshar," Miss Bellwether, leaning against a wall, dryly informs Lemuel, "is an exchange student from Syria. Unlike some of our home-grown, garden-variety students, he not only manages to stay awake in class, he does homework."

"That is a totally hype question," Lemuel tells Izzat.

"Sir, I look forward eagerly to your response."

The eyes of a boy dozing in the back row flutter open. "Izzat's a certified airhead," he says loudly. The girl in the second row giggles again.

"Hey, I do not need this," Lemuel tells the student in the back row. He stares down the boy, who shrugs and goes back to sleep. Lemuel addresses Izzat. "Here's the deal. There is a practical side to working out the decimal expansion of pi to three billion places that I will not go into. There is also a theoretical side, which I *will* go into. The decimal expansion of pi, at least up to the three billion, three hundred and thirty million, two hundred and twenty-seven thousand, seven hundred and fifty-three places I am familiar with, appears to be the most random sequence of numbers ever discovered by man. My guess is that you could calculate the value of pi from now to doomsday without discovering a method to its meandering madness; without reaching a point where you can predict the next number in the sequence. Of course there will be occasional flashes of what I call random order, which, in theory, is a constituent of pure, unadulterated randomness; something that is truly random will naturally have random repetitions. Which is why, around the three hundred millionth decimal place, eight eights turn up. Further along, ten sixes appear. Somewhere after the five-hundred-million mark, you stumble across a one-two-three-four-five-six-seven-eight-nine, in that order."

The pencil shoots into the air again. "Sir, you seem to be saying that if a sequence of numbers is really random, it will have random repetitions."

Lemuel performs a mock bow. "Rock 'n' roll."

"Sir, how can you tell the difference between random repetitions, which indicate that a sequence is truly random, and nonrandom repetitions, which indicate that a sequence is not random at all but chaotic?"

"Hey, Izzat, can you run that up the flagpole and salute it again?" cracks one of the boys in the back row.

"Another totally hype question," Lemuel concedes. "I suspect you are looking forward eagerly to my response."

"Sir, I am."

"Nonrandom repetitions, run through a software program devised by me, reveal what those of us in the business of chaos call a strange attractor, which is a mathematical portrait of the order that is thought to be at the heart of a chaotic system. Random repetitions, run through the same software program, reveal . . . beans."

"Sir, beans?"

"Check it out. Beans. Zilch. Zip. Zero. Nada. Nothing. Which is the tip-off that we should as a sign of respect take off our hats and light candles and talk in whispers because we may be in the presence of pure, unadulterated randomness."

"Sir, you speak about pure, unadulterated randomness as if it were a major religion, as if it were the work of God."

"Pure, unadulterated randomness," Lemuel fires back—the words originate in some heart of the heart of an unexplored Brooklyn in him—"is not the *work* of god. It *is* God."

Lemuel's eyes burn with revelation. The Rebbe had been right after all. Randomness *is* His middle name.

"Fucking Yahweh," he murmurs.

"Sir?"

After class Izzat is in no hurry to arrange the papers in his crocodile attaché case, and only gets up from his seat when he is alone in the room with Lemuel. With great diffidence, he approaches the guest lecturer.

"Sir, would it be possible to have a private word with you?"

"Hey, didn't I see you smoking dope on the stairs at Delta Delta Phi in a previous incarnation?"

"Sir, that is entirely conceivable."

"Weren't you condemned to thirty dollars or thirty days for demonstrating against the nuclear-waste dump?"

"Sir, you are clearly blessed with a memory for faces."

Lemuel shrugs a shoulder. "So what is your question?"

"Sir, may I ask when your contract expires at the Institute for Advanced Interdisciplinary Chaos-Related Studies?"

"Ask. Ask. Everyone else wants to know, why not you?"

"Sir, when *does* your contract expire?"

"When does the semester end?"

"Thirty-one May."

"Thirty-one May is when my contract expires."

"Sir, what will you do then? Return to the St. Petersburg flat you share with two couples on the brink of divorce?"

Lemuel hikes his trousers and his eyebrows. "You seem to know things about me that are not in my official biography in the Institute's glossy three-color catalogue. So where is this conversation going?"

"Sir, my father, the minister of the interior—"

"Your father is minister of which interior?"

"Of the Syrian Arab Republic, sir. When I informed him I would be attending your guest lecture, he sent me an urgent coded fax explaining the practical side to working out the decimal expansion of pi to three billion decimal places—"

"Your father, the minister of the interior of the Syrian Arab Republic, understands the practical side to working out the decimal expansion of pi?"

"Sir, my father holds advanced degrees in mathematics from the Massachusetts Institute of Technology. He did his master's thesis on common knowledge and his doctoral thesis on game theory. Which explains how he came to be in charge of my country's encryption and decryption service. Which also explains how he understands your remarkable contribution to the art of cryptography. I only grasp it imperfectly, sir, the mathematics being clearly over my head, but you seem to have devised a computer program that dips with near-perfect randomness into three billion, three hundred and thirty million, two hundred and twenty-seven thousand, seven hundred and fifty-three decimal places of pi in order to extract a random three-number key, which is then used to encipher and decipher secret messages."

"Hey, your father, the minister of the interior, keeps his ear to the ground."

Izzat smiles timidly. "Sir, my father, the minister of the interior, is known to have excellent sources of information in the Central Asian republics of the former Soviet Union. Which explains how he recruited many of your scientific colleagues. Thanks to my father, the minister of the interior, the Syrian Arab Republic now employs former Soviet missile technicians, rocket-booster engineers, laser and telemetry specialists, nuclear physicists. You name it, sir, the Syrian Arab Republic has it."

"I need this conversation like a hole in the head."

In the hallway, gongs ring melodiously. "Sir, in the inimitable words of my fraternity brothers at Delta Delta Phi, check it out. My father—"

"The minister of the interior—"

"—has instructed me to offer you political asylum in the Syrian Arab Republic."

"If I needed political asylum, Syria would be the last place on the planet Earth I would go to. What a chuckle. Political asylum. In the Syrian Arab Republic."

"Sir, you are leaping to conclusions without being aware of the advantages of obtaining political asylum in the Syrian Arab Republic."

"Name me an advantage. To political asylum. In the Syrian Arab Republic."

"Twenty-four-hour access to a Fujitsu parallel supercomputer to pursue your work on pure, unadulterated randomness. A numbered Swiss bank account with an initial balance in seven figures—my father, the minister of the interior, is talking British sterling. A centrally air-conditioned duplex penthouse all to yourself in downtown Damascus. A fully staffed condominium in Dayr-az-Zawr dominating the Euphrates valley, which is said to have a milder climate than Miami. Ah, it is obvious from your expression that you are sensitive to weather. Coming as you do from a city a snowball's throw from the Arctic Circle, who can blame you for being tempted by Florida or its equivalent? Which brings me to the last item on my father's list: all the black beluga your heart desires."

Glancing out of the window Lemuel spots Rain, the French horn strapped diagonally across her back on a braided sling, hurrying toward a practice session of the marching band.

"What my heart desires is not black beluga."

"Sir, knowing my father, you only have to identify what your heart desires and it will be yours."

Lost in a painful fiction, Lemuel focuses on a horizon beyond the horizon. "My heart desires . . . to know what happened to my *Royal Canadian Air Force Exercise Manual.*"

"Sir?"

Word Perkins, the Institute's factotum, surprised to see light seeping under Lemuel's door so late, pokes his head into the office without bothering to knock. "Caught you burnin' midnight oil, huh, professor from Petersboig? Still tryin' to catch that there serial killer with yaw computer?"

Lemuel makes a mental note of "midnight oil." At a delicate point in his programming, he continues to punch codes onto the computer screen.

Working the night watchman's shift, Word Perkins is eager for an excuse to take a break. "I'm glad you asked," he says, firing a preemptive shot across Lemuel's bow. "Lotsa folks wanna know how someone winds up whit a handle like Woid. Here's the deal. My ol' man was a Baptist deacon in the Bronx," he explains, orbiting the circle of light cast by the desk lamp. "I was the foistbawn a twelve. So my papa went an' called me Woid after the Gospel accordin' to Saint John. 'In the beginnin' was the Woid . . .' "

Lemuel looks up from the computer keyboard. "So can you say me the rest of the passage?"

Word Perkins hefts himself onto the edge of Lemuel's desk, reaches into his pocket to turn up the volume on his hearing aid. "Sure I can," he admits. " 'In the beginnin' was the Woid, an' the Woid was whit God, an' the Woid was God.' "

" 'The Word *was* God,' " Lemuel repeats slowly.

"That's what the man went an' said."

"What word was God?"

"Search me."

"Search you? Hey, I dig it. If I was to search you, right? I still would not discover what word was God."

"Huh?"

"On the other hand, if you was to search me you might discover what word was God." Lemuel smiles triumphantly. "Randomness is the word. That was God."

Baffled, Word Perkins removes the blue policeman's cap he wears when he is working as night watchman and scratches over an oversized ear, dislodging flakes of dandruff, which float toward the ground.

"Fucking Saint John," Lemuel says excitedly. He adds quickly, "Hey, no offense intended toward the saint in question, right? But what a pisser he must have been. Think of it. In the beginning was randomness, and randomness was with God, and randomness *was* God."

Word Perkins's eyes narrow into a suspicious squint. "This randomness that was God, it ain't got nothin' to do whit cross-country skiin', huh?"

Lemuel shakes his head. "Not."

Word Perkins accepts this with a careful nod; the penny has dropped. "I went an' made a fool outa myself the night you breezed into Backwater, didn't I? Tellin' you this was a randomnists' paradise 'cause a all the snow we got us."

"You are less of a fool than most," Lemuel assures Word Perkins. "You admit it when you are wrong. Besides which, Backwater turned out to be a randomnists' paradise after all."

"If it ain't about snow, what is this randomness that was God all about?" Word Perkins sucks in his cheeks. "Bein' as yaw a visitin' egghead at the chaos school, I'll lay odds randomness's gotta got somethin' to do whit chaos."

"Randomness and chaos are related, but not the way you think. Chaos is the opposite of randomness, Word. In its heart of hearts, chaos contains the seed of order. Even if we cannot see it, the order is there. Pure randomness, on the other hand, conceals in its heart of hearts—"

"I'm startin' in to get it. The randomness that's got nothin' to do whit snow conceals disorder."

"Not so much disorder, which implies a deliberate effort to avoid order, but a simple, elegant, perfectly natural absence of order." Lemuel is talking to himself now. Pieces of a puzzle are falling into place. "Yo! The Rebbe, who is viscerally uncomfortable with randomness, who sees it as a vice, discovered traces of randomness in God, which is why he loves God but does not like Him. Me, I see randomness as a virtue, so when I discover traces of God in randomness, it permits me to like Him even though I am not a hundred percent sure He exists."

Word Perkins is confused. "How can you like somethin' that don't exist?"

"I can say you it is not easy." Lemuel plunges into the labyrinth of his own logic. "Dostoevsky got it wrong when he had Ivan Karamazov say that if God was dead all things would be permitted. It is because God is *alive*, because He is randomness incarnate, that all things are permitted. Don't you dig it, Word? Goddammit, if He can be when and where He will be, then, since we are made in God's image, we can too."

"Yeah, well, what I 'preciate about you, professor from Petersboig, is you don't own what you know, you spread it around." Word Perkins slips off the desk and starts for the door. "Don't think I didn't get a kick outa our little yak, but I gotta move on whit my rounds. Holler when yaw ready to call it a day, huh? so as I can double-lock the front door behind you." His cackle reverberates in the long corridor. "We don't want no unauthorized person or persons sneakin' in an' monkeyin' whit the Institute's chaos, do we?"

"Not," Lemuel agrees absently, swiveling back toward the computer screen.

He punches some computer codes into his workstation, sits back to watch an endless series of digits parade across the screen; the Institute's Cray Y-MP C-90 supercomputer, programmed from Lemuel's keyboard, is comparing the two most recent serial murders with the eighteen murders that came before. The supercomputer is coming at the crimes from different directions, comparing the ages and occupations and physical descriptions of the victims, the time of day of the murders, the day of the month, the phase of the moon, the scenes of the crimes. Working from the case files of the two new murders, Lemuel—searching for the seed of order buried somewhere in all the disorder—has programmed in additional elements: the height and weight of the victims, the color of the clothing they were wearing when they were murdered. Scrambling and rescrambling numerical equivalents, sorting through the endless variations on a theme, the supercomputer fails to detect a trace of order in the clutter of randomness.

Frustrated, still convinced he is missing something, Lemuel glances anxiously at the wall clock; according to the worksheet posted outside the Director's office, he can access the Institute's supercomputer from his workstation until midnight, at which point the Cray is scheduled to go offline for routine maintenance of its cooling system. Stabbing at the keyboard, punching in more computer codes, he programs the

Cray to come at the problem from yet another direction, then sits back and stares at the screen as a new series of numbers begins to flash across it. Each victim appears to have been selected at random; the software fails to turn up a seed of order, a method to the madness of murder. All the supercomputer comes up with is . . . disorder.

Disorder . . .

Not so much disorder, he remembers telling Word Perkins, because disorder implies a deliberate effort to avoid order. . . .

The numbers flashing across the screen blur. A pulse throbs in Lemuel's forehead. He knows what is missing from the computer study of the twenty serial murders. Yo! What is missing is what he discovered in pi somewhere around the three hundred millionth decimal place, namely, eight eights. What is missing is the faintest trace of *occasional order*, which is an essential ingredient of pure, unadulterated randomness. My God, Lemuel thinks, I could kick myself I didn't see it before; this is definitely the kind of information I need rattling around in my brain. If the serial murders were characterized by a simple, elegant, perfectly natural absence of order, which is to say if they really were random, they would contain random repetitions. Granted the sampling is small, but somewhere in the twenty murders the serial killer would have struck at the same time of day or the same day of the month; he would have murdered someone who had the same age or occupation as a previous victim; he would have killed two people wearing red flannel shirts.

Which means the murders were not random at all, but rather the work of someone who is trying to make them appear random. But why would the killer go to such lengths to make the murders *appear* random? There can only be one answer. The common denominator in the serial killings, the thread running through the crimes, has to be the killer's unspoken theory that if he or—why not?—she appeared to select victims randomly, the police would never look past randomness for the motive, and the crimes would be impossible to solve. Which suggests that the opposite is true: Since the victims were not selected at random, one of the crimes must be easy to solve.

But which one? All Lemuel has to do is go back into the case files and look beyond randomness for a motive in each murder. One of the murders will betray a motive so apparent that the killer had to mask the crime as just another in a series of random or motiveless murders.

Lemuel keys the supercomputer, calling up the original files starting with the first murder. All of a sudden the screen goes blank. Then a message appears: "Your connection to Cray has been cut," it says. Lemuel glances at the clock. It is twenty-five to twelve. He should still have another twenty-five minutes of access to the Cray. He punches in his personal code and tries to network with the supercomputer, but all he gets is a flickering "Sorry. Access denied." Furious, he grabs an Institute directory from a shelf, runs down the list with his thumbnail until he finds the number of the Director. He snatches the telephone off the hook and dials the number. After seventeen rings the Director comes on the line.

"Goodacre here."

"L. Fucking Falk, one of the world's preeminent randomnists, is on this end of the line. Remember me? I am supposed to have access to the Cray from eight at night until twelve. I am supposed to be able to burn midnight oil."

"Are you inebriated? Do you have the slightest idea what time it is?"

"I can say you it is eleven thirty-eight, give or take thirty seconds. Which means I should have another twenty-two minutes of computer time. You have been squeezing me out of the Cray loop ever since we had our little conversation in your office about me and Rain. First I could only network in the afternoons. Then in the evenings. Now I have to come in at night if I want computer time."

The Director clears his throat. "Can I inquire what chaos-related project you are working on?"

Lemuel clears his throat. "I can say you the sheriff asked me to do some correlating of his serial murders—"

"You are correlating serial murders?"

"Right. To see if they are really random crimes."

There is a moment of strained silence. Finally the Director says, "I would like to submit that solving serial murders on Institute computer time is not what you were brought all the way from St. Petersburg to do."

Lemuel holds the phone away from his face and stares at it. The Director's voice, tinny, continues to issue from the earpiece. "You are supposed to be patrolling your famous Pale, looking for the randomness that is a footprint of chaos. Instead you wind up free-lancing for the sheriff on the Institute's supercomputer. Do you have the slightest idea what computer time costs? People kill for half an hour's access to a Cray Y-MP C-90 . . ."

Lemuel feels himself being sucked into a flamboyant fiction. In his mind's eye he is A. Nevsky, barring the Nazi-helmeted Teutonic Knights from crossing a frontier, which happens to be a frozen lake. Various shots of the ice splitting into floes under the enemy's feet, of horses losing their footing and slipping off into the water, of Teutonic Knights, dragged down by their heavy armor, disappearing beneath the surface of the wintry water. Long ground-level shot of mist rising from the churning lake. Pan to a triumphant A. Nevsky surveying the scene. On the now calm lake, from A. Nevsky's POV.

Fresh from having defended a territory at its goddamn frontier, Lemuel brings the phone back to his lips and cuts the Director off with a primal yowl. "People also kill for tenure at the V. A. Steklov Institute of Mathematics. So what does this tell us about *Homo mathematicus* that we are better off not knowing?" Suddenly toast, A. Nevsky reverts to his L. Falk voice. "Hey, doorknob, murder is generally considered to be chaos-related," he mutters. "If I am lying," he adds with a bitter snicker, "I am dying."

Distracted, Lemuel closes down his workstation, locks his office and heads for home. Making his way down the corridor, he notices the light is extremely dim, particularly on the landing. He could have sworn the corridor was better lit when he turned up earlier in the evening. Could half a dozen bulbs have burned out between then and now? He gropes for the swinging door leading to the stairs.

Two figures materialize out of the shadows on the landing.

"Falk, Lemuel?"

Startled, Lemuel shrinks back. "What do you want?"

"Your money *and* your life."

Lemuel gasps. The second shadow, taller, leaner, meaner than the first shadow, so it appears to Lemuel, laughs under its breath. "You oughtn't to go and say things like that, Frank. It could scare him shitless. The last thing in the world we want to do is scare him shitless."

"It was probably a joke," Frank announces solemnly.

"Ha ha," Lemuel says weakly. "Like who are you? How did you get into the building?"

The second shadow says, "Mr. Word Perkins let us in after he got a look at our credentials."

"What credentials?"

"We are both armed with pistols," Frank says. "The pistols are equipped with silencers."

Lemuel's palate goes chalk dry. In the dark, he can feel the two men looking at him in the peculiar way people who are armed look at people who aren't. "Hey, you are making another joke, right?"

"We have come all the way from Reno, Nevada, to have a discussion with you," says the shadow named Frank.

"About what?" Lemuel tries to keep the fear out of his voice. "What about?"

"About your future," Frank replies. "Isn't that what we want to talk to him about, Fast Eddie?"

"It is," Fast Eddie agrees. "We have come all this way to make sure he has a future."

"You are not here about the random murders?"

"Do we look like we are here about random murders?"

Fast Eddie strikes a match and holds the flame to the tip of a thin cigar. Lemuel notices that both men are wearing fedoras. "The handful of murders we have personal knowledge of," Fast Eddie explains, his words filtering through a cloud of cigar smoke, "have not been random."

Lemuel yells into the stairwell, "Yo, Word!"

A faint echo spirals back up from the ground floor. "Yo, Word!"

Sucked into an agitated fiction that fills his head like a disjointed nightmare, Lemuel hears a voice spiral up from his lost childhood. *Tell us where your father hides his code book.* Backpedaling until his back is flat against a wall, mopping perspiration from his forehead with a sleeve, he cries out, "For God's sake, Word, where the hell are you? You are going to get yourself in deep excrement if you let an unauthorized person or persons monkey with the Institute's chaos."

"We are not interested in the Institute's chaos," the shadow named Fast Eddie says quietly. "We are interested in *your* chaos."

"Lots of people we know have been telling lots of people we know about you."

"About me?"

"Sometimes it seems as if all anybody upstate New York wants to talk about is you."

"All roads lead to Backwater," Fast Eddie says with a laugh.

"What are people saying about me?"

Frank takes a step in Lemuel's direction. "That you can make num-bers dance."

"It turns out you can read other people's mail," Fast Eddie remarks.

"There are certain people—federal prosecutors, FBI lawyers, CIA agents—who write things about the organization we work for."

"We got no problem getting our hands on what they write," purrs Fast Eddie. "The trouble is it's always in gibberish. A-x-n-t-v, r-l-q-t-u, z-b-b-m-o. You get the drift?"

"Random five-letter groups," Lemuel says weakly, "mean that the original was enciphered." He is sure the two men in the shadows are wearing steel-toed shoes.

"We hear on the grapevine you can read gibberish."

"We hear on the grapevine the gibberish in question uses a U.S. government code system known as the Data Encryption Standard. The people who encode messages they do not want us to read use a secret number, called the key, to garble the message. The people who decode the messages use the same secret number to ungarble the message."

"We figure if you could figure out the key, we could ungarble the message and read the gibberish."

"What kind of name is Falk, Lemuel?"

"Russian." Lemuel swallows hard. "Jewish."

"We are an equal-opportunity employer, isn't that the situation, Frank?"

"You do not by any coincidence happen to have Italian blood? You do not by an coincidence happen to *parlare Italiano*?"

"I told you it does not matter if he speaks Italian," Fast Eddie in-forms his colleague. "The gibberish we want him to read is in En-glish."

"I was only trying to get a fix on his qualifications," Frank says defensively.

"Let us put cards on the table," says Fast Eddie. "The organization we work for would like to employ you. You could have a title—something along the lines of 'officer in charge of reading gibberish.' Now, we got branch offices all over the country. As for deciding where you want to work, you can pick your poison. Reno, Nevada, has a dry climate which is supposed to be very good for people with asthma and bronchial problems. Florida is sunny all year around, people who live there swear by it. Sùre, New England gets cold in the winter, but the autumn is supposed to be very colorful."

"You need an apartment, you got an apartment. You need sharpened pencils, you got sharpened pencils. You need a secretary—I am talking young, I am talking good-looking, I am talking long legs and short skirt—you got a secretary."

"Normally I work with a computer. . . ."

"You need a computer, you got a computer."

"Whatever they are paying you here, we will triple it."

"There are no deductions for medical care and retirement."

"We personally look after your health. You never retire."

In the dark, Lemuel clears his throat. "Like it is not that I do not appreciate the offer, right? It is more a question of having a lot of irons in a lot of fires."

"You want to be extremely careful you do not get burned by none of them," warns Fast Eddie.

"Concerning our offer," says Frank, "I would like to have the opportunity to persuade you."

Lemuel is astonished to hear the A. Nevsky in him say, "You think you have a big enough vocabulary?"

Frank takes Lemuel's insolence in stride. "In my line of work," he says pleasantly, "we got a saying: 'One bullet is worth a thousand words.' "

"He is probably making another one of his jokes," Fast Eddie assures Lemuel.

"Look, this is an important decision," Frank says. "Do not feel you have to give us an answer right away."

Fast Eddie reaches out of a cloud of cigar smoke and punches Lemuel playfully in his upper arm. "Yeah, take your sweet time. Think about it a minute or two before you say yes."

Chapter Four

Territory, you haven't forgotten my rule of thumb, right? has got to be defended at the goddamn frontier. Which is why I wasn't about to let L. Falk get away with a remark like that.

"Where do you come off saying I planned the whole thing?" I shot back. "You're listed on the masthead as a consenting adult."

Talk about a feeble defense. "I consented to try your dope," is what he mumbled. "I did not consent to what came after."

"You didn't say not, neither. You didn't push her away."

"I did not want to be rude. I did not want to hurt her feelings."

I was, I openly admit it, getting hot under the collar even though I wasn't wearing a collar. I was bare-assed, as they say in Backwater, nude, as they say in movie land. In the bathtub. Having a morning-after-the-night-before conference. With the *Homo chaoticus* in my life.

"What a chuckle," I said in a tone which made it clear I was not in a chuckling mood. "You pass out doing dope.

When you wake up, Shirley's going down on you and you don't want to be rude? Hey, test-fly another one."

To tell the God-honest truth, you could have knocked me over with a feather when L. Falk agreed, the night before, to join us, us being Dwayne and Shirley and yours truly, Backwater's legendary Tender To. L. Falk saw my hollowed-out *Hite Report* open on the table when he came back from the office, my cardinal New Year's resolution about never doing your own dope doesn't apply to Fridays, it was around midnight, the three of us were pretty mellow, we'd been smoking and yakking for hours. He watched Dwayne, who has talent in the tips of his fingers, I am speaking from first-hand knowledge, hand-rolling thick Thai truffles. Shirley lit a new one from what was left of an old one, took a long drag and held it out to L. Falk.

Like this was not the first joint he'd been offered, right? but he had up to then always found an excuse to say no, he was too tired, he was too busy following erotic bands of randomness to their psychotic origins, lah-di-dah, he had to be up and out to deliver a guest lecture on apple pie at the crack of eleven, whichever. But that night he seemed more . . . frustrated than usual, probably because of the altercation—hey, *altercation* has to be in the same league with *averted* and *menstruate*, right?

Where was I? Altercation. I was saying as how L. Falk was pretty strung out from this fight he went and had with What's-His-Face, the führer at the Chaos Institute. In my head I have this picture of L. Falk staring at the joint very intently, the way Eve might've eyeballed the first Golden Delicious, he wanted to try it but he was afraid there was a worm in it. He glanced over at me. I shrugged one of my curvaceous shoulders. He shrugged one of his heavy shoulders. He reached out and took the joint.

"So what do I do?" he asked me.

"Tell Lem what to do, babe," Dwayne told Shirley.

Shirley plunked herself down on the couch next to L. Falk, draped a leg over his thigh and an arm over his shoulders and gave him the beginner's course in dope-smoking. "You insert A into B," she said. "A is the joint. B is your mouth."

I got to admit we thought it was hype, Dwayne and Shirley and me, watching him inhale and hold the smoke in until his eyes watered. Even Mayday seemed to have a smile on her face. L. Falk batted the smoke away with the back of a hand and told us the dope wasn't having any effect on him, he didn't feel different, he suspected my world-famous Thai truffle might have come from someone's backyard in the heart of the heart of Brooklyn. Then he started in giggling. When I asked him what he was giggling at, he said something about how he was gonna take his sweet time before saying yes. Shirley pressed one of her tiny tits into his arm and asked him what he was saying yes to. Slurring his words, L. Falk explained he was saying yes to Yahweh-made randomness, which implied a not to man-made randomness. He started rambling on about how he could kick himself for not seeing it before, it was exactly the kind of information he needed rattling around in his brain.

Shirley probably figured if she could keep him talking, she could keep him smoking. She passed the joint back to L. Falk and asked what information he had in mind. Still giggling, he informed us he had just about solved the serial murders. He said the lesson he had learned from the serial murders was applicable to randomness in general. He said the fact that you set out to manufacture randomness, I think I'm getting this right, right? means the randomness you manufacture has not been selected randomly. He got the hiccups, took another drag on the joint and held his breath until the hiccups went away. Giggling some more, he said what was missing from man-made randomness was randomness. Which was another way of saying, this is still L. Falk talking, not me, that randomness, like God, had to be discovered, as opposed to invented.

Shirley was hanging on his every word and nodding as if he was supplying her with information she couldn't live without. Dwayne caught my eye, nodded toward Shirley, then stuck his tongue out and wiggled it around suggestively.

You didn't need to be a shrink to see what was rattling around in Shirley's brain.

"Dwayne and me, we both saw Shirley had the hots for you," I was explaining to L. Falk in the bathtub. I started running more hot water, I like to sweat when I soak, when I noticed L. Falk's circumcised periscope peeking through the bubbles of the bubble bath.

Just thinking about what he was thinking about had turned him into a *Homo erectus*.

Watching my *Homo* turn *erectus* was turning me on. I stoked both our fires. "So you didn't not like it, right?"

L. Falk seemed to wrestle with the question, I could see the wheels turning in his head, I could see the smoke coming out of his ears.

"Come clean," I urged.

"I can say you, at the time I did not not like it. Which I think means I liked it."

"So describe it."

"You want me to describe it? Out loud?"

"Yo," I said. "Everything," I said. "From E to Z."

You would've thought I'd gone and ordered up periscope.

L. Falk's lids drifted over his eyes, which I took to mean he wasn't only remembering, he was reliving. Go with the flow.

"I was dreaming," he said dreamily, "In my dream, I was hovering over Backwater like a cloud in trousers, that is a line from a Mayakovsky poem, blocking out the sunlight, when I felt something warm and moist close over my you-know-what."

"Hey, go ahead and say it."

He took a deep breath. "Penis."

I reached through the bubbles with my toes to fondle his periscope. His left foot floated toward me and docked against my butterfly tattoo. I gave a good imitation of a bitch in heat.

"And then and then and then?"

"And then Shirley came up for air, 'I'm not very good at this,' she told me. 'My mouth's too small.' "

"Shirley doing her fishing-for-compliments act. Rock 'n' roll."

"I tried to reassure her. I told her she was doing great. 'I'm not as good as the Tender To,' she said with a sigh. 'The Tender To's fantastic.' I asked her how she knew how good you were. 'From Dwayne. He says Rain gives incredible head. She has a big mouth.' 'They have made love together, Dwayne and Rain?' I asked her. 'Geez, I thought you knew or I wouldn'ta shot my mouth off. We all been into the occasional major merge. Dwayne and Rain. Me and Rain. Dwayne and Rain and me, *à trois,* as the French fries say. Haven't you ever made it *à trois?*' "

I slid the heel of my foot along L. Falk's thigh. "Like have you?"

"*À deux* already strains my capacities."

"You didn't go and tell that to Shirley?"

"I can say you I did. 'You'll love it, Lem,' Shirley promised me. 'Three's a trip you want to take. You get confused. After a while you lose track of who's doing what to who. It gets very . . . busy, if you see what I mean.' "

"I told her I saw what she meant," L. Falk remarked in the tub, "but I did not really see what she meant."

"Fast forward to the X-rated scenes," I ordered impatiently.

"We ran out of conversation and she went back to what she had been doing. After a while I asked her if she was trying to bring me off with her mouth. I heard the words 'why' and 'not' drift up through her naturally wavy hair."

"Fucking Shirley," I said in admiration. In jealousy, too. I honestly didn't mind her making it with my squeeze, I just didn't feature her making it with him better than I make it with him. Besides which I happen to know, bear in mind I am a professional, her hair is not naturally wavy.

"Afterward," L. Falk went on, "I could not think of anything to say, so I said thank you. I told her I thought it was a very elegant gesture to take a friend's . . ."

"Hey?"

". . . penis into your mouth. Shirley curled up alongside me and slid a stick of gum between her teeth and told me it was no big deal, all she did was insert A into B, I should not give it a second thought, the pleasure was mostly hers, she liked sucking the occasional unfamiliar cock, what with variety being the spice and all. Of life. Or words to that effect."

This was definitely not the moment to educate L. Falk about dudes who thanked you afterwards, as if you were the Tender To who serviced their goddamn yacht. "You guys sure were courteous," I said, my voice dripping sarcasm. "Maybe you should collaborate on a book of etiquette. You could call it *The Greenhorn's Guide to Polite Oral Sex.*"

L. Falk was so caught up in reliving the scene he missed the sarcasm, but he wasn't about to let some new slang slip past his ear. " 'Greenhorn' means what?"

"A greenhorn is a new immigrant who doesn't know his ass from his elbow and thinks it's physically possible to wear his heart on his sleeve. In other words, it's someone who's innocent about anatomy. Which is why he needs a guide to oral sex, forget polite."

L. Falk shoe horned *greenhorn* into his vocabulary with one of those slow, solemn, pursed-lip nods that professors own the patent to.

"So where was I?" he asked himself. "Shirley said she really wanted to show me she could write her name backward. She made it sound important. She said the human race was divided into those who could write their name backward and those who could not. But by the time I came up with a pencil and some paper, she was snoring away. So I tiptoed into the living room."

I stepped up the antisubmarine patrol in the general vicinity of his periscope. "You're only up to the M in your E to Z."

"Which is when I spotted the pile of clothes on the couch. The TV was on with the sound turned off, there was one of those late-night shows where some girls go off with some men and then they talk dirty about each other and try to guess who said what about who. I fingered the clothing—your miniskirt, your body-hugging ribbed sweater, your purple tights, your gray Calvin Klein underpants. I think my hearts, the one in my chest, the one on my sleeve, skipped several beats when I saw Dwayne's pinstriped button-down shirt, his designer jeans, his silk boxer shorts."

"Oooooooooh."

"I started folding the clothing over the back of the couch, I live in a kind of permanent chaos, I go slumming in order when I can find any, when I heard sounds coming from the bathroom. I padded down the hallway to the door."

"Which is warped and never quite closes . . ."

"Through the crack I could see the two of you in the

tub. You were kneeling between his outstretched legs, which were pink and hairless. You were reaching over his shoulder to wash his back. Your nipples were centimeters from his granny glasses. His left hand was cupping your right knocker. His right hand was caressing your left hip."

"You definitely have an eye for detail. So did you get off on seeing me bare-assed with another dude?"

"I could not believe it," L. Falk murmured so softly I had to strain to catch his words. "It was extraordinarily beautiful . . . I felt as if I was watching you with me. . . . At the same time I had trouble breathing."

"I love it that you were looking," I told him, and I meant every word. If you are what the French call a voyeur, you like to be, pardon the conjugation, voyied.

"I went back to the bedroom and stretched out alongside Shirley. I lay there in the dark, contemplating the blackness of the night, squaring circles, following elusive threads of randomness to their chaotic origins . . . most of all listening. I heard Shirley exhale between snores, I heard the wind whistle past the window, I heard the wind harp hanging from a branch of the tree tinkle, I heard the church bell toll the half hour." L. Falk cleared his throat. "I heard the floorboards squeak. I heard the couch in the next room open. I heard the soft gasps that escape from the back of your throat when you fuck. . . ."

"I love it you were listening," I whispered.

"So now it is your turn to describe everything from E to Z."

It will go on the credit side of my ledger when I'm nominated for sainthood that I didn't leap at the opportunity. I told L. Falk I wasn't absolutely convinced he was ready to hear the dirty details; he might lose his cool, he might freak out. He smiled a razor-thin smile which came across as one-third uncertain, two-thirds curious.

"I will freak out if you do not tell me the dirty details. Telling me everything from E to Z proves that the core conspiracy is with me."

Core conspiracy! Goddamn L. Falk! There were still parts of him I had not been to yet.

So I thought, What the hell, you want someone to act like a consenting adult, treat him like a consenting adult. "I wanted to go back to the couch in the living room," I be-

gan, monitoring his vital signs, so far so good, "but Dwayne
was worried you'd come barging in. He wasn't sure how
you'd take it, seeing the two of us. In the act. So we went
on into your office and pushed aside the Nordic skier and
opened the couch—hey, we really have to oil the hinges on
it one of these days. Then we sort of hugged awhile, me
looking out the window at the light in the steeple of the
Seventh-Day Baptist Church on North Main, him advertising his erection by pushing it into my butt. Then Dwayne
said something like, 'We might as well do this Hollywood-
style, huh, babe?' Dwayne has this Rudolph Valentino side
to him. He lifted me up and carried me to the bed. Jesus,
L. Falk, the goddamn bath's getting cold. Anyhow, I don't
remember all the details."

"Add hot water. So were you wearing the T-shirt that
does not cover your navel?"

"Yo. I put it on after the bath like I always do. Somewhere along the way it must have disappeared, because I
don't remember taking it off, but I remember him kissing
my nipples . . . Then he went down on me."

". . . does Dwayne give good head?"

". . . yeah. As a matter of fact he does. Give good head.
He makes you feel he's doing it because he likes cunts, not
because giving head happens to be next on the menu. He
makes you feel like you don't need to go and douche with
yogurt."

". . . was he wearing his granny glasses?"

"Jesus, you ask a lot of questions. Dwayne always wears
granny glasses."

"If he was wearing his granny glasses, it meant he could
see the Siberian night moth in the sea of freckles under
your knocker."

"Hey, Dwayne's no greenhorn, he knows his way around
the female body without granny glasses. Anyhow, after that
I sucked his nipples, but you'll be gratified to know they
didn't get erect like when I suck your nipples."

When I hesitated, L. Falk hit me with, "You are only up
to the M in your E to Z."

"Right. M . . . So then I went and sucked him a bit."

"How long is a bit?"

"Five minutes . . . eight on the outside."

". . . did he do the dirty deed in your favorite position?"

Looking back, I can see we should have stopped while we were ahead. He was pushing me past where it was safe to go. I don't like to be pushed. Maybe that's why I decided to get clinical, which was my way of pushing back. I suppose you could make a case that I wanted to hurt him.

So much for my nomination for sainthood.

"Okay, after you hear the answer, do me a personal favor and remember you asked, right? So where was I? When I finished sucking him, which might've lasted ten or twelve minutes now that I think of it, I rolled over onto my stomach so he could fuck me from behind. But he rolled me back onto my back and fucked me from in front. Very slowly. The way someone who's sure his erection will last forever fucks. I folded my legs back and dug my heels into his butt."

". . . did you come off?"

"Sure I came off. The juices were really flowing."

". . . did you like fucking Dwayne?"

"I more than liked fucking Dwayne. I loved fucking Dwayne. It's fly to fuck with a friend, especially if the friend in question happens to have a beautimous body. I don't understand why more people don't do it more often. I got this theory, I remember telling you about it the night of the Delta Delta Phi bash, you always love the person you're fucking while you're fucking. You lose yourself in the act, you stop growing old, you stop dying."

L. Falk let this pearl sink in. After a while he cleared his throat several times, which I interpreted to mean he was about to drop an economy-sized A-bomb.

"So what ever happened to monogamy?" is what he muttered with his ventriloquist's lips.

So what ever happened to monogamy! What a chuckle, right? when you need to educate a consenting *Homo chaoticus* as to the facts of life. What is it with men, they have this incurable double standard? I mean, he sure as hell wasn't into monogamy while Shirley was going down on him. So he hears me fucking with a friend, what could be more natural? and all of a sudden he's pitching new, improved monogamy.

I wasn't looking for a fight, so I tried to pass the whole thing off as a joke. "I prefer knotted pine."

Dudes have gone and told me I don't know how to deliver punch lines. L. Falk provided the living proof when he lobbed his next observation into the conversation. "Monogamy has nothing to do with mahogany," is what he said. "What you need is a good dictionary," is what he said.

A good dictionary!

Me.

Go figure.

So there we were, eyeing each other across a tub that suddenly felt as if it was filled with ice cubes, his periscope sunk below the surface of the ocean that had come between us, on the threshold of our second fight.

"So don't beat around the goddamn bush," I remember telling him, "come right out and say it. You think I'm uneducated, right?"

"I think you are educated . . . differently. You know how to fuck, but you do not know how to make love. I can say you it is possible to make love and still not miss the violence, the orgasm. I can also say you I think there is nothing wrong with you that cannot be corrected."

I vaulted out of the tub and shuddered like a dog to get the water off and wrapped the only body I'll ever have in a beach towel. "What do you say we go directly to the heart of the heart of the goddamn problem," I sneered, I must have raised my voice an octave or two because L. Falk's eyes took on the startled gawk that made him look like a bird about to take to the wing. "Just because you get to fuck me doesn't mean you get to fix me. I mean, I am not broken." I tried to chill out, I half succeeded, which means I half didn't. "Jesus, L. Falk, for a while back there I thought we had something going. . . ."

He followed me out of the tub. "We had something going," he said with maddening calmness, there's nothing more infuriating than dudes who get cooler as you get hotter. He opened the medicine chest and took out the Swedish safety razor that bitch with the sagging tits gave him. I couldn't believe my eyes. He was going to goddamn *shave*. With *her* goddamn razor.

"J. Alfred Goodacre was not out to lunch after all," he mumbled. "Who I fuck *is* chaos-related. In America the Beautiful, fucking is chaos-related."

Talk about sunny-side-ups over easy, the doorknob still didn't know which side was up. "Fucking is definitely a form of chaos," I agreed angrily. "That's what makes fucking fun. Hey, how did you describe chaos? It's determined, right? but it's unpredictable. Like that's me. I'm determined. I'm unpredictable. Check it out. I'm goddamn chaos!"

I stomped out of the bathroom and threw on some glad rags and padded barefoot into the kitchen to make myself some mango chutney and yogurt. After a while L. Falk came through the door, whistling to hide his nervousness. I'd never seen him whistle before, I did not take it as a positive, forget auspicious, sign. Mayday must've also been worried by the whistling; she kept her head down but her raw pointed ears jerked straight up like antennas. L. Falk was wearing his faded brown overcoat and carrying his Red Army knapsack in one hand and his duty-free shopping bag in the other. He kneeled down in front of the drier and opened the porthole and began sorting through the dry laundry. His socks and underwear and a shirt or two he stuffed into the shopping bag.

I have to admit my heart was pumping blood to beat the band, but I was goddamned if I was going to give him the satisfaction of knowing it. "Going somewhere?" I asked so casually you'd've thought I was vaguely curious about the time of day.

He avoided my eye. "I am going to take one of those nonstops to the most Florida city I can find," he announced huskily. "Dayr-az-Zawr on the Euphrates is a hot possibility—I heard on the grapevine it is more Florida than Miami. I am going to check into a fully staffed cockroach condominium and never check out."

With that, L. Falk . . . up and walked out . . . of my entire goddamn life.

Hey, it was no big deal. It's not like he's the last *Homo chaoticus* on earth, right? Besides which Mayday and me, we're already used to living without him . . . Like the thing I'll miss most, even though I still have my trusty Hitachi Magic Wand to fall back on, is the safe sex . . . That and the bleeding heart he wore on that goddamn sleeve of his . . . And the weird way he had of starting sentences with "I can say you" and then babbling on about pure, unadulterous what's-its-face which, if I read him right, doesn't exist except in his imagination. Jesus, the way he went on and on about it, you'd think randomness was some kind of goddamn religion.

Read it and weep, the Gospel according to Saint Fucking Lemuel.

As for the drums in my ear, I can say you I am one hundred and ten percent sure it was pure coincidence they came back the day, the hour, the minute L. Falk walked out the door with his goddamn duty-free shopping bag thumping against his thigh.

Rat-a-tat-tat, rat-a-tat-tat, rat-a-tat-tat.

Pretty soon I'll wear see-through shirts and nobody . . . nobody will want to look.

Me.

Toast.

Fucking L. Fucking Falk.

Patrolling the apartment over the Rebbe's head in the early hours of the morning, pausing occasionally to discard one of the sheriff's serial-murder files and pick up another, Lemuel becomes aware of faint high-pitched shrieks drifting down the hill from another Delta Delta Phi bash. He has an irresistible urge to drop what he is doing—the solution to the serial murders will still be there tomorrow—to climb Mount Sinai, to dance a slow with Rain, to feel her breasts against his chest, to feel her thighs against his legs, to smell her lipstick.

Imagining the bash, Lemuel feels himself being sucked into a fiction that is two-thirds exhilarating, one-third irritating. Close in on Lemuel, sitting with his back against a wall in a murky basement room. Pan through a haze of marijuana smoke and zoom in on tiny images on the television screen. Three silvery figures appear to be impaling themselves on one another. On Lemuel, glancing to his left. On what he sees. Rain, in a corner, hikes her miniskirt and deftly impales herself on the enormous, hey, go ahead and say it, penis, right? of the young man reclining on the cushions next to her.

Lemuel recognized the blond beard, the earring, the granny glasses. The penis in question is attached to Dwayne.

"Shirley adores you," he hears Dwayne say. "Don'tcha, babe?"

Shirley, nude, as they say in movie land, presses her tiny tits into Rain's back, reaches around her, unbuttons her shirt and starts to caress the night-moth nesting under her right knocker. Shirley giggles awkwardly. "You'll love it, angel," she whispers hoarsely in Rain's ear. "Three's a trip you want to take."

"Rain, babe, why don'tcha dial back and run that part again on slow?" Dwayne urges.

The fiction in Lemuel's mind's eye skids backward. With a jerk the impaled figures disengage, the miniskirt comes down like a curtain. The image freezes for an instant, then the tantalizing ballet begins again, this time in slow motion.

Behind the images, there is a voice-over. "How many times has a dude got to repeat something before it sinks into that thick skull of yours?" Lemuel could swear he hears Rain murmur between the soft gasps that originate in the back of her throat. "It's me, goddamn chaos. Check it out. This may be as close to pure, unadulterous what's-its-face as you're ever going to get."

Close in on Rain, backlit, light shimmering through her dirty-blond hair, as she arches her body in a languorous stretch and melts back into Shirley's thin bare arms.

"If I'm lying," Rain breathes, "I'm dying."

Visions of disorder press like a migraine against the back of Lemuel's eyeballs. "Fucking Occasional Fucking Rain," he groans. "I cannot live with her, I cannot live without her."

Standing on a wooden box, his shirtsleeves turned back to his bony elbows, his suspenders trailing down the sides of his shapeless trousers, the Rebbe is scrubbing dishes when Lemuel shows up for supper. *"Hekinah degul,"* the Rebbe calls to his guest. He notices Lemuel sniffing the air. "That's bacon you are getting a whiff of," he admits. "There is a culinary snobbery that claims the expression 'kosher food' is an oxymoron. As the Diaspora's preeminent practitioner of *nouvelle* kosher cuisine, I am the living proof that 'kosher' is not incompatible with 'food.' Which is why, to give it flavor, I am roasting the guinea fowl wrapped in strips of bacon."

Lemuel grunts. "I thought religious Jews did not eat bacon."

"Who said anything about eating it? I only smell it. I happen through no fault of my own to be addicted to the odor of bacon. The yeshiva where I studied as a child was situated behind a twenty-four-hour diner. In the summer we had to open the windows to breathe, so all day long we read Torah and smelled bacon cooking on the griddle. I came to associate the two. When I smell bacon, I think Torah. When I think Torah, I smell bacon. Oy vey."

"Who invented kosher?"

The Rebbe rinses a dish in running water and sets it on the slotted plastic drier reserved for meat dishes. "Torah instructs us, 'Thou shalt not cook lamb in its mother's milk.' From this molehill our Talmudists created a mountain called kosher, and I am its faithful climber. I possess, feel free to count them if you think I am exaggerating, I will not be offended, six sets of dishes: two for meat and dairy every day, two for meat and dairy on Shabbat, two more for meat and dairy on Passover. Only to set the table I need to consult a scorecard."

"If you carry kosher to its logical conclusion," Lemuel observes dryly, "you would need two sets of dentures, one for meat, one for dairy."

The Rebbe stacks the last of the dishes. "In kosher, as in all things, it is important to draw the line between the ritual and the ridiculous."

Waving Lemuel to a seat at the kitchen table, he distributes paper napkins swiped from the Kampus Kave, glances at his watch, darts to the oven and removes a sizzling roast guinea fowl wrapped in slices of bacon. He carefully peels away the slices of bacon and drops them into the plastic garbage pail lined with pages from *The Jewish Daily Forward*. Sharpening a knife, he sizes up the guinea fowl as if he is about to perform open-heart surgery.

"Thank God for Noah," the Rebbe mutters under his breath as he begins to dissect the bird. "Before the Flood, everyone was vegetarian. Then Yahweh gave Noah the good news. I'm talking Genesis 9:3. 'Every moving thing that liveth shall be meat for you.' "

Lemuel clears his throat. He has an announcement to make. "I want to say you I appreciate your discretion, Rebbe. I have been here five weeks today and you have not hit me with any questions."

"The fact you moved back upstairs speaks unfortunately for itself," the Rebbe says without looking up. "For a shiksa," he adds, rolling his head mournfully, "Rain has a sensational ass."

Lemuel is following his own thoughts. "If anybody was at fault, it was me. I do not love, I cannot live with, chaos."

"Funny you should talk about living with chaos. I am in the process of finishing the rough draft of the last thesis I will do for the Institute before I follow my Star of David to Brooklyn," the Rebbe explains. "I call it *Torah as Crapshoot*." He looks up from his carving, winks both his eyes at Lemuel over his silver-rimmed spectacles. "Snappy title, even if it's me who says so. I am toying with the idea of maybe expanding the thesis into a book-length book, in which case I am going to retain the movie rights. With a hot title like that, you never know how many millions could come your way. Today a modest chaos-related yeshiva in the heart of the heart of Brooklyn, tomorrow a chain of chaos-related yeshivas linking Jewish outposts in the Diaspora." He spoons two boiled potatoes and some shriveled peas onto a plate. "Leg, or maybe breast?"

"Breast, thank you, Rebbe."

"Left or right?"

"Left or right?"

"Where's the advantage to being a consenting adult if you don't consent?"

"That sounds like something Rain might say."

"It does. She did. I was telling her about Onan being a pioneer in coitus interruptus when she came out with it."

Lemuel eyes the two breasts without enthusiasm. "Left. Right. Either or."

Using his fingertips, the Rebbe drops a guinea fowl breast onto the plate, sets it in front of his dinner guest and starts to prepare his own plate.

"My launching pad for the paper, I take it for granted you want to know, is the story of the scapegoat—I'm talking Leviticus 16:8–10." Inclining his head, closing his eyes, absently curling a sideburn with a fingertip, the Rebbe recites from memory: " 'And Aaron shall cast lots upon the two goats; one lot for the Lord, and the other lot for the scapegoat. And Aaron shall bring the goat upon which the Lord's lot fell, and offer him for a sin offering. But the goat, on which the lot fell to be the scapegoat, shall be presented alive before the Lord, to make an atonement with him, and to let him go for a scapegoat into the wilderness.' "

Setting down his dinner plate, the Rebbe flicks on the radio, plays with the dial to tune in the classical-music station from Rochester, then joins Lemuel at the table. He cocks his head toward the radio, listens for a moment, identifies the music.

"I'd recognize that with my ears closed. It's Ravel's 'Valses Nobles et Sentimentales.' The music haunts me—it was playing on the radio the night I lost my cherry."

Rolling his head in time to the music, the Rebbe meticulously half-fills two long-stemmed crystal glasses from a bottle bearing the label "Puligny Montrachet," clinks glasses with his guest. *"Le'hayyim,"* he growls. He closes his eyes, sips the wine, rolls it around in his mouth, swallows, nods in satisfaction. "It is maybe a little on the young side, I could have let it breathe another hour or two, a good wine you can never open too early, but it beats Manischewitz. . . . About the scape-goat," the Rebbe continues, talking and chewing at the same time, "there is a Jewish legend about Azazel, some say he was a fallen angel, some say he was a demon, either or, it doesn't change the story. Every year on Yom Kippur two male goats were chosen by lot, one for the Lord, the other, a scapegoat, for Azazel. The high priest, I don't envy him the job, transferred all the sins of the Jewish people onto the scapegoat, after which the animal, no doubt staggering from the weight on its back, was driven into the wilderness and stampeded off a cliff to its death."

The Rebbe peers at Lemuel over the drumstick he is gnawing on. "You are probably wondering, it is a relevant question, by all means ask it, what coded signal Yahweh is sending to the resident scholars and visiting professors at the Institute for Advanced Interdisciplinary Chaos-Related Studies when He decrees that the goat must be selected by lot, which is to say, at random. My thesis makes the case that Leviticus 16:8–10 should maybe be seen as the heart of the heart of Torah, more important even than the manifesto of monotheism in Deuteronomy 6:4, *'Shema yisro'eyl, adoynoy eloheynu, adoynoy ekh-o-o-o-d.'* . . . 'Hear, O Israel: The Lord our God is one Lord.' In Leviticus 16:8, Yahweh, a consummate poker player, He normally holds His cards close to His vest, always assuming He wears a vest, Yahweh, as I was saying, tips His hand. He wants to persuade us to embrace what looks to us like randomness, and inasmuch as His randomness is a footprint of you-know-what, to embrace chaos. If I'm on to something, and I think I am, He wants us to learn to live with chaos even if we are not comfortable with it."

"I do not see . . ." Lemuel blinks rapidly. He begins again. "How can it be possible to live with something if you are not comfortable with it?"

The Rebbe picks with a fingernail at some guinea fowl caught between two teeth. "It becomes possible when you grasp that it is chaos which gives zest to life."

He spots a single tear welling in the corner of one of Lemuel's bloodshot eyes. Embarrassed, he peels his spectacles away from his face, noisily fogs the lenses with his breath and occupies himself polishing them with a napkin.

"What is your opinion of bacon-wrapped guinea fowl?" he asks, eager to move on to a safer subject. "You know the Yiddish joke about guinea fowl? When a Jew eats a guinea fowl—ha!—one or the other will be sick."

Neither man laughs.

Sighing, the Rebbe settles back into his chair, concentrates on the music coming from the radio. "In your intellectual hegira, you have maybe stumbled across Ravel's maxim?" When Lemuel hikes a shoulder, the Rebbe cracks a lopsided smile. " 'Order. Routine. Chaos. Joie de vivre'—that's his maxim." Suddenly his bulging Talmudic eyes burn with secular discovery. "Could it be . . . do you think it's within the realm?"

"Could what be? Is what within the realm?"

The Rebbe's palm slaps against his forehead. "I could kick myself I didn't see it before, I could kick myself harder for seeing it now, who needs this kind of information rattling around in his brain?"

"For God's sake, what kind of information—"

"The Gospel according to Ravel is pointing us in the direction of an awkward conclusion, namely, that chaos is not the pits, but only a pit stop."

Carried away by the logic of what he is proposing, the Rebbe bounds from his chair, circles Lemuel waving his drumstick at him. His corkscrew sideburns dance in the air.

"Here we are, 5,752 years down the rocky road from Creation and the Garden of God, which happens to be, count them, 3,304 years after Yahweh personally hand-delivered the itemized list of do's and don'ts to the first Jewish mountain climber to conquer Mount Sinai, and we are still blind to the moral in Ravel's music, deaf to the handwriting on the wall. Consider the mouth-watering possibility, I'm flirting with probability even, that you weren't out to lunch when you gave that insolent after-lunch speech to the resident scholars and visiting professors at the Institute, when you startled them with the suggestion that chaos was maybe only a way station."

The embroidered yarmulke slips off the back of the Rebbe's head. He snags it in mid-air. "The real terminus," he goes on, waving the drumstick with one hand, the yarmulke with the other, "I catch a whiff of it when I read Torah, I feel it in my gut, I feel it in my groin, may be joie de vivre! Oy, Lemuel, Lemuel," he rasps, swept away on a tide of emotion, "consider also the possibility, I'm flirting here with heresy, so what, I'll take the plunge, that joie de vivre is maybe only a fancy French handle for pure, unadulterated randomness."

Breathing heavily, smirking in embarrassment, his hands spread wide, his sweaty palms turned up, the Rebbe backs away from his dinner guest—backs away from the idea also. "I was talking hypothetical, it goes without saying. Any idiot knows there's no place in the heart of the heart of Brooklyn for pure, unadulterated randomness."

Lemuel whispers huskily, "You almost reached the Promised Land, Rebbe. For God's sake, don't pull back now. I can say you Yahweh is not as uptight as you think. Go with the flow. Make the leap."

The Rebbe looks as if he has swallowed bacon. "What leap are we talking about?"

"The leap of faith. Pure, unadulterated randomness has to exist or nothing makes sense. If it exists, it has to be the work of God. Hey, it *is* God!"

"You are off your rocker," the Rebbe declares, patrolling the room. "If pure, unadulterated randomness, alias joie de vivre, were really the terminus, life would be bursting with succulent alternatives. Faced with such a feast, we would go crazy, not to mention hungry. Nobody would get an act together. Painters, terrorized by an infinity of possibilities, wouldn't paint, architects wouldn't architect, girls wouldn't give in and go to bed with boys, you, Lemuel, would never nibble on a drumstick again. Your left, right, either or would miss the point, would miss the violence of having to choose, would miss the orgasm that comes from having chosen. Oy, what words can I find to make you see the light? We think we are tossing lots for the scapegoat, but Yahweh has loaded the dice, which is another way of saying He selects the scapegoat for us. You were right all along: Yahweh's randomness is fool's randomness, which means His randomness is a footprint of chaos. Which means, thank God, that everything under the sun is determined even if it's beyond our power to predict what will come next. Left, right, either or works because your choice is determined; therefore you don't have to choose. Oy, how could it be otherwise? Where would the Yahweh of Torah, this visceral avenger we know and love but don't particularly like, where, I ask you, answer if you can, would He fit into the big picture if pure randomness existed, if nothing were determined, if we had to pick and choose a thousand times a day, if we, as opposed to God, were the real masters of our destiny?"

The Rebbe snatches a tabloid from a pile of newspapers he uses to line the garbage pail, flops into his chair, riffles angrily through the pages. "Under my roof even food for thought turns out to be kosher," he mutters. Something in the newspaper catches his eye. "Oy vey," he mumbles, his nose buried in the racing section, "there's a mare named Messiah running in the fifth at Belmont. Whether she'll win by an eyelash or limp in last has already been determined. But can I risk *not* betting on her?"

Chapter Five

"To lose one's cherry" rings a bell. Lemuel wonders where he could have come across the expression. Certainly not in his lost *Royal Canadian Air Force Exercise Manual.* Nor does it sound like the kind of thing King James would have come up with in 1611. Which narrows it down to Raymond Chandler and *Playboy.* Lemuel's intuition tells him *Playboy* is the more likely suspect, which suggests that losing one's cherry has sexual implications. But what exactly did the Rebbe lose when he lost his cherry while Ravel's "Valses Nobles et Sentimentales" was playing on the radio? Having lost this cherry of his, did the Rebbe then re-place it with another cherry? In America the Beautiful people cried over spilt milk (an expression Lemuel picked up from Dwayne when they were touring the E-Z Mart one day and discovered a puddle of milk near the refrigerated-food section), but was it appropriate to cry over lost cherries? He makes a mental note to look up the idiom in the *Dictionary of American Slang* and add it to his repertoire. He can picture Rain's face when she hears him respond to her "Z'up" with, "I went and lost my cherry."

Sinking wearily into a desk chair, Lemuel forces himself to concen-trate on the sheriff's serial-murder files. Details pile up like slag on a heap. Many come equipped with a riddle.

Item: A handkerchief bearing someone else's embroidered initials jutting from the breast pocket of the serial killer's first victim.

Item: Corrective contact lenses in the pocket of a victim with twenty-twenty vision.

Item: A ring, filled with keys that did not fit any known door in the victim's life, clutched in a dead woman's hand.

Item: A tiny battery-powered hearing aid in the pocket of a victim who was not deaf.

Item: A seven-inch cesarean scar on the stomach of a woman with no history of pregnancy.

Item: A package of undated, unsigned, explicitly heterosexual love letters hidden under the garbage pail liner of a victim who detested women and was thought to be celibate.

Item: Seventeen gold coins buried in ice cubes in the freezer of a victim who qualified for food stamps.

Item: A vial of heart stimulants in the pocket of a victim with no record of a cardiac ailment.

Then there are fragments of fetishes: drawers filled with unwashed socks, closets filled with unshined shoes, cartons filled with women's underwear, shoeboxes filled with false teeth or ivory dildos or fingernail and toenail clippings, a valise brimming with faded pornographic photographs of consenting adults engaged in impolite oral sex.

What does it all mean? Are the killings really chaos-related, as Lemuel suspects? Will the elusive threads of fool's randomness lead him to the chaotic origin of the crimes? Will they lead him to the single detail that will solve the puzzle and expose the criminal? Persuaded he is on the right track, he plows on, rummaging in the lives of the victims with the single-mindedness of someone plunging through the decimal expansion of pi toward infinity.

Well past midnight, Lemuel begins to have difficulty focusing on the print in the files. He strolls into the kitchen, lets the water run for a minute before filling a glass and drinking. (Old habits die hard: In Petersburg, you had to let the water run for four or five minutes to get past the rust.) Returning to the living room, he swallows a yawn, flicks on the Sony, catches the tail end of the WHIM news bulletin.

"Weather in the tri-county on this next-to-last day of April is gonna be out a sight. If you're tuned in, Charlene, honey, you wanna go and inflate the boat and put it in the water. Blue skies up above, everyone's in love, up a lay-zee river with meeeee. Oh-oh. They're going ballistic in the control booth, which means we got us a hot phone call from one of our regulars. Hallo."

"Like I happened to have the radio on, right? which is how come I caught you telling Charlene to go and put the boat in the water."

"Hey, where you been hanging out? We haven't heard from you in weeks."

"I been busy putting patches on my see-through shirts."

With a pang, Lemuel recognizes the voice of the caller, crouches in front of the radio, turns up the volume.

"So what's bugging you tonight?"

"Nothing's what's bugging me. It's just the word *boat* made me nostalgic."

"Did you use to own a boat when you were a kid?"

Rain can be heard snickering. "Me? Own a boat? You need a clue or two. I can't even swim."

"I don't dig how you can be nostalgic for a boat if you never owned a boat."

"Hey, if you can be passionate about someone who doesn't exist, why can't you be nostalgic for something you never had? Which explains why some dudes are nostalgic for group sex or incest or hot pastrami sandwiches on pumpernickel. Me, I happen to be nostalgic for boats. I always wanted to own one and sail off to the horizon."

"What's holding you back?"

"What's the use? I had this friend who happens to be an expert on horizons, he knows more about them than you and me put together. He says when you reach the horizon, he was speaking from personal experience, right? there's always another horizon on the horizon."

"The trip could be a chuckle even if you never reached the horizon. Isn't that so, Charlene?"

"Not. If you buy into America, you buy into the idea that it's the getting there that counts."

"You sound kinda down in the mouth."

Lemuel, crouching, grabs a pencil and scratches "down in the mouth" on the back of an envelope.

"I go with the flow. Sometimes the flow turns out to be upstream."

"Can you play that back for me slow like? Pay attention, Charlene, honey. Rain's got herself what the heavy hitters call a worldview which is definitely not mainstream. She goes with the flow even if it's upstream. Ha ha. Hey, you still with us, Rain? Rain? Well, what'd'ya know? She must a been phoning from a booth and run out of quarters. Well, if you've just joined us, you're listening to WHIM Elmira, the station where consenting insomniacs listen to sleepers describe their X-rated dreams. I'll take another call . . ."

Gazing into the Sony, trying to conjure up an image of Rain in the phone booth, Lemuel feels himself being sucked into a frightening fiction. Medium shot of Rain in the booth, the phone cradled between her neck and shoulder blade, rummaging in her pockets for a quarter, then hanging up in disgust when she can't find one. Close in on Rain as she discovers the phone booth is jammed shut by a coiled boa constrictor. She starts to pound on the sides with her small fists. Her breath fogs the glass, obscuring her face. Lemuel could swear he hears her muffled cries: "Hey, Mayday, Mayday. I'm trapped in the goddamn booth, right? I want out."

Lemuel's mind's eye zooms out for a long shot. The telephone booth is lost in the heart of the heart of a lush garden. "I'm trapped outside the Garden of God," he hears himself moan. "I want in."

On the radio, a caller with a vaguely familiar rasp to his voice is on the phone. "I couldn't help overhearing your previous interlocutor mention incest," he says. "If God was really against incest, He would maybe have created two couples instead of one in the Garden of Eden. Or better still, two Edens situated within commuting distance of each other, each garden with one biologically unique couple in it. If He didn't do this, we can assume it wasn't because of a shortage of clay—I'm talking Genesis 2:7, 'And the Lord God formed man of the clay of the ground.' We can likewise assume it wasn't because He couldn't come up with a spare rib."

"You don't want to go and miss this, Charlene, honey. I got a live one on the line making the case incest is best."

"I'm not arguing it's best. I'm only suggesting that God may have been sending a coded signal to the resident *shlimazels* and visiting *shlepps* of the planet Earth when He created one couple in one garden—"

The host cuts off the caller. "So I'll bite: What coded signal was God sending when He created one couple in one garden?"

The man on the phone can be heard blowing his nose a nostril at a time. "Like Moses," he finally says, "I can maybe climb a mountain and catch a whiff of the Promised Land, I know it's right over the horizon, I feel it in my gut, I feel it in my groin, but I will never actually get to kiss the ground. . . ."

"I must've missed something: What's kissing the ground of the Promised Land got to do with incest and one couple in one garden?"

Over the radio, the hum of the phone line is replaced by the shrill pitch of a dial tone.

Lemuel senses the sheriff come to life on the other end of the phone line. "You went'n what?"

"I went and solved the serial murders," Lemuel says again. "I spent the last three nights combing though the files. I know who the killer is."

"Where the hell are you?"

"In Backwater. On South Main. In the apartment over the Rebbe."

"Lock the door," the sheriff orders excitedly. "Don't open it for no one except my man Norman. He'll be 'round to fetch you 'fore you can skin uh cat."

"Fetch," Lemuel repeats with interest. "Skin a cat."

Twenty minutes later a blue-and-white cruiser with a yellow light pulsating on the roof pulls into the driveway under Lemuel's French doors. A moment later there is the pounding of boots on wood. Lemuel hears the Rebbe's voice calling up the stairs, "Where's the fire, Norman? You're knocking over stacks of books with the name of God in them." There is an insistent knock on the door. Lemuel unlatches the chain and opens it.

Norman touches two fingers to the brim of his hat. "Sheriff sent me over," he explains. "Told me to bring you in dead or alive." Flashing a sheepish grin, he flexes his knees to adjust his testicles. "Don't get nervex—he specified alive was his first choice."

"I will fetch the file folders and be with you before you can skin a cat."

Downstairs, Norman holds open the rear door of the car. Ducking, Lemuel slides in. He is surprised to discover two men sitting in the car, one in front, one in back. The one in front, square-shouldered, square-jawed, unsmiling, twists in his seat.

"Mitchell, with two l's," he announces. "FBI."

The pale man sitting next to Lemuel regards him through tinted eyeglasses as he offers a soft, pudgy hand. "Doolittle," he introduces himself. "I work for A.D.V.A., which is a subdivision of PROD, which is a division of N.S.A."

"Hey, you definitely have an eye for initials," Lemuel says uneasily.

Norman slips into the driver's seat, turns the key in the ignition, switches on the headlights and the overhead pulsating light, flicks the compass attached to the dashboard with the nail of his third finger, then starts down the driveway toward the street. "Sheriff figured as how you'd want to have a private word with these here gents while I was driving you in," he says over his shoulder.

"Let me fill you in real quick-like," Doolittle tells Lemuel. " 'N.S.A.' stands for the United States National Security Agency, which is in the business of cryptoanalysis and traffic analysis. 'PROD' is short for the Office of Production, which is in the business of signal intercept. A.D.V.A., which I happen to run, is so secret I can't tell you what the initials stand for. We're in the business of taking the intercepts provided by PROD and breaking Russian-language cipher systems."

With an effort Mitchell twists in his seat again. "I pulled down a C-minus in my college math survey course," he tells Lemuel. "What you do for a living is Greek to me. Doolittle here informs me that you do it better than anyone else in the world. What we want, what would give us pleasure is for you to come in from the cold and do it for the good guys."

"Funny you should talk about the good guys," Lemuel says. "My whole life I have been waiting for that piece of information to rattle around in my brain. So I will bite: Who are the good guys?"

Mitchell does not look as if he appreciates Lemuel's sense of humor. "We're the good guys, sport," he says with a tight smile. "The bad guys are no longer players. We deported the Russian woman with the washed-out brassiere, we deported the Oriental man who chats folks up with a stiff upper lip, we deported the Syrian exchange student who tried to talk you into relocating to a mosquito-infested metropolis on the Euphrates, we have taken the two spaghetti types from Reno into custody for doing sixty in a fifty-five-mile-an-hour zone and resisting arrest when we tried to show them the error of their ways. You will not be hearing again from any of them in the foreseeable future."

"On the off chance someone is interested," Norman calls over his shoulder, "the straight stretch of Interstate right after the next bend is pointing like an arrow toward Jerusalem." He taps the compass with a fingernail. "Six degrees south of east, magnetic, as opposed to true. The sheriff and me, we went and calculated it on a Mercator map a the world in the office atlas just in case the Rebbe gets himself re-arrested again."

Doolittle and Mitchell exchange puzzled looks. Doolittle turns back to Lemuel. "All this foreign hustle and bustle in Backwater came across as a seven on the Richter scale located in the FBI's Rochester office, which Mr. Mitchell here heads," he explains. "That's how we discovered you were in the country."

"We know who you are, sport," Mitchell says.

"You know more than I do," Lemuel remarks under his breath.

"We also have a pretty good idea," Doolittle says, "thanks to an MIT alumnus who is a key player in a major Middle East franchise, exactly what it is you do." He extracts a three-by-five file card from the breast pocket of his tweed jacket and reads aloud: "Falk, Lemuel, forty-six, member of the Soviet Academy of Sciences, divorced, Jewish, atheist—"

"Hey, I am no longer an atheist. Studying chaos, I found traces of randomness, which could be footprints of God. . . ."

Doolittle looks up, nods once, then goes back to the card. "Di-vorced, Jewish, we'll skip atheist, it doesn't influence the situation one way or the other. Tenured professor of pure randomness and theoret-ical chaos at the V. A. Steklov Institute of Mathematics in Leningrad."

Lemuel mumbles, "There is no Leningrad anymore," but Doolittle cranks up his voice a notch and plows on as if he has not heard him.

"Falk," he says, consulting the card, "appears to have devised a computer program that dips with near-perfect randomness into three billion, three hundred and thirty million, two hundred and twenty-seven thousand, seven hundred and fifty-three decimal places of pi in order to extract a random three-number key, which is then used to en-cipher and decipher secret messages."

With a screech of wheels, Norman swings the cruiser off the Inter-state, past a sprawling trailer park, past a drive-in movie with *The Ten Commandments* flickering on the screen, onto a narrow, winding dirt road. "I'm taking a long cut," he calls over his shoulder, "so you gents can finish your conference before we get where we're going."

"I have given a lot of thought to the relationship between the going and the getting there," Lemuel mutters. "It is within the realm that the going without a getting there is the ultimate trip."

"How's that again?" Mitchell inquires.

"We want you to come on board the A.D.V.A. flagship as a senior researcher," Doolittle is saying. "We want you to break the military and diplomatic ciphers you created for the Russkies. What's in it for you? This is the question you could and should be asking."

"So what *is* in it for me?"

"I'm glad you asked. A new identity so the bad guys from Reno can't find you; a six-figure salary; a rent-free three-bedroom ranch-style house within commuting distance of our base, which is situated at Fort George Meade, Maryland; a Mercedes sedan with tinted windows; a permanent visa; a green card; eventual American citizenship are part and parcel of the offer."

"Part and parcel," Lemuel repeats with interest.

"A free one-way steerage-class ticket back to Russia," Mitchell pipes up from the front seat, "is part and parcel of the offer if you turn us down." Doolittle starts to interrupt, but Mitchell waves him off. "It's better for everyone concerned if we don't mince words—"

"Mince words," Lemuel repeats with interest.

"If you decide not to accept our generous offer," Mitchell continues, "we send you packing with a note addressed 'To Whom It May Concern' stapled to your forehead which reads: 'This is to certify that Falk, Lemuel, forty-six, a member of the Soviet Academy of Sciences, divorced, Jewish, atheist, was extremely helpful in aiding a secret United States government agency break Russian-language ciphers.'" Mitchell drapes a mean smile over his face. "You can lay money on it, sport, they won't make the mistake of letting you out of the country a second time. You'll spend the rest of your natural life queuing for recycled toilet paper and swiping sausages made of sawdust and cat meat from the V. A. Steklov Institute canteen."

"We have almost got to where we was going," Norman calls. He bounces the cruiser over railroad tracks, deftly maneuvers it into a back alley and brakes to a stop next to a back door. A naked bulb over the lintel illuminates a wooden sign that reads: "County Sheriff."

Lemuel clears his throat. "Let me risk a wild guess," he says. "You want me to take my sweet time before making a decision. You want me to think about it a minute or two before saying yes."

"I will definitely enjoy working with you at A.D.V.A.," Doolittle notes. "In addition to your other qualifications, you obviously have a sense of humor."

Sheriff Combes's beer belly swells over his tooled leather gun belt as he sinks back into his swivel chair. "I'm all ears," he announces, sucking pensively on a twenty-five-cent cigar.

"All ears is something I can relate to," Lemuel fires back. "I used to be all toast."

The sheriff, eyeing Lemuel across the desk, fixes his professional squint on him. "What language are we talkin' today?" He waves a beefy hand to clear a tunnel in the cigar smoke so he can get a better look at the man who claims to have solved the serial murders. "Use the King's English, talk turkey," he orders.

"Talk turkey?"

"Get down to brass tacks."

"Brass tacks? Hey, what language *are* we talking today?"

"Who's the perpetrator who went'n murdered all those folks?"

Lemuel sifts through the file folders, extracts one and begins to walk the sheriff through his theory. "You need to start off by understanding that the serial murders are chaos-related," he says. "The victims were not selected at random, even though to the naked eye the crimes may appear random. If the serial murders were really random crimes, right? they would exhibit a telltale pattern of random repetitions—for instance, two victims wearing red flannel shirts; for instance, two victims with the same age or occupation. The failure to come up with this telltale pattern means the killer set out to simulate randomness—he painstakingly selected the victims for their apparent randomness."

"Why did he wanna go'n stimulate randomness?"

"The answer is as plain as the nose on your face, no offense intended," Lemuel tells the sheriff. "He wanted to convince the police that the crimes were random in order to throw them off the track."

"I'm still all ears."

"Once the police assumed randomness was the motive for the crimes, they would start looking for the nut case responsible for a series of serial murders, they would not dig very deep into the possibility that one of the victims had been killed for a motive other than randomness. At this point, the perpetrator could murder the one person

he really wanted dead, but dared not kill unless and until that particular murder could be disguised as just another in a series of random
murders."

The sheriff takes this all in with a skeptical nod. "I reckon," he says,
without specifying what he reckons.

"Using game-theory concepts, I calculated that the serial killer
would murder the person he really wanted dead about two-thirds of
the way through the list of victims, and then kill a third again as many
people to keep up the appearance of a serial murderer stalking the
tri-county. So I began seriously sifting through the files at murder
number twelve. At murder number fifteen, I hit pay dirt—I discovered
the real victim of the serial murderer."

"The fifteenth victim was Purchase Honeycut, the self-styled tri-
county used-car czar," the sheriff recollects. "Made somethin' of uh
splash when they found his corpse."

"According to the file you gave me, Honeycut owned the Purchase
from Purchase dealership on the Interstate outside of Hornell. Buried
in the same file was a little-noticed detail: Honeycut had a silent partner, none other than his brother-in-law, Word Perkins, the handyman–
night watchman at the Institute for Advanced Interdisciplinary
Chaos-Related Studies."

"Bein' uh silent partner is not a crime. How about motive?"

"Honeycut and Word Perkins made out a notarized agreement stip-
ulating that if one of them died, the business would revert to the living partner. When they started out twelve years ago, the dealership
was worth peanuts. Since then, Honeycut divorced Perkins's sister and
built up the Used-Car Bazaar to the point where it is worth a small fortune. Check it out. The dirty details are all in the fine print of the
state police report. Since the police were looking for a serial murderer, the notarized agreement got lost in the shuffle."

The sheriff scratches several fingernails across the stubble on his
cheek. Distracted by the sound, Lemuel says, "There is more."

"Hit me."

"I beg your pardon."

"Give me the more."

"Honeycut's body was discovered in an automobile graveyard off
Route 17."

"He was found slumped over the steerin' wheel of uh wrecked

Toyota, the entry wound from uh .38 caliber dumdum bullet rubbed with garlic in his left ear," the sheriff recalls.

"You definitely have an eye for detail, Sheriff. So do you remember what was in his jacket pocket?"

The sheriff nods his heavy head carefully, almost as if he is afraid of dislodging a thought. "Uh hearin' aid, which was peculiar inasmuch as Purchase Honeycut wasn't deaf."

"But Word Perkins was. Is." Lemuel brings up a grunt of satisfaction. "From a psychological point of view, there is a certain logic to a deaf man shooting his victims in the ear."

The sheriff rocks forward until the edge of his desk bites into his stomach. "There wasn't no blood splattered around the vehicle, which meant Honeycut was shot somewhere else an' his body dumped in the Toyota."

"Let us, for the sake of argument, slip into a plausible fiction." Lemuel closes his eyes. "The two partners have been getting on each other's nerves ever since Honeycut divorced Word Perkins's sister. One night Honeycut turns up at Word Perkins's apartment in Hornell. Maybe they quarrel about money—Honeycut has been milking the dealership and Word Perkins feels he is not getting a fair share of the profits. Maybe they quarrel about politics—Honeycut is a lifelong Republican, Word Perkins is a reform Democrat. Either or, it does not alter the dynamics of the story. Honeycut does not give a centimeter. Word Perkins pulls out a pistol. 'I never could stomach folks who own what they know,' he shouts. Honeycut backs away, holds up a hand, desperately tries to talk him out of pulling the trigger. 'You will never get away with it,' he pleads. 'The police will suspect you the instant they discover you inherit the dealership on my death.' Word Perkins cackles cruelly. 'I have already killed fourteen people, each victim carefully selected to make the murders appear random. You will be the fifteenth.' Honeycut sees he cannot save himself, but he can return from the grave to point an accusing finger at his killer. So he slips a spare hearing aid lying around on a table into his pocket in order to send a message to the police."

"What we gotta do now," the sheriff says excitedly, snatching the telephone off the hook, punching buttons, "is go'n see if the power of the hearin' aid found in Purchase Honeycut's pocket matches the hearin' deficiency of the alleged perpetrator. If it does, we'll drive over to Hornell, we'll advise Mr. Word Perkins of his right to remain silent, then we'll beat the shit outa him till he talks."

Lemuel wanders into the outer office and helps himself to a cup of water from the cooler. A teletype machine clatters away in a corner, spitting out paper, which accumulates in a carton on the floor. Two deputy sheriffs are playing gin at a desk near the door. A third is straddling a bench, spit-polishing his knee-length leather boots. Lemuel can see that the deputy's socks have holes in the heels. Norman is nowhere in sight, but his voice drifts over a partition. He appears to be chatting with someone on the phone.

"Sheriff sure as heck expects to be involved. . . . No, no, he ain't got nothin' 'gainst the state police makin' the actual arrest, but it has got to be clear it's the sheriff that went an' investigated the tip, it's the sheriff that went an' broke the case, it's the sheriff that went an' ordered the arrest. . . . Yeah. . . . He ain't forgot the nuclear dump deal. . . . Sheriff figures he owes you one, so he's not 'gainst sharin' the photo credit. . . . When we march her out, how about the sheriff'll be on one side and one of your boys on the other. . . . Right or left, it don't make no difference to him. . . . No problem, she can be handcuffed to the state police officer as long as the sheriff has got a firm grip on her other elbow. . . . Yeah, wheelin' an' dealin', buyin' an' sellin', we're talkin' drugs, we're talkin' LSD, we're talkin' amphetamines, we're talkin' all kinds of shit." Norman delivers a horselaugh into the phone. "Would you believe in a hollowed-out sex book called *The Weight Report* or *The Height Report,* though what weight or height's got to do with sex I sure as heck don't see. . . . No, we don't expect as how the incriminating evidence'll be hard to find. I actually been up to her place once on department business, I don't remember an awful lot of books floatin' around. . . . Right. Right. Rendezvous at the Kampus Kave on South Main at eight. We'll hit them up for a lasagne on the house before we arrest the perpetrator. Yeah, see you."

The sheriff materializes in the doorway of his office. "Norman," he brays.

Startled, the deputies playing cards, the deputy shining boots look up. Norman bolts from his cubicle.

"I reckon as how I went'n solved the serial murders," the sheriff announces. " 'Member the hearin' contraption we found in the pocket of Purchase Honeycut? Well, actin' on uh tip from uh civic-minded citizen, here present, I went'n checked it out with the Hearin' Center in Hornell. The power of the hearin' aid matches the audio deficiency of the handyman over at the Chaos Institute, who by coincidence turns out to have inherited the used-car dealership of the late lamented Mr. Honeycut."

"Are we gonna go an' bring the state police in on the arrest?" Norman wants to know.

"No way. Their Bureau of Criminal Investigation has done diddly on these murders. We went'n solved em. We get to get the credit." The sheriff hikes his gun belt up on his stomach. "I want you to hold the fort, Wallace," he tells the deputy who has been shining boots. "Bobby, Bubba, 'long with me'n Norman here, we're gonna pick up uh signed'n sealed arrest warrant, after which we're gonna go'n get our pictures in the newspapers. You're welcome to tag along, Mr. Falk. You went'n earned it."

Lemuel can barely keep his voice reined in. "I need to get back to Backwater. . . . I have important computer business to attend to."

"Come on, Lem," Norman coaxes. "The least you can do is get yourself on the tube again."

"Hey, no, really—"

"Maybe you oughta keep us company," the sheriff decides. "What with you bein' the one who went'n risked his life on the nuclear-dump deal, we got us uh better chance of hittin' network prime time with you on board."

Chapter Six

I can say you, when it comes to watching someone being arrested, I am, if only it could be otherwise, not a vestal virgin. I have already described the young lady I fell wildly, eternally, achingly in love with as she was being dragged by her hair across the cobblestones in front of the Smolny Institute. Also how I was hauled in for questioning when the second of my two signatures turned up on a petition. I did not look forward to witnessing the arrest of what the sheriff, with the bureaucrat's genius for dehumanized jargon, called the perpetrator. (I suppose it is easier to arrest people, easier, in the end, to execute them, if they do not come equipped with a handle.) The trouble was I could not worm out of it without alerting Norman to the possibility he had been overheard making arrangements to bust Rain.

So now I'll do the arrest of the alleged perpetrator.

I will start with the weather. In the great scheme of things, April showers are supposed to lead inexorably to May flowers, but someone had not gotten the word. It was a raw, soggy May evening, the result, no doubt, of trivial turbulence created by a night moth flailing its wings in a reach of Siberia. Swollen teardrops of rain were exploding against the windshield faster than the wipers working at breakneck speed could clear them away. Which is why what I witnessed was blurred, first by the rain, later by the teardrops which spilled from my eyes, I will tell you why eventually.

I was in the backseat of the sheriff's cruiser as we eased into Purchase Honeycut's Used-Car Bazaar on the edge of Hornell. The other cruiser, with Bobby and Bubba in it, drove up the ramp across the lot, blocking that entrance. The four headlights illuminated the one-story, all-glass building.

Norman picked up the car microphone. "Seen hide nor hair of the TV boys yet?" he asked Bubba over the radio.

I was jotting down "hide nor hair" on the back of an envelope when static erupted on the radio:

"—Jus' 'rivin' now—"

A white truck with "Channel 8 News" printed on the side pulled up to the curb outside the lot. A man leaped out and started filming with a shoulder-mounted camera that also bore the "Channel 8 News" logo.

"Here's where we earn our paychecks," the sheriff said, climbing out of the car.

He was wearing a yellow fireman's raincoat and carrying a battery-powered bullhorn and a revolver, which he kept out of sight behind his back. He gestured for me to wind down my window.

"Go'n stay put," he told me, "in case the perpetrator decides to resist gettin' hisself arrested." He raised the possibility of a shootout with a gleam in his eye, as if he was measuring the size of the headlines to come.

The sheriff checked to make sure the TV people were filming, then waved the bullhorn in the direction of Bubba and Bobby, who drew pistols and started forward. Walking in lockstep, he and Norman began wading through an enormous puddle toward the glass building with the neon "Purchase from Purchase" sign sizzling over the front door as if it was electrocuting horseflies.

A figure loomed in the open glass door.

The sheriff and his three deputies froze in their tracks. The sheriff raised the bullhorn to his lips. "I'm Chester Combes, the county—"

He was drowned out by an ear-splitting squeal from the bullhorn. "Like I was sayin', I'm Chester Combes, the county sheriff? I was sorta countin' on havin' uh word with you, Word."

" 'Bout what?" the man at the door shouted into the rain.

" 'Bout the demise of Purchase Honeycut an' nineteen other serial-murder victims."

Word Perkins cackled wildly. "A nitwit like you couldn't a figured it out all by himself. I'll lay odds you hadda have help from the visitin' professor who don't own what he knows—who went an' loaned you the answer."

I could see Word shielding his eyes with his hand and peering into the headlights. "I know yaw out there, huh, professor from Petersboig," he called.

Sinking down into the backseat, I watched the sheriff scratch the nape of his neck with the barrel of his revolver. "You wanna be sure an' edit out the part where he calls me a nitwit," he told the TV reporters through the bullhorn. He turned back and took a step in the direction of the sizzling neon sign. The other deputies closed in from different directions.

"Word Perkins," the sheriff bellowed through the bullhorn, "you're under arrest. It's my duty to warn you anythin' you say may be used in evidence against you. . . ."

Through the drops of water streaming down the front window, I could see the perpetrator reach up and snatch the hearing aid out of his ear. Then in one flowing motion he stepped back and slammed the glass door shut and stooped and turned the key in the lock at the base of the door. The sheriff and his deputies charged up to the building. The sheriff kicked at the glass door, but it did not give. He brought his revolver out from behind his back and pointed it at the man standing inside.

"I'm directin' you to open up or I'll open up," he blustered through the bullhorn.

Word Perkins shrugged and shook his head to indicate he could not hear what the sheriff was saying. Backing away, he turned and disappeared into an office with glass partitions. I could see him wrench open a metal filing cabinet and fling out several fistfuls of paper before coming up with an object wrapped in a piece of cloth. Walking slowly, lost, so it seemed from a distance, in the eerily silent world where you cannot hear your own footsteps, he made his way back into the showroom and confronted the sheriff and his three deputies through the locked door. The television cameraman came up behind the sheriff and filmed over his shoulder.

Word Perkins peeled the cloth away from the object as if he was skinning an orange. The object turned out to be a snub-nosed revolver. The sheriff and the three deputies dropped into a tense crouch, their pistols thrust forward. Word Perkins calmly removed a bullet from the folds of the cloth and rubbed its nose against what would later be identified as a clove of garlic. Thumbing the bullet into the chamber, he brought the pistol up and jammed the barrel into his left ear.

"You don't wanna go'n do that," the sheriff cried over the bullhorn, but of course the perpetrator could not hear him.

I rolled my window all the way down and stuck my head out to get a better view, but the scene was still blurred. Tears over which I had no control were flooding from my bloodshot eyes, I was crying like I had not cried since . . . since . . .

Through my tears I could see Norman whirl around and block the lens of the television camera with his hand, God bless him for this delicacy, even a perpetrator is entitled to a certain amount of privacy when he blows his brains out. I also looked away. In my mind's ear, dear God, if only it had been a fiction I could slip into and out of like the sleeveless sweater my mother knitted me when she got out of prison, in my mind's ear I heard the muted, brittle explosion, it sounded like a sharp dry cough coming from behind a closed door, I saw the faceless men who had been searching the apartment lunge toward the bathroom, I saw one of them kick the door off its rusted hinges, I heard my mother emit a sound so inhuman it stabbed my eardrums. And then I was pushing through the men standing around the bathtub and sinking to my knees next to their thick-soled, steel-toed shoes and gaping at the syrupy fluid oozing from between the thick lips that had so often teasingly kissed me on my child's lips.

My father . . .

My father was clutching the German Luger he had brought back from the Great Patriotic War and had produced, along with the *Royal Canadian Air Force Exercise Manual,* every time he told the story of how he had personally liberated Poland, as if the existence of these two trophies proved he had been there. Tactful as always, he had climbed into the bathtub before shooting himself so as not to stain our precious East German linoleum with blood. His unblinking eyes were riveted on mine, they contained, it seemed to me then, it seems to me now, a melancholy reproach, an unspoken question. Why did you do it? his eyes asked. And then he was staring at me. I do not know how at the age of six I knew such a thing, he was, this is a true detail, staring at me without seeing me. Which was when I put two and two together and figured out what the word meant that my parents had refused to explain me.

The word was death.

I also figured out what had happened to my lost turtle and my lost goldfish and my mother's youngest brother, my crazy uncle Hippolyte who brought me striped candy canes every time he came over until one day he stopped coming over and my mother burned all the snapshots of him in the family album. Maybe it was all that information clicking into place in such a short span of time which overloaded my cerebral circuits; maybe it was the sight of one of the faceless men closing my father's eyes with his soiled, sausage-thick fingers—whatever the reason, my head started spinning from all the questions which suddenly had inconvenient answers.

I do not usually have an eye for detail, but in this case I am able to reconstruct the scene as clearly as if the whole episode took place yesterday. By the age of six I had already developed the lifelong habit of avoiding the chaos of the moment by slipping into fictions. I remember holding my breath, hoping against hope this was a fiction I could slip out of.

I lost all hope when the faceless men stuffed my father's body into a bloodstained burlap sack and dragged it down the stairs, the elevator as usual was out of order, and pitched it into the back of an open truck. Gazing down from my apartment window through the tears streaming from my eyes, they turned bloodshot from crying so much, they would stay that way for the rest of my interminable life, I could see the burlap sack rolling from side to side as the truck pulled away from the building.

With the advantage of hindsight, I can identify this as the precise moment my childhood ended. After the suicide of my father, I was never young again. Emotionally speaking, I froze in my tracks. The emotions I experienced that day are the emotions which dominate my life today. If I loathe and fear chaos, it does not come from nowhere.

For some people it is always too late to have a childhood, forget happy.

Where was I?

Another brittle explosion reached my ears. I wheeled around in time to see the sheriff kick away the lock he had shot off and push through the glass door. Inside, a rag doll of a body lay motionless on the floor. Overhead, the "Purchase from Purchase" sign sizzled irritably. Automobiles roared up to the curb. Tires squealed. Journalists brandishing cameras and microphones and klieg lights and tape recorders crowded up to the door, elbowing each other to get a better look at the late unlamented perpetrator. Exploding flashbulbs strobe-lit the scene. The sheriff, his pistol and bullhorn dangling along the gold stripes of his trousers, emerged from the glass building. He walked with a jerky gait, as if every second frame was missing from the film. He answered a few questions, shook his head, gestured with his chin toward me.

The next thing I knew the cruiser with me huddled in the backseat was adrift in a sea of reporters. Flashbulbs detonated in my face, a long television camera snaked into the car through the open window, its lens whirring in and out as it tried to focus on my tear-streaked face.

"Can you tell us how you figured out the identity of the serial killer?"

"I can say you I used game theory, also the theory of randomness, to prove the perpetrator was trying to make his crimes look random. This discovery led directly to the serial killer."

"What'd he say?"

"Come again?"

"Would you run that past us once more looking straight into the camera?"

"It is as plain as the nose on your face. The conscious effort to produce randomness negates randomness."

"What is it about randomness that grabs you?"

"Whether the universe is random or determined shapes up as the ultimate philosophic question. Our view of the structure of the universe, of why we are passengers on the planet Earth, depends on the answer. The quest for a single example of pure, unadulterated randomness can thus be seen as the search for God."

"What are you, some kind of religious nut?"

"Say, aren't you the visiting professor at the Institute for Chaos-Related Studies who stopped the bulldozer at the nuclear-waste site?"

"Could you comment on how it feels to solve a crime that stumped the police?"

Before I could open my mouth, a journalist called, "Could you tell us how it feels to be responsible for someone's suicide?"

"Would you say whether you ever killed anyone before?"

A cry burst from my heart of hearts: "For God's sake, I was only six. I wasn't even a consenting adolescent, forget adult."

"What did he say?"

"He said he was only sixty."

"He doesn't look a day over fifty."

"Would you share with us your secret to looking younger than you are?"

"Do you follow a special diet?"

"Do you exercise regularly?"

"Did you have plastic surgery?"

"What about hair implants?"

"Is there any truth to the rumor that you lied about your age to avoid the draft in the Soviet Union?"

"There is no Soviet Union anymore," I started to explain, but my words were drowned out by a barrage of questions.

"Would you give us your views on a common European currency?"

"Would you give us your views on the European Common Market?"

"Would you give us your views on euthanasia?"

I wanted to say them I was more familiar with the predicament of youth in Europe, but it was obvious nobody would have paid the slightest attention to my answer.

"What do you think of American crime?"

"What do you think of American criminals?"

"What do you think of America?

"Can you tell us if you've learned anything from your visit here?"

I managed to slip a word in. "I learned to wear my heart on my sleeve. I learned how a city on the Euphrates can be more Florida than Miami."

"Are you seriously suggesting it's safe to put fluoride in drinking water?"

"Are you for or against family values?"

"What's your position on infidelity?"

"What is your position on incest?"

"If God was really against incest," I started to explain, "He would have created two Edens within commuting distance of each other," but I might as well have been whistling into the wind.

"Do you agree with those who claim that serial murder is a search for serial orgasm?"

"Speaking as an expert on chaos, do you think premature ejaculation can be cured?"

"Does theoretical chaos hold out hope for men who can't achieve orgasm?"

I could barely speak; I felt the words catch in my throat. "It is a matter of getting a jump start," I managed to say, "of being downwardly mobile. . . . The next thing you know, whoooosh, you are pushing the speed limit on the Interstate."

"Are you saying you're against the fifty-five-mile-per-hour speed limit?"

"He fielded that question last time we interviewed him," an anchorwoman noted.

A siren wailed in the distance, its pitch rising as it approached. The heads of the journalists craned toward the sound. "Thank you for the interview, Mr. Falk," one of the reporters called through the open window. The television lens zoomed back until it was nesting in the camera. The journalists scurried away to film the arrival of the white truck with the pulsating light that sent tiny orange explosions skidding across the rain-soaked road.

The sight of the orange light released in me a flood of memories. I thought of the truck spewing sand onto the icy road the night I arrived in Backwater and the tiny orange explosions on the ice-lacquered pavement, I thought of the ice storm that had been caused by the Siberian night moth, I thought of Occasional Rain jump-starting my battery, I thought of her warm mouth closing over a part of me it had not been to before.

Could it be, was it within the realm that I had fallen wildly, eternally, achingly in love with a girl who actually existed?

Shaken, shaking, I stumbled away from the sheriff's cruiser. Drifting between the used cars in the lot toward the street, I heard Word Perkins's demented cackle reverberating in my brain.

In the beginnin' was the Woid . . .

The rain had let up, a damp darkness shrouded the scene. Down the block the journalists thronged around the white truck. Norman and Bobby and Bubba, looking like ghostly angels in the harsh white light of the kliegs, pushed through the crowd with a stretcher containing the perpetrator gift-wrapped in the sheriff's yellow slicker. They came up behind the tailgate and folded back the wheels under the stretcher and maneuvered the corpse into the back of the truck and closed the doors. Norman rapped his knuckles twice on the side of the truck.

The siren started wailing again, at first feebly, then with an intensity that reminded me of my mother's inhuman shriek. I pressed my palms against my ears, dampening the sound. At least Word Perkins would not be disturbed by the noise, I thought.

. . . the Woid was whit God.

As the truck pulled away from the curb and started down the street toward me, I caught sight of letters gleaming over the windshield. They read:

AMBULANCE

I racked my exhausted brain, but could not recall anything even remotely resembling this in my *Royal Canadian*

Air Force Exercise Manual or my other English sourcebooks.
Nor did it strike me as being Lilliputian.
Which meant it was a new language.
The King's English had slipped into chaos.

The sheriff detonates the head of a match with his thumbnail and holds the flame to the tip of the cigar jutting from his mouth. "I'd go an French-kiss uh horse's arse," he allows, interrupting himself to suck the cigar into life, "just to see the faces on the Criminal Investigation boys when they catch the evenin' news." He exhales, bats away the smoke. "You gotta hand it to the perpetrator," he rambles on. "Killin' hisself the way he did went'n saved the county the expense of uh trial, not to mention eventual incarceration."

Norman is unusually subdued as he wheels the sheriff's cruiser onto the Interstate, direction Backwater. "Believe it or not, I never seen no one blow his brains out before," he announces.

"I seen uh perpetrator once," the sheriff says, sinking back into his memories, "it was up in Boston, I was only uh depety sheriff at the time, he got wind he was gonna get arrested an' rigged uh garden hose from the exhaust into his car, then locked hisself in an' started up the motor. He went'n killed hisself listenin' to uh Judy Garland tape." The sheriff's eyes screw up into a nostalgic squint as he hoarsely croaks the words. " 'I'm al-ways chay-sin' rain-bows . . .' That song was still playin', back 'n' forth, back 'n' forth, when we busted into the car. Funny how a tune can stick in your head."

Sheriff Combes twists in his seat belt to talk to Lemuel, who is lost in the darkness in a corner of the backseat. "You bein' un-American an' all, I don't expect as how you're familiar with rainbow chasin'."

Lemuel says moodily. "I have chased a rainbow or two in my day."

Norman says, "If rainbow chasin's anything like ambulance chasin', it's against the law."

They cruise the Interstate without a word for half a dozen miles. Norman breaks the silence. "Word Perkins rubbing the dumdum with garlic before he shot himself to death proved the perpetrator was the perpetrator."

"Garlic, hell, goin' an' killin' hisself is what proved he was the perpetrator," the sheriff says. "Perpetrators who didn't perpetrate don't blow their brains out."

"There are exceptions to your rule," Lemuel remarks darkly.

"Why would a perpetrator kill himself if he's not the perpetrator?" Norman asks innocently.

Before Lemuel can respond, an eighteen-wheeler coming from the other direction blinds Norman and the sheriff with its brights. Norman flicks his headlights several times, then raises an arm to shade his eyes. "Son of a bitch," he swears.

Bubba's voice, crackling with static, bursts over the car radio. "What'cha say I hang a U and nail the fucka?"

The sheriff glances at the luminous dial of his wristwatch. "We're late already," he says into the microphone. "If we don't show up at the Kampus Kave before they polish off their lasagnes, the state cops'll go an' arrest the perpetrator theirselves."

Lemuel catches a glimpse of Norman's eyes in the rearview mirror. The deputy sheriff is peering into the mirror, trying to penetrate the darkness in the backseat. "I just thought of somethin'," he says, "namely, old Lemuel back there used to share an apartment with the broad who cuts hair in Backwater."

Lemuel realizes Norman is on the verge of putting two and two together, realizes also that the deputy sheriff is simple-minded enough to decide it equals four. "What's-Her-Face and I broke up in April," he says quickly. "I have not seen . . . hide nor hair of her since."

"Lemuel here is a bona fidee hero," the sheriff says, trailing after his own thoughts. "I'm gonna go 'n' put him in for uh citizens' medal for assistin' the law enforcement authorities."

The cruiser speeds past the sign planted at the spot where the countryside ends and the village of Backwater begins. Lemuel catches a glimpse of it through the car window. "Backwater University— Founded 1835. Home of the Institute for Advanced Interdisciplinary Chaos-Related Studies." Underneath someone has spray-painted the words "Chaos sucks!"

Could it be . . . Is it within the realm . . . Has he stumbled across another, until now unsuspected, property of chaos? Or was the graffiti merely a chapter heading in *The Greenhorn's Guide to Polite Oral Sex*?

Norman spots the Rebbe's house and starts to slow down. Lemuel leans forward. "Can you drop me downtown?" he asks casually. "I am scheduled to access the supercomputer over at the Institute until midnight."

A minute later Norman eases the cruiser up to the curb behind the two state police cars parked in front of the Kampus Kave. The cruiser with Bobby and Bubba in it pulls up behind them. The sheriff corkscrews in his seat and offers a three-fingered handshake over his shoulder.

"I'd give uh hell of a lot to know what you do on that computer of yours when you're not solvin' serial murders."

Lemuel, pushing open the door, says, "It is a relevant question, I am glad you asked it. What I do is plunge through the decimal expansion of pi toward infinity."

"Uh-huh," Norman grunts.

"Don't it make your head swim?"

One foot out the door, Lemuel says, "Compared to the high you get from infinity, marijuana is kids' stuff."

Lemuel starts down the block toward the Institute, glances back to make sure the coast is clear, doubles back and peeks through the "e" of the "Kampus Kave" on the window. Molly, all smiles, is distributing toothpicks to the four state troopers and a television cameraman as they slide out of the booth and shake paws with the sheriff and his deputies.

Lemuel realizes he does not have an instant to lose. He lumbers diagonally across Main Street, passes the twenty-four-hour laundromat, turns into the unpaved alleyway, takes the steps of the narrow wooden staircase two at a time. His chest heaving, he presses his ear to the door. Hearing nothing, he feels for the key hidden over the cement lintel. When his fingers close over it he feels a surge of relief. His hand trembles as he tries to fit the key into the lock. He fills his lungs with air, steadies his right hand with his left, inserts the key and opens the door.

The room is awash in the eerie light cast by the projector with the piece of mauve silk over it. Mayday, curled up on her blanket, stares at Lemuel with unblinking eyes filled with cataracts and reproach.

Lemuel bends down and strokes the dog's head. "Hey, it is me, L. Fucking Falk," he whispers in the dog's ear. "I did not go to Miami-on-the-Euphrates after all."

On the phonograph, a needle is scratching in the end grooves of a record. Lemuel spots garments flung carelessly over the back of the couch and instinctively begins to fold them—a pleated miniskirt, a body-hugging ribbed sweater, sea-green tights, gray Calvin Klein underpants. His hearts, the one in his chest, the one on his sleeve, skip several beats as he folds a pin-striped button-down shirt, a pair of designer jeans, silk boxer shorts.

From the bedroom come the soft gasps that originate in the back of the throat of someone fucking.

Lemuel listens for a moment, then stepping silently over the dog, snatches *The Hite Report* from the shelf. Grasping it in his suddenly clammy hands, he backs out of the room, locks the door behind him, puts the key back on the lintel.

He just has time to duck between a garage filled with Spring Fest floats and an abandoned building before headlights appear at both ends of the alley. Twisting and turning to avoid potholes, four automobiles crawl slowly toward each other along the unpaved road and meet under the staircase leading to Rain's loft. The headlights snap off. Car doors slam. Metal taps echo on the wooden steps. Knuckles drum on the door.

"Anybody home?" The voice has Norman's unmistakable twang.

"Call again, Norman."

"You in there, Rain?"

A naked electric bulb flickers on over the lintel. The door opens. A familiar voice reacts to the presence of the law enforcement contingent. "Z'up, Norman? Z'up, Sheriff?"

"Miss Occasional Rain Morgan," the sheriff intones, "we got us a signed, sealed warrant to search the premises."

Norman adds, "You could save us all a lot of pain by handing over the hollowed-out sex book called *The Weight Report.*"

From inside the loft, a man's voice calls, "What's the deal, babe?"

Rain can be heard groaning, "Oh, shit, this is all I needed."

The sheriff, his three deputies, the four state troopers and the reporter filming the scene with a shoulder-held camera crowd into the loft.

Gripping *The Hite Report* under his arm, Lemuel disappears down the dark alleyway.

Lemuel lets himself in the front door of the Rebbe's house, wipes the soles of his shoes on a shabby carpet in the vestibule before making his way into the living room. He hears the sound of a radio coming from behind the closed door of the kitchen. Still clutching Rain's hollowed-out book, wondering if *The Hite Report* has the sacred name of God buried somewhere in its pages, he looks around at the Rebbe's waist-high leaning towers of books stacked, spine outward, snaking along the walls of the room and on up the stairs. Back in the alleyway, he flirted with the idea of flinging the book and its contents into a garbage bin, but decided against it; the book, which surely had Rain's fingerprints all over it, might be discovered and turned over to the police. Better to hide it, but where? The last place anyone would look for a book, he reasoned, was in a pile of books. And the first pile that leaped to mind was the Rebbe's collection of books with the name of God in them.

Lemuel just manages to slip *The Hite Report* into a stack of books halfway up the staircase when the kitchen door swings open.

"Lemuel?"

The Rebbe, looking more Lilliputian than Lemuel remembers him, pushes through the door into the living room and snaps on the overhead light. Hunched over like a parenthesis, his coiled sideburns dancing in agitation, his beetle brows skydiving toward each other in anxiety, he peers up the stairs. When he speaks his voice is uncommonly hoarse, as if he has cheered too much. But for what? Or against what?

"For hours I have been asking myself, Where could the schlimazel be?"

"Better late than never."

"How could you do it?"

"How could I do what?"

"I thought I was your friend."

"You are."

"I thought you trusted me."

"Hey, I do."

"Then explain, if it's within the realm, why you didn't confide in me."

"Confide what, for God's sake?"

The Rebbe lowers his voice to a croaking whisper. "We sat at the same table, we shared the same bread, we drank the same Puligny Montrachet. The least you could have done was tell me about the codes."

Lemuel shuts his eyes. "Not you too!"

"Everybody in Backwater, also everybody outside of Backwater, seems to know about it except me. What have I done that I'm the last to learn? Do I deserve this?"

"Who spilled you the beans?"

"A little birdie spilled me the beans. Oy, Lemuel, Lemuel, if you had taken me into your confidence, I could have saved you a lot of *tsouris.*" The Rebbe advances onto the first step. "I still can." He mounts another step. "Save you a lot of *tsouris.*"

Lemuel begins to massage his eyelids with his thumb and third finger. "Do not tell me you work for an intelligence agency."

"Being a spy is like being a Messiah."

"Do not tell me you work for the Israelis."

"I don't actually work for them." The Rebbe inches higher on the staircase. "I am what they call a headhunter and I think of as a hearthunter. When I come up with a warm body who's a hot prospect, I remove the enciphering instructions they gave me from its hiding place"—the Rebbe points with his beard to a particularly high pile of books near the kitchen door—"and send a coded picture postcard to an address in Israel. Air mail. Don't look at me like that. I am not ashamed to be part of the international Jewish conspiracy. The world is crawling with anti-Semites, which is to say with people who hate Jews more than necessary. It is a matter of life or death for the pro-Semites to read their mail."

"Why me?"

"If not you, who? I beg you, Lemuel, do not turn a deaf ear to the handwriting on the wall. A day doesn't go by, an hour even, when I don't patrol the back pages of the newspaper looking for little articles that indicate the start of a new Holocaust. You are trying not to smile at things that strike you as absurd. Your cynicism is an insult to the parents who raised you. Read it and weep. 'Seven hundred thousand Jews reportedly exterminated in a Polish backwater called Oświecim.' That was how *The New York Times,* which calls itself a newspaper of record, which prints all the news that fits, broke the story of what the Nazi bastards were up to, it was on a back page, the crossword puzzle was more prominent, the front page was otherwise occupied with a hot scoop on summer vacations."

Lemuel settles down onto the carpeted step. "I can say you, Rebbe, I have had it with code books. I have had it with subtexts."

The Rebbe sinks to his knees on the step below. "Lemuel, Lemuel, everything in life is coded. The Torah I love more than oxygen, the whisperings of lovers, the rantings of a rebbe, your left, right, either or, novels even, novels *especially*, they all have a subtext. If there is no subtext, the absence of a subtext is the subtext, it makes a statement, it says, It is important for me to convince you what you see is what you get. As your former shiksa lady friend would say, get a life. In this *meshugge* world, between the experience and the language available to describe it—ha! between joie de vivre and its exegesis—there is an abyss. Codes, subtexts are the bridges across the abyss."

"At this point in the spiel dudes usually tell me what is in it for me."

"Oy, you haven't deciphered my subtext. Nothing is what's in it for you. If you go to Israel to help the Jews make and break codes, you will reside in a cramped, noisy apartment in Tel Aviv, Petersburg compared will look like a paradise lost. Like everyone else in the Holy Land you will live on bank overdrafts to make ends meet. You will vacation on a polluted seashore crawling with snot-nosed kiddies kicking sand in your face. But you will serve Israel, and through Israel, Yahweh."

"I am still not one hundred percent sure He exists."

The Rebbe plunks himself down next to Lemuel. "So where is it written you cannot serve God while you are searching for Him?"

"Tell me something, Asher. Do you really believe the dude exists? Come at the problem from another direction: Have you discovered Him or invented Him?"

The Rebbe's bulging eyes flash. He fixes Lemuel with a fierce regard. "When you see a three-piece suit, you *discover* the tailor, you don't *invent* him. Why should it be different when you see a rose in bloom, a bird in flight, a swirling tempest of ice paralyzing the East Coast, a footprint of chaos in the dunes of time?"

Sighing, he pulls the enormous handkerchief from the inside breast pocket of his jacket, opens it with a theatrical flourish, mops his brow. At length he says, "I caught you on the tube tonight. Thanks to you, they nailed the serial murderer to his cross, so to speak. You are once again a local hero." One of his hands comes to rest on Lemuel's forearm. "I saw you cringing in the back of the car, I heard you say the quest for a single example of pure, unadulterated randomness is the search for God. So what are you waiting for, Lemuel? Go for it. Do what I couldn't bring myself to do. Make the leap."

Lemuel squirms uncomfortably. "What leap are we talking about?"

"The leap of faith. Okay, Torah is maybe a can of worms. Was it David who killed the goy Goliath—I'm talking 1 Samuel 16–17—or some local hero named Elhanan—I'm talking 2 Samuel 21:19. Either or, Torah is still the work of God and the word of God, Blessed be His holy name. The subtext, the codes, what's written between the lines, are His handiwork too. You and me, Lemuel, we maybe approach Torah from opposite directions, but in your heart of hearts you are as kosher as I am. It is no accident your name means 'devoted to God.' "

"You put on a good show," Lemuel says tiredly.

"Every word comes from the gut," the Rebbe says quietly.

Suddenly aggressive, Lemuel asks, "Like what is in it for you if I sign on the dotted line?"

"Ask, ask, I am not insulted. What is in it for me is a bonus for every recruit I sign. Where do you think I get the seed money to start a yeshiva in the heart of the heart of Brooklyn, from a goy bank?" The Rebbe manages a smile that is both lopsided and delicate. "What is in it for me is finding grace in the eyes of Yahweh." Rocking gently, he recites, " 'He brought me forth . . . he delivered me, because he delighted in me.' " Out of habit, he coughs up his source. "I'm talking 2 Samuel 22:20."

There is a sharp knock on the front door. Suddenly alert, the Rebbe eyes Lemuel. "You are maybe expecting someone?"

"Not."

The Rebbe heaves himself off the step, pads through the vestibule to the front door, opens it a crack. The first thing he sees is a shoe wedged between the door and the jamb.

From his place on the steps, Lemuel hears a muffled argument. Seconds later Mitchell and Doolittle, trailed by five FBI clones in tight-fitting three-piece suits, push through the vestibule into the living room. Wringing his hands, the Rebbe brings up the rear.

Mitchell spots Lemuel on the staircase. "Small world, isn't it, sport?"

"You want to hear something hilarious," the Rebbe broadcasts in a high-pitched voice, "these guys, who barge into a private house without an invitation, without kissing the mezuzah on the doorpost of my gate, without wiping their feet even, these guys with the razor-sharp creases in their trousers think I am maybe the agent of a foreign country."

"We don't think," Doolittle corrects him. "We know."

"If the Syrians turn up in Backwater," one of the clones remarks, "can the Israelis be far behind?"

The clones spread out and begin rifling through drawers. The Rebbe grabs the sleeve of one of them. "You can't do that."

With a snap of his wrist, Doolittle unfurls a paper in front of the Rebbe's face. "A circuit court judge disagrees with you."

"*Chazak,*" the Rebbe mutters to himself. "Be strong."

Mitchell settles onto his haunches and starts to leaf through the top book on a leaning tower at the bottom of the stairs. "What's with all these books?"

"I've collected them over the years," the Rebbe explains. "They have the name of God in them." He swallows hard. "It's against Jewish law to destroy a book containing the name of God."

"If we have to," Doolittle vows, "we'll examine every book in the house."

"It will take days," the Rebbe says hopefully.

"Time," Mitchell announces, shaking a book by its spine, "is what we have on our hands."

Doolittle motions for the agents to start searching the books piled against the walls. Mitchell looks up at Lemuel. "Join the movers and shakers, sport. Tell us where he's hiding the incriminating evidence." He dangles a book upside down by its spine and jiggles it. "You haven't forgotten who the good guys are, have you? Show us whose side you're on."

Halfway up the steps, Lemuel is trembling like a leaf in a tempest. In his mind's eye, dear God, if only it had been another one of his fictions, he hears a voice whisper in his ear: "You want to show Comrade Stalin whose side you're on, don't you, sonny? Tell us where your father hides his code book."

He hears his answer spiral up from his lost childhood. "What is a code book?"

Cowering in a corner, he watches, spellbound, as one of the faceless men slits open his parents' mattress with a bread knife and starts to gut it. Two others tear clothing out of the armoire and pass it to a third man, who cuts away the linings from his mother's coats and dresses before flinging the garments onto a heap in a corner.

"Be strong," his father calls across the room. "There is nothing for them to find."

One of the faceless men looks Lemuel's father in the eye. "Talking while the flat is being searched is not permitted," he says coldly. Lemuel's father lowers his gaze.

When the armoire is empty, the faceless men begin to dismantle it, stacking the pieces against a wall. Lemuel feels bile mount to his mouth, starts toward the kitchen to spit it into the sink. Someone grabs his arm.

"Let him go," his mother pleads. "He is only six."

When Lemuel slips back into the bedroom, the faceless men are lifting the back of the armoire away from the frame. One of them notices a loose flap of wallpaper above the floorboards. He squats, peels the paper away from the plasterboard, reaches into a crack and comes out with a book. Lemuel's father glances quickly at the boy, who is barely able to breathe.

The agent in charge leafs through the pages, which are dog-eared and full of underlined words and phrases. "It is in English," he notes. He reads an underlined phrase aloud. " 'Stretching abdominal muscles in this manner fifteen minutes a day . . .' " He turns to the title page. " *'The Royal Canadian Air Force Exercise Manual.'* " He looks up. "This is clearly a code book, used for enciphering and deciphering secret messages," he announces. He adds the book to the letters and photograph albums in a barrel with the words EVIDENCE and THIS SIDE UP stenciled on the wood.

Lemuel's father shakes his head in frustration. "You don't understand. I brought the book back from the Great War. A Canadian pilot I liberated from a prisoner-of-war camp gave it to me. I shared the book with my son, Lemuel. I use it for exercises. He uses it to study English."

"If the book had not been hidden in the wall, your story might ring true," says the agent in charge.

Lemuel's mother whispers urgently to Lemuel's father, who says, "We made the mistake of telling the boy that English books were not permitted. When he saw you searching the living room, he must have crawled under the armoire and hidden it in the wall so he could continue his study of English." His father smiles tensely across the room at the boy. *"The Royal Canadian Air Force Exercise Manual* is his most prized possession."

Suddenly everyone in the room is staring at Lemuel, who is cowering in the corner. "Is it true you study English from this book?" one of the faceless men demands.

Lemuel, trembling like a leaf, shakes his head. Choking on sobs that block his respiration, he whimpers over and over, again and again, "It was not me who hid the code book."

Lemuel's mother begins to weep. The back of his father's hand brushes against the back of his mother's hand. "With your permission," his father tells the faceless men, "I will collect my toilet articles in the bathroom."

"It is my book!" Lemuel hears himself blurt out—dear God, he has been wandering in a wilderness for forty years, but better late than never.

Suddenly everyone in the house is staring at Lemuel. "What book are we talking about, sport?" Mitchell asks.

Lemuel pulls the hollowed-out *Hite Report* from the pile of books and offers it to Mitchell. Doolittle and Mitchell exchange triumphant glances. The Rebbe starts to climb the stairs, but one of the clones bars the way. Mitchell takes the book, opens it, touches the vials and paper satchels inside with a fingertip.

"It's a drug stash," he decides, clearly surprised.

"I recognize that b—" the Rebbe starts to say, but Lemuel cuts him off.

"You want to let me deal with this in my own way, Asher. I beg your pardon for abusing your hospitality. I needed a place to hide it."

"Why are you telling these crazies the book is yours?"

"Because in deep ways it is true."

"I thought we came here to arrest an Israeli agent," one of the clones gripes.

"We have nothing against landing a big fish," Doolittle says.

"Consider the possibility," the Rebbe, insulted, reprimands Doolittle, "that calling an alleged Israeli agent a small fish can be construed as anti-Semitism."

Lemuel aims one of his half-smiles at the Rebbe. "Do not worry your head about me, Asher. I can say you I have become a consenting *Homo chaoticus*. The chaos that accompanies me like a shadow, sometimes it is behind, sometimes in front, I still do not love it, but I think I am ready to live with it."

"You are in deep shit," Mitchell warns Lemuel. "Drug dealers have been known to rot in jail for years."

"In jail," Lemuel points out, "I would not be able to map intricate statistical variations in large samples of data, which is the weak link in even near-randomness. I would not be able to break any cipher being used in the world today."

"Sounds to me like we're in a negotiation," Mitchell tells Doolittle.

"I think we have the makings of a deal here," Doolittle says carefully.

"Let's get it straight," Mitchell recapitulates. "If we were to forget about *The Hite Report*, you'd come in out of the cold and work for the good guys?"

Doolittle nails down the fine print. "You'd break ciphers for A.D.V.A., which is a subdivision of PROD, which is a division of N.S.A.?"

"There is a condition," Lemuel says. "Get off the Rebbe's case."

"Don't take the fall for me," the Rebbe implores Lemuel. "I have friends in high places."

"Name one, sport," Mitchell sneers.

The Rebbe draws himself up to his full five feet, two inches. "Yahweh."

Mitchell doesn't seem impressed. "What agency does he work for?"

Lemuel asks with a straight face, "Yo! You never heard of Occasional Yahweh? The Dude is out to lunch most of the time, which explains a lot of things in the back pages of *The New York Times* like the Holocaust, but He is definitely a mover and a shaker. There is not much that goes on in the corridors of power He does not know about."

The Rebbe's sideburns cavort in the air. "Glory be to God," he proclaims. "You have made the leap." His wrists shoot from his starched cuffs as he thrusts his arms heavenward and addresses Yahweh one-on-One. " 'Our soul is escaped as a bird out of the snare of the fowlers,' " he exults. " 'The snare is broken, and we are escaped.' "

"He's talking gibberish," says one of the clones.

"What I'm talking," the Rebbe corrects him with a biblical gleam in his shining Talmudic eyes, "is Psalm 124:7. Selah."

Chapter Seven

Dudes who've aced introductory psychology have told me there is more to shoplifting than meets the eye, but I honestly don't see it. I don't feel like I'm defying parental authority, lah-di-dah, when I score the odd item from a supermarket shelf (when my dad said he was minding the store, he was talking about a B-52 bomber), I don't feel I'm expressing a death wish neither, if anything the contrary is the case, I am expressing a life wish inasmuch as I always eat what I steal.

So I happened to be patrolling the aisles of the E-Z Mart, slipping the occasional luxury item over my lecherous shoulder into the hidden compartment in my cloth backpack, it was the day of the summer solstice, the single hand on my Swiss watch which tells the phase of the moon and the season was leaning against the "S" of "Summer." The semester had officially ended right after L. Falk disappeared from the face of the earth three weeks before. I'd run into the Rebbe on the street and casually asked if his housemate had relocated to Miami-on-the-Euphrates. I suspected the Rebbe knew more than he wasn't saying and crowded him, which is how I learned about my *Hite Report* winding up in the hot hands of the FBI.

Where was I?

In two days I was going to trade in my glad rags for a rented cap and gown and graduate with what Dwayne calls a summa cum softa degree, which is his way of reminding me of my straight C average. I'd more or less made up my mind to hang out in Backwater after graduation, I was even toying with the idea of adding a second chair to Tender To for washing hair, why not go with the flow, right?, and was scoring the makings of a feast to celebrate the decision. I had a tentative date with Zbig, the Polish-origin nose tackle, I'd been rehearsing his last name to get the pronunciation right, it's something like Jed-zhor-skin-ski, give or take a syllable.

Dwayne, with Shirley in tow, had moved on to a mother of an E-Z Mart in Rochester, it's so huge customers go for vacation cruises in the aisles, which meant the E-Z back in Backwater had got itself a new manager. I was naturally concerned he'd be tighter than a duck's ass on water when it came to shoplifting and tried to put the fix in with Dwayne.

"Sure I know who my successor is, babe, I'm the one who talent-scouted him, but I'm not about to lay this information on you," is all I could worm out of him. Shirley also wasn't talking while the flavor lasted. "Dwayne'd kill me if I was to shoot my mouth off," she giggled, "wouldn't you, angel?"

So you can picture what a bombshell it was, right? when this dude in a knee-length white medical-type smock came up the aisle behind me and jiggled my backpack. I whirled around so fast I caught his clipboard on the side of the head. "Yeooooow!" I howled. When it comes to defending frontiers, offense is the best defense, so I let him have a blast from both barrels. "You airhead—what are you trying to do, guillotine me for shoplifting? What ever happened to the goddamn punishment fitting the goddamn crime?"

I wobbled back and batted my seaweed-green eyes as if I was having difficulty bringing him into focus, I rubbed my head more than it needed to be rubbed, I looked up into this grubby gray mask of a beard trying to decide if the person hiding behind it would figure me for someone with a lawyer friend up the sleeve who'd file a tort claim for her.

I noticed the eyes above the beard smiling at me, I noticed the smile in question was two-thirds faintly amused.

The beard moved. "Yo. What are you scoring?"

It took a microsecond for the guttural tone of the voice to penetrate.

"What are *you* scoring?" I shot back as if we were both reading from a script.

"I can say you I am not scoring nothing. I am not even playing."

"Hey, don't be a doorknob. Score something. Everyone knows supermarkets pad their prices to make up for shoplifting. Which means someone's got to shoplift to make sure they don't profit by people not shoplifting." The freckles on my face felt like they were on fire. "L. Fucking Falk! What are you doing here?"

"I am the new E-Z manager. Dwayne went and put the fix in. He convinced them I knew more about stocking the store than the computer."

Aside from the white coat and the beard, there was something different about him. His hair was longer, and flying off in all directions, he badly needed my professional services, but that wasn't it. Hey, that wasn't it at all. It was more the way he occupied his space, right? It was more the laid-back slope to his shoulders, as if a weight had been lifted from them.

"What's with the beard?" I asked.

"You could chalk it up to experience," he said. "I do not want to have the experience of being recognized if certain Mafia types turn up in Backwater looking for someone who can read FBI mail."

I meandered after him through the aisles while he ticked off things on his clipboard. "Quaker Oats, After Eights, Skippy's Peanut Butter had a good run for their money in the last twenty-four hours. We could probably use more suntan and after-shave lotions, underarm and vaginal deodorants, sunglasses and visor caps. What a chuckle. In Russia we used to say the shortages would be divided among the peasants. Here we punch codes into the overnight order and the stuff turns up on the doorstep the next morning." At this point he said something I will repeat even though I didn't one hundred percent understand it. "American the Beautiful," is what he said. "It turns out the streets are paved with Sony Walkmans after all," is what he said.

He yammered on about how easy it was to run a supermarket. It seems like L. Falk wasn't plugging into the E-Z's supercomputer to keep the store stocked; he was doing it with his super clipboard and his super pocket calculator and a natural talent for spotting shortages. The two hours of supercomputer time set aside for the Backwater E-Z Mart he was using, this is L. Falk talking, right? to spiral into the heart of the heart of something called pie deeper than anyone had ever gone before, deeper than anyone dreamed you could go, he was already at six billion five hundred million decimal places and the E-Z supercomputer was still spitting out numbers, plummeting toward infinity through pie's inky depths where no light penetrated.

Talk about knowing it like a poet!

The way L. Falk described it, you'd think he was suffering from a terminal case of rapture of the deep. Seems like he'd given up trying to invent pure, unadulterous what's-its-face, since what was missing from man-made randomness was randomness, but he still hoped to discover it on the horizon beyond the horizon. He said he figured if he kept at it a lifetime, he might be able to work this pie thing out to a trillion decimal places, why not? And as long as he didn't stumble across traces of order, as long as he didn't find a shadow of a pattern, as long as the repetitions were random repetitions, I ought to be getting this right, right? I heard it often enough, it meant pure, unadulterous you-know-what remained a distinct possibility. Here he added something about flirting with probability.

By this time L. Falk was so wound up there was no stopping him. Accessing the E-Z's supercomputer from his workstation the night before, he had calculated pie out another 250 million decimal places and come across twenty-three twenty-threes. This particular random repetition looked so hype he'd gone and torn off the printout and kept the paper, he happened to have it in his pocket, he'd be glad to show it to me. He held it up like it was a sacred scroll, I actually still have it, it was filled with numbers. Sure

enough, sitting smack in the middle of the numbers were
twenty-three twenty-threes:

```
01424518457255225922457819062652833828 95
84184755512154275945768524815465826366497
28358004256137933428104937232323232323232
3232323232323232323232323232323237502154679
45484225874134679815594672863215542798641
2130772643565428784949457842164352461 2457
3791255420299379
```

Don't ask me how, I finally managed to slip a word in
edgewise. I pointed out that twenty-three was how old I was,
and half L. Falk's age. Hey, I said to tease him, maybe someone's trying to tell you something.

The fact that I'd spotted it freaked him out, his words
tripped over each other as they spilled from his mouth. It
turns out each parent contributes twenty-three chromo-
somes to a baby. Ditto for DNA, whatever that is, where
something called bonding irregularity occurs every twenty-
three angstroms. Ditto for the tilt of the earth on its axis,
which is twenty-three degrees. Also there are twenty-three
axioms in geometry discovered, I remember L. Falk stressed
the word discovered, by some Greek joker with the unlikely
name of U. Clid. L. Falk started getting into things more up
my alley. In something called Tantra, man's sex cycle turns
out to be twenty-three days, the number representing a
woman turns out to be two, the number for a man, three.
Do we chalk these all up to coincidence? he wanted to
know. Or has God planted a coded signal six billion five
hundred million places out in the decimal expansion of pie
telling us He exists?

I badly needed to change the subject, my head was reel-
ing, I was getting high on twenty-threes, so I asked L. Falk
where he'd been hanging out since he left Backwater, it was
a detail the Rebbe had omitted.

L. Falk took a chill pill. "You do not want to know."

"Sure I want to know, which is why I asked. Why don't
you come back to the loft and fill me in over potluck supper?"

"I would like to see Mayday again."

I laid some bad news on him. "Mayday died in her sleep the day the Rebbe left for Brooklyn. I like to think she decided I didn't need her anymore. Just before Dwayne moved to Rochester, he helped me bury her in the field where they were going to put the nuclear-waste dump."

"Hey, I'm sorry.... About supper, are you sure I would not be interrupting anything?"

At that moment in the history of the universe I couldn't have pronounced Zbig's last name if my life depended on it. "Like I got nothing lined up for tonight."

Over sunny-side-ups, which were not over easy for the first time in my culinary career, lah-di-dah, I finally got around to thanking him for removing *The Hite Report* before the sheriff showed up with his search warrant. "I knew it was you even before the Rebbe told me how you handed over my *Hite Report* to protect him."

"How did you figure it out?"

"I found one of your two signatures—the clothes you folded over the back of the couch. You must've heard me and Dwayne going at it, right?"

He nodded.

"So?"

Then he said something which took my breath away. "Just because I had the good luck to fuck you does not mean I get to fix you. Besides which, you are not broken."

We were into mango chutney and yogurt when he filled me in on where he'd been for the last three weeks. Turns out he'd been whisked by helicopter to some fortress in Maryland which had two, count them, two barbed-wire fences surrounding it and a rain forest of antennas on the roof and the longest corridor in the history of corridors, it was three football fields long if it was a centimeter according to L. Falk, which makes Dwayne's E-Z up in Rochester look like a pocket playground for kids. Whoever it was that ran the joint had gone and set L. Falk up in a room without windows but with round-the-clock access to a Cray something or other, whatever that is, and then told him to break codes.

Hey, I didn't even know he could make codes.

I asked L. Falk how he'd wormed out of it. Which is when he explained more than I needed to know about codes. At this fortresslike fort in Maryland, he'd mapped statistical vibrations in large samples of data, I think that's what he said, and broken Russian and Syrian and Iranian and Iraqian codes and winged the messages on up the chain of command. It turned out he was telling the dudes in another fortress called the Pentagon what they didn't want to hear, namely, that Russian submarines couldn't submerge and Iraqian long-range missiles could only go short range and their short-range missiles couldn't get off the ground and Syrian artillery shells had faulty fuses and the Iranian atomic bomb wouldn't see the light for another fifty years, this was the optimistic view, and the economies of all of them were so screwed up they were crawling over each other to get American aid. The dudes at the Pentagon started sputtering like fuses when they read all this, L. Falk guessed it was not the kind of information they wanted circulating during budget-hunting season. They'd put the heat on some dude named Doolittle, who'd gone and started proceedings to extradite L. Falk back to Mother Russia, a process that would take six months, according to the lawyer L. Falk checked with.

"You could stay in America if you wanted to."

"How?"

"Become American."

He laughed. "I am allegoric to guns, buying one would make my eyes water."

"Don't be a doorknob—there are other ways of becoming American besides buying a gun."

"Name one."

"Ask for sexual asylum. Marry someone who's already American."

"Do you have a particular dude in mind?"

I swear to God, the idea popped into my head at random, the words slipped out before I'd thought them, they amazed me as much as they amazed L. Falk.

"There's always the Tender To."

He looked at me very strangely. "So are you proposing?"

I treated myself to a deep breath and let a "why" and a "not" drifted up through my naturally straight hair. I mean, I wasn't completely against the idea even though I knew from personal experience that marriage, like sex, was what L. Falk would call chaos-related.

"Look at it this way," I remember telling him. "The first

guy I lived with was a barber, right? He taught me how to cut hair, we opened a his-hers styling emporium in Albany, when clients started to wait for me even if he was free, he up and moved out. The second guy I lived with taught me how to fuck. When I became better at it than him, he moved out too. I'll skip over my ex-husband, the less said about bird killers the better. In my experience men can't stand being outperformed. One of the things I like about you is you can live with me doing some things better than you."

He let this percolate in his brain a while, I could tell from his expression he wasn't buying a word of it, then he said, very slowly, very angrily, very quietly, I had to strain to hear him, "If you please, stop bullshitting me. Stop bullshitting yourself. If you are really ready to marry someone who is toast, say why."

He was right on, of course. I glanced at him, he was staring at me across the table with an anxious half-smile, so I decided to come clean, if there's a better way of getting a consenting *Homo chaoticus* to consent, I'm not familiar with it. So here is roughly what I told him.

"The way I see it, a dude who plunges toward infinity isn't toast— how could he be when he's doing something that's never been done before? I don't really follow all the dirty details, right? but what I do get is you're on a trip with no hope of a getting there, which is the toughest kind to take, you need to be goddamn gutsy to get involved in something like that. Marriage, when it works, is also a trip without a getting there. It's what the dudes over in the art department call a work in progress."

Suddenly, I don't know why, I hadn't done any dope in weeks, I had this weird feeling I was plunging toward infinity myself, picking up speed, pushing the limit on the Interstate, whooshing past a line of eighteen-wheelers with psychedelic twenty-threes splashed across their sides, I couldn't've stopped if I'd wanted to. Which I didn't.

"So I sorta thought, hey, as long as we're going in the same direction, we might as well travel together." He was teetering, he needed one last nudge. "In case you're interested," I remember adding, "I have a last but not least."

I could see he wasn't not interested.

"Okay, here it is, my last but not least. I never met anyone in your category before."

"What is my category?"

"An erection is not the single most original thing you have going for you. . . . Jesus, do I have to go and spell it out?"

He didn't say anything, which I took to mean he needed it spelled out.

I closed my eyes and took another deep breath and opened my eyes, I could see I hadn't lost my audience, L. Falk was still hanging on my every word, which I took as an auspicious, even positive, sign. "The fact is . . . I love you to death, L. Fucking Falk." The freckles on my face were burning again. "So what do you say we stop beating around the goddamn bush? Would you or wouldn't you? Like to? Get hitched? With yours truly, the Tender To?"

"You are asking me," L. Falk must've been repeating the question to make sure he had decoded it correctly, "if I want to marry you, right?"

I remember blowing air through my lips in exasperation. "Like do you or don't you? Will you or won't you? R.S.V.P."

He watched me like a bird ready to take to the wing at the first sign of second thoughts. After what seemed like an ice age, he cleared his throat.

What he coughed up was a jubilant "Yo!"

I can say you the first time I got married, the ridiculous overwhelmed the ritual. I remember standing there in a thirdhand suit with threadbare patches on the threadbare elbows, shifting my weight from foot to foot on a motheaten carpet, gazing up at the faded color photograph of the paramount *Homo sovieticus* hanging askew on the peeling wall as the ceremony, if that is what it was, droned on. I remember feeling Vladimir Ilyich's cramps pinch my intestines. "Do you or don't you?" the painted *babushka* doll presiding over the one-minute ceremony in the Leningrad Palace of Marriage insisted impatiently. I remember tearing my eyes away from V. Lenin. "Do I or don't I what?" I asked. The woman who was destined to become the mother of my daughter, she was already twelve weeks pregnant, jabbed me in the ribs. Behind us, my future ex-father-in-law, the rector at the V. A. Steklov Institute of Mathematics, leaned forward and provided me with some stage coaching. His voice had an exasperated edge to it, I was not on his short list of prospective sons-in-law. "Do you or don't you take my daughter to be your wedded wife?" is what he whispered.

"I always said you had an ear for detail," Rain observed when I told her the story of my first wedding, we were waiting at the foot of the carillon tower for the Rebbe to show up and join us in wedlock. "So what did you do?"

"Hoping against hope to get a meal ticket, and eventually tenure, by marrying the rector's daughter, I let a barely audible 'why' and 'not' float up from my paralyzed vocal cords. The *babushka* doll pronounced us man and wife. My future ex deposited a dry kiss on my chapped lips, a down payment on ten years of listless, lustless marriage, and pulled me toward the door."

"I'll bet someone went and threw goddamn rice."

"As a matter of fact, her father, the rector at Steklov, stood on the steps of the Marriage Palace flinging Vietnamese rice he had bought on the black market."

"Poor fucking Russian birds," Rain said.

"Poor fucking Russian birds," I agreed, though I had in mind a larger category of victims.

Lugging my Red Army knapsack and my duty-free shopping bag, I had moved back into Rain's loft the evening of the day she proposed marriage to me. We quickly settled into a routine, with Rain cutting hair at Tender To until noon and showing up at the E-Z in the afternoon to score supper. I worked the day shift distributing cartons, keeping the shelves stocked, searching for the order I knew to be lurking beneath the appearance of disorder, and went in evenings to access the Mart's supercomputer and continue my headlong plunge through the decimal expansion of pi toward infinity. Every second Saturday, weather permitting, we would kick Rain's Harley into life and buzz up to Rochester, me piloting, her head glued to the back of my new flight jacket, there is nothing like a motorcycle to make you feel ten years younger, for some chaos-related fucking, which Rain calls lovemaking these days, with Dwayne and Shirley. I would lie awake next to Shirley listening to her snore, listening to the traffic on the beltway, listening to the planes roar off the runway, listening most of all to the soft gasps escaping from the back of Rain's beautiful white throat in the next room. Sometimes I would pad into the living room and finger their clothing. Once, talk about coded messages, I found Rain's blue jeans, her ribbed sweater, her Calvin Klein underpants, Dwayne's chinos, his turtleneck sweater, his plaid boxer shorts all neatly folded over the back of the couch. I winged a playful message back at her—I unfolded everything. Later, waiting for the frozen pizzas to heat in the oven, I caught Rain smiling wistfully at me, reminding me, as if it was something I could forget, where the core conspiracy was.

Hanging out under the carillon tower, keeping an eye peeled for the Rebbe, Dwayne studied the storm clouds gathering overhead. "If he doesn't show soon, the wedding's gonna hafta be postponed."

Shirley batted her eyelids innocently. "Does that mean we get to get one of Rain's checks?"

"The bus ride up from New York probably wore the Rebbe out," I guessed. "One of us ought to go down to the cockroach motel and make sure he's not sleeping."

We had filled out the marriage license as soon as we received the results of the blood test. Without thinking I tried to sign with my second signature, you never know when you might need to deny being married, right? but at the crucial moment I discovered I could no longer write my name backwards and wound up signing my real signature on the dotted line. That night Rain phoned up the late-night talk show to say she would not be calling in anymore.

"So which horizon are you finally sailing off to?"

"Here's the deal. . . ." "Here's the deal. I'm in love, I'm starting out on a trip that has no end, it's called marriage."

"Well, different folks have got different strokes. Two's a trip some couples need to take. If you're listening up, Charlene, honey, don't get any ideas in that gorgeous head of yours. Two for tea, tea for two is great lyrics for a song. As a lifestyle, it needs work."

Rain went straight up the wall. "You can go and ram . . ." "You can go and ram your advice to Charlene, who probably doesn't exist, right? I mean, what girl in her right mind would want an inner eyelid for a squeeze? You can ram your advice up your asshole, asshole."

The sky over Backwater was growing darker by the minute. I was beginning to wonder if my second wedding would be called on account of rain when Shirley clambered onto the first crossbeam of the carillon tower and spotted the Rebbe. "I see him, angel," she called excitedly to Dwayne, who was peeing behind a tree. "He didn't sleep through it after all."

The Rebbe, you want an educated guess, must have come up the hill along the footpath running behind the Kampus Kave; must have, while passing the exhaust fan in the kitchen window, smelled bacon, because when he arrived at the carillon tower, short of breath, red in the face, sweat staining his starched collar, he was definitely thinking Torah.

"I didn't sleep a wink all night," he groaned, judging from the bags under his eyes he was not exaggerating. He set the new E-Z Mart canvas shopping satchel I had given him on the ground, he took off his black fedora and wiped the sweatband with the tip of his tie. "I teased meanings out of passages in Torah that have mystified rabbinical brains for a thousand years, I skimmed the Babylonian Talmud looking for clues."

"Clues as to what?" Rain wanted to know.

"Clues as to how an ordained Rebbe, a Brooklyn Or Hachaim Hakadosh no less, can join together in holy matrimony a Jew to a Catholic, even if she is lapsed."

I knew the Rebbe well enough to understand the problem was not academic. In ways I could never get a handle on, he cared about the do's and don'ts that What's-His-Face brought down the mountain, he believed the ritual needed to be protected from the ridiculous.

Dwayne, buttoning his fly, ambled over. "You make lapsed sound like a venereal disease," he teased the Rebbe.

Shirley slid her hand into the rear pocket of Dwayne's jeans. "He must have come up with something, angel, or he wouldn't have showed."

"To tell the truth," the Rebbe said, "I had just about given up, you can only read so much in one night, when it suddenly came to me. Rain could convert! At which point there would be nothing standing in the way of my marrying you."

"Hey, I don't mind being Jewish if it'd make life easier for the Rebbe," Rain said.

"I thought you needed to be circumcised to be Jewish," Shirley said.

"Only the males of the species are circumcised, babe," Dwayne informed her.

Shirley seemed disappointed. "There he goes again, opening his fly and exposing his Harvard education."

"I read somewhere it takes months to convert to Judaism," I told the Rebbe. "Your bus for Brooklyn leaves in two hours."

He looked at me with a gleam of satisfaction in his bulging eyes. "You have maybe forgotten the story I told you after the faculty lunch, the one about Rebbe Hillel and the goy."

Turning toward Rain, he ordered her to stand on one foot. Without a word she followed his instructions. "Whatever I say, you say," he told her. " 'That which is hateful to you . . .' "

Balancing easily on one foot, taking the whole thing very seriously, Rain said softly, "Like 'that which is hateful to you.' "

" '. . . do not do to your friend.' "

" 'Do not do to your friend.' "

"This is the whole Torah," the Rebbe explained solemnly. "The rest is commentary."

Rain digested this with a thoughtful nod. "I get it. This is what the Torah boils down to. Everything else is window dressing."

Shirley looked at Dwayne. "Well, I don't get it."

"You want to dial back and run that past us again on slow?" Dwayne asked.

"I have taught her the heart of the heart of Torah," the Rebbe said. "For an ultra-un-Orthodox Jew like me, someone who understands Torah as well as Rain has to be Jewish."

You must be wondering, you are too discreet to put the question into words so I will preempt: Did this dope-smoking Rebbe really swallow his own blah-blah-blah? Does he really believe disorder is the ultimate luxury of those who live in order? Does he really think chaos is at the heart of the heart of Torah?

Hey, do not make the mistake of thinking you can tell a rebbe by his cover. I love the little guy; he looks more like

a messiah every time I see him. In ways I have not really figured out yet, he is holier than all of us put together. I do
not doubt, when he sees a three-piece suit, that he looks
around for a tailor. I do not doubt that he discovers Him.
So the answer to your unasked questions is yes to all of the
above. I myself think there is a serious possibility the Rebbe
may be an exalted person—someone who weeps without
making a sound, who dances without moving, who bows
down with his head held high.

If I close my eyes, I can see the Rebbe reaching out awkwardly to touch Rain's shoulder, I could tell he enjoyed the
physical contact, he may be exalted but a saint he is not.
"Being Jewish," he informed her with great formality, "you
are free, according to the laws handed down to Moses by
God, to marry a Jew."

"Let's go with the flow," Rain said happily.

Through his E-Z contacts in Rochester, Dwayne had gotten hold of one of those *Nonstops to the most Florida cities* billboard ads and strung it up on the side of the carillon tower
as a sort of in joke. Rain and I, with Dwayne and Shirley
forming a parenthesis, gathered under the ad, facing the
Rebbe. I felt Rain's arm slip through mine, I felt her breast
press into my elbow. Over our heads, the pigeons nesting
among the bells of the tower set up a throaty clamor. In my
mind's eye I imagined they were standing on one foot and
discussing the merits of birds of different feathers flocking
together.

The Rebbe fished yarmulkes from his shopping satchel
and handed them to Dwayne and me. Eyeing the threaten-
ing sky, it looked as if a thunderstorm would break overhead any instant, he said, "So we'll dispense with the
traditional canopy, the storm clouds are canopy enough,
and maybe use the abbreviated version of the ceremony, it's
not as if anybody present is a virgin."

From the seemingly endless depths of the shopping
satchel he produced a wine opener and a dusty bottle of
Château Montlabert 1979, deftly removed the cork, savored
the aroma of the wine on the cork, then half-filled a wineglass and raised it in a toast to the bride and groom. Rocking gently back and forth on the balls of his feet, he
intoned, *"Borukh atoh adoynoy, eloyheynu melekh ha'oylom,*

boyrey pri hagafen. Blessed art Thou, God, King of the universe, Creator of the fruit of the vine."

He sipped the wine. "Blessed are Thou, God, King of the universe, who has sanctified us by His commandments and given us the laws of marriage."

He motioned for me to produce the ring and slip it on Rain's finger. "Repeat after me," he said, glancing again at the storm clouds. *"Hareï at mekudeshes . . ."*

"Hareï at mekudeshes."

". . . li betaba'as zo kedas . . ."

"Li betaba'as zo kedas."

". . . moyshe veyisro'eyl."

"Moyshe veyisro'eyl."

"What language is he talking, angel?" Shirley asked Dwayne behind our backs.

"Lilliputian," I said under my breath. "It is the mother tongue of one of the lost tribes of Israel."

"Behold, you are sanctified to me by this ring," the Rebbe intoned, "according to the law of Moses and Israel."

When I hesitated, he nodded vigorously for me to repeat it.

Still clinging to Rain's hand, I turned to her. "Behold, you are sanctified to me by this ring . . ." I cleared my throat.

"So what are you nervous about?" she whispered. "You've been married before."

"That is what I am nervous about," I whispered back.

I started to slip into a fiction, but caught myself at the last instant. It dawned on me that the chaos of the moment was infinitely more interesting.

I took a deep breath and completed the ritual sentence. ". . . according to the law of Moses and Israel."

The Rebbe's head bobbed gleefully, his coiled sideburns cavorting in the air. "With these words the delicious deed is done. Under Jewish law the bride is considered a married woman, the groom a married man."

"Hey, I don't feel different," Rain announced.

Shirley burst into tears. "It's . . . so . . . fucking . . . fly."

Fighting back tears, Rain reached up and with a strength I did not know she possessed pulled my head down to hers. She pressed her lips fiercely against my cheek, when she spoke I felt her breath singe my ear.

"I swear to Christ I'll be there when you need me."

"Me also," I whispered back, I was too emotional to say more, it is not every day you marry someone you are wildly, eternally, achingly in love with.

The Rebbe, his enormous Adam's apple bobbing, tilted back his head and polished off the glass of Château Montlabert in one long gulp, then wound a piece of cloth around the wineglass and placed it on the ground.

"Stomp on it," he told me. "It brings good luck."

I stomped on the glass with my heel, shattering it into a million fragments.

"Mazel tov!" cried the Rebbe.

"Check it out," whooped Dwayne, caught up in the excitement.

"Hey, I am freaking out." Rain laughed nervously. "Totally."

An elated "Yo" was all I managed to cough up.

The Rebbe, it turned out, had not completed the ceremony. "One of the perks of being a Rebbe," he said, holding out a palm, feeling the first drop slap against it, "is you get to deliver the homily to a captive audience."

Behind me, I could hear Dwayne muttering to Shirley, "Chill out, babe."

"I can't," she sobbed. "I think I want to become Jewish, I think I want the Rebbe to marry us too."

"What better way to celebrate a beginning," the Rebbe said, davening impatiently, "than to go back and take a quick look at the Big Bang. 'In the beginning God created the heaven and the earth. And the earth was *tohu-vavohu*. I'm talking Genesis 1:1. The *schlimazel* King James translates this, 'the earth was without form.' But *tohu-vavohu* happens to be the Hebrew word for 'chaos.' The ... earth ... was ... literally ... chaos!"

"Tohu-vavohu," Rain murmured, "sounds like the most Florida city in the Pacific. Hey, maybe we could honeymoon there sometime."

"Are you hanging on my every word, Lemuel and Rain?" the Rebbe forged on, he did not appreciate interruptions. "You don't have to be an Eastern Parkway Or Hachaim Hakadosh to maybe know chaos didn't sneak through the door uninvited, it was also created. Knowing Yahweh, we can assume it was within His power to create night and day and grass and trees and seasons and sun and fish and fowl and Eden and Adam without first creating chaos. So what coded signal was Yahweh sending down through the ages to Jews being joined together in holy matrimony when He created chaos before He moved on to Creation with a capital C?"

If I live to be a hundred and six, which is how old I was when Rain jump-started my battery, I will never forget the Rebbe's talmudic eyes bursting with biblical originality. He absently slipped a finger between his starched collar and the welt on his neck as he supplied the answer to his own question.

"You want an independent opinion, He was maybe telling us what every artist instinctively knows, namely that there is no such thing as creation without chaos." Heavy drops of rain started to spatter at our feet, Shirley and Dwayne exchanged worried looks, the Rebbe lunged toward his punch line. "So, my darlings, if you are lucky enough to get a whiff of honest-to-God chaos in your life as a couple, don't run away from it, run toward it, embrace it, use it, for God's sake."

Dwayne sensed the Rebbe had run out of words. "Now, babe!"

He and Shirley pulled recycled paper bags from their pockets and began pelting us with fistfuls of bird seed. Instantly the carillon tower came alive with blurred wings as waves of pigeons beat down to peck at the ground. Below, in the valley, a prong of lightning split the sky, followed immediately by a slow roll of thunder. The rain began in earnest.

I took off my sport jacket and held it over Rain's head. The sight of the pigeons fluttering down from the tower made my hearts beat faster—I understood that the trivial turbulence created when wings flail the air sets off tiny ripples that amplify with time and distance to bring, into the life of a Russian theoretical chaoticist no longer on the lam from terrestrial chaos, Occasional Rain.

Go figure.

The Debriefing

Stone is the head of an elite arm of the Joint Chiefs of Staff—and a seasoned professional in the psychologically sophisticated art of debriefing. When Oleg Kulakov defects from Russia, handcuffed to a sealed diplomatic pouch, it's Stone's job to find out if he's genuine. As Stone uncovers Kulakov's darkest secrets, he penetrates Russia itself to learn the chilling truth—a truth that tears his own world apart.

ISBN 978-0-14-311440-6

Walking Back the Cat

This mesmerizing espionage thriller unfolds in New Mexico, where a Soviet era KGB agent has been living under deep cover. Reactivated by a new controller for some particularly brutal "wetwork"—murder—the agent's suspicions are aroused. Fearing a double-cross, he begins, in espionage lingo, "walking back the cat"—retracing the operation to find the source of the deception. *ISBN 978-0-14-311357-7*

The October Circle

Set against the backdrop of the Russian invasion of Prague during the Cold War, *The October Circle* is one of Littell's most riveting early works. Seven of Bulgaria's cultural elite—all disillusioned communists—and one American drifter find themselves staging an extremely dangerous protest that will set off a wave of repression and threaten to repay their heroism with death. *ISBN 978-0-14-311299-0*

Vicious Circle

This suspenseful and brilliantly topical thriller looks at the cycle of political violence in the Middle East. In the tradition of John le Carré and Graham Greene, Littell dissects the culture of violence by searching the corrupted consciences of the people ensnared within it.

ISBN 978-0-14-311266-2

The Company

Robert Littell seamlessly weaves together CIA history and fiction to create a multigenerational, wickedly nostalgic saga that tells the story of agents imprisoned in double lives, fighting an amoral, elusive enemy.

ISBN 978-0-14-200262-9

The Amateur
Charlie Heller is an ace cryptographer for the CIA, a quiet man in a quiet back-office job. But when his fiancée is murdered by terrorists and the Agency decides not to pursue her killers, Heller takes matters into his own hands.   *ISBN 978-0-14-303814-6*

The Sisters
Centering on Francis and Carroll, two enigmatic and extremely dangerous CIA legends dubbed "the Sisters Death and Night," *The Sisters* masterfully unveils an abyss of artful deception. By luring a former head of the KGB sleeper school into betraying his last and best assassin, Francis and Carroll set off a desperate race against time as he tries to stop his protégé from committing the Sisters' world-shattering crime.
ISBN 978-0-14-303821-4

Legends
Martin Odum is a one-time CIA field agent turned private detective in Brooklyn, struggling his way through a labyrinth of memories and past identities—"legends" in Agency parlance. But who is Martin Odum? Is he a creation of the Legend Committee at the CIA's Langley headquarters? Is he suffering from multiple personality disorder, brainwashing, or simply exhaustion?   *ISBN 978-0-14-303703-3*

An Agent in Place
Deep in the vastness of the Pentagon and the bowels of the massive KGB center in Moscow are old Cold Warriors who refuse to fade away. Yet how can they wage their battles when there are no enemies anymore? Their answer is Ben Bassett. Sent to Moscow as a lowly embassy "housekeeper," Bassett meets a fiercely independent, passionate Russian poet, Aïda Zavaskaya, and falls under her spell. Together they become pawns in a dreadful game that leads to the clandestine heart of the Soviet system itself.   *ISBN 978-0-14-303564-0*

The Once and Future Spy
When "the Weeder," an operative at work on a highly sensitive project for the Company, encounters an elite group of specialists and a clandestine plan within the innermost core of the CIA, disturbing moral choices must be weighed against a shining patriotic dream.
ISBN 978-0-14-200405-0

The Defection of A.J. Lewinter
For years an insignificant cog in America's complex defense machinery, A.J. Lewinter, a scientist, is now playing both sides against the middle. As Russia and America each struggle to anticipate its opponent's next move, Lewinter is swept up in a terrifying web of deceit and treachery.
ISBN 978-0-14-200346-6